my secret vice

MOUNTAINS & MONUMENTS SERIES

ALICIA WILDER

Rocket Books

For the ones who speak out and take up space

content warning

This book includes characters who promote decriminalizing cannabis, a substance that in the United States is currently legal for recreational use in 24 states and for medical use in 38 but remains a Schedule I controlled substance under federal law. Possession of as little as 4 ounces of cannabis can still result in a criminal charge and imprisonment in some states. According to the ACLU, Black individuals are 3.73 times more likely than white to be arrested for cannabis.

This romance novel deals with sexism and discrimination, two unfortunately common obstacles to love.

There is also explicit language and sexual content between consenting adults.

Cindy

THE FIRST QUESTION is the one I dread: "What happens if you can't pass this legislation, congresswoman?"

Our White House minder had tried to herd me and the rest of the delegation right past the cluster of media behind a rope set up to pen them in but I'd stopped to talk to them. My cause benefitted from their attention.

"Is this your first time at the White House, congresswoman? How do you feel?" The questions are shouted to avoid being drowned out by the white noise of the blades of the Nighthawk helicopter churning air on the South Lawn of the White House.

"Do you want to run for president, Representative Wight?" Plans to run for president are cheaper than a craft cocktail in this town; the press knows that. I ignore this question.

"Do you have plans to primary the president's reelection ticket?"

Trying to keep a steady, meaningless smile on my face because of all the photographers, I glance at the rest of my congressional delegation—all men—watching Marine Two land 20 feet away.

The vice president's helicopter normally would only land on the White House lawn in an emergency. They wanted a show of force ahead of our summit meeting. It's meant to turn me and the others into peasants asking for favors, to make me less certain of *my* demands. It's a hollow gesture, like chocolates and flowers given in lieu of treating someone well.

Although newly elected last year, I am familiar with the power dynamics and how those in control tend to use them to intimidate others.

The massive, military helicopter; the green, landscaped expanse of the White House lawn with the historic building behind me; the gaggle of press aiming their phones at me and the helicopter all adds up. It might be a show, but it's got a lot of weight behind it.

"I'm glad to be here as a voice for the vulnerable people who need this legislation most," I shout over the chop of the rotors. This video clip—me with my hair flying, attempting to keep my skirt held down—will appear on social media within minutes. I need to set the right tone. "I'm privileged to speak for them in this meeting today. They're why I was elected and that's what I'm focused on now."

I use my peripheral vision to check on my colleagues, all more seasoned lawmakers than I am. The faces of the members of House leadership are impassive and none of them are fidgeting, smoothing their clothes or hair. They all act experienced, but I know that's not true. Negotiations at the White House are rare when one party holds all branches of government. There is no one more jaded than a mediocre white man with power, and this is a whole cluster of them.

Fake it 'til you make it, Cindy. I represent the contrarians, the fresh blood flowing into Congress this session, bringing with it new ideas and more diversity of perspectives. I'll remain uncowed by this setting, these men with their satisfaction in their power. I'm here to shake them up.

It's a *fun* mission. That's why my heart is pounding to the beat of the helicopter's rotors, and nearly as loud.

I wish I'd worn pants. Or at least an A-line skirt instead of this swingy one that I'd thought would subtly signal youth and daring. The red seemed like a power move for the solo woman selected for the summit. Instead, it's a symbol of inexperience that could lead to a wind-driven media catastrophe.

My long, dark hair, currently a halo around my head, is going to be a mess. I'm worried the brisk wind, stirred up by the rotors and causing my eyes to water, will transport my makeup to the mild crow's feet around my eyes. It'd be just my luck if there's no time to tidy up before we jump into the pool of photographers. Part of my media appeal is my youth. At almost 45, I'm not that young, but when the median age of House members is 58, I benefit from comparison.

The helicopter is finally winding down and a Marine in dress uniform is opening the side door. Out pops the vice president, as casual as if this is his normal commute, his fading black hair close-cut and unruffled. He's wearing a dark suit and a bright red tie that could rival my own loud outfit. He returns the officer's salute and walks toward us, his long legs eating up the grass of the White House lawn, suit coat and tie flapping behind him. His athletic build belies his 50 years and his tanned skin shows fewer lines than the average politician. Every inch the "disturbingly handsome bachelor in the White House," as the *Daily Mail* wrote about him when he took office five years ago. His pant legs reveal a glimpse of red socks, likely one of the novelty pairs the vice president is known for wearing. Camera shutters click nearby.

The huddle of journalists start calling out. "Mr. Vice President, do you expect to reach a deal today?" and "Mr. Vice President, do you have a date tonight?"

"Have you and Representative Wight met before, Mr. Vice President?" another reporter calls out.

He waves at them, face impassive, and keeps going, through a side door and into the White House. A young man in a suit, wearing a blue staff badge on a lanyard around his neck and boredom on his face, gestures for me and my group to follow him.

"Did you vote for the president's ticket, Madame Congresswoman?" I hate when people call me that. It's so stodgy and makes me sound like I'm part of the establishment now.

I turn back to the reporters, not about to miss this opportunity. I voted for the more progressive ticket and hope to again, I tell them.

"Not even in the general?" a reporter with a stain on his tie asks. He's trying to catch me in an unforgivable sin: not holding your nose to vote for your own party.

"I don't believe in party over principle. I voted for change, not the status quo," I say. It's a line one of my staff members wrote in a speech and it always goes over well. With voters, anyway; less so with elected members of my party.

That sets off another flurry of questions, but it's time for me to rejoin the others. As I turn to walk with the group back into the White House, my heels sink into the lawn. The heat of embarrassment slides down my neck and around my breasts. Perhaps I'm going to step right out of my shoe and be forced to stand there hopping with one bare foot on the White House lawn. In front of all these people I need to impress. Then the shoe comes loose, still on my foot, and I keep going with a minor stumble.

Hopefully, I recover that smoothly from any stumbles in the upcoming meeting.

* * *

Alex

Exiting the helicopter, I dread the day ahead. I salute the Marine holding my door, as usual trying and failing to meet the young man's eyes. The disciplined Marines assigned to the White House never make eye contact, even though I was one of them not that many years in the past.

All eyes are on me. It's the curse and the blessing of being vice president. I don't have to work hard to gain attention, but I do have to do everything in public view. Including pull a power play on the people I'm meeting with this afternoon. And co-host an important fundraiser later with a woman who is the wife of one of the president's most obnoxious and wealthy donors. Those two things usually go hand-in-hand.

"You should give all the women in attendance red roses," my aide Deena said on the helicopter. My staff hadn't even remembered it was Valentine's Day until I reminded them. It isn't exactly a high-priority occasion in Washington, given that it's not a holiday for government workers or a deadline for legislation. Joke's on me for being a romantic. Now I'm stuck playing Cupid at the last minute.

Marguerite will make the perfect hostess. And I need a perfect hostess on my arm, hosting my event at *her* house because it's not "appropriate" for a single man to host a $10,000-a-plate fundraiser at his bachelor pad. Even if the bachelor pad is the residence at the United States Naval Observatory.

Not that I'm bitter. I expected to have fewer "should"s and "must"s in my life at this point, that's all. Still, looking out across the White House lawn from the door of the white-topped Marine Two, it's obvious what I've lost in control, I've gained in accomplishments.

As I walk toward the White House across the immaculate lawn, one scarlet dress among a sea of gray and black suits catches my eye. Ah yes, the lone woman in the delegation, author of the bill we are here to discuss and leader of the group of junior lawmakers that the press is calling the Freshman Six. Elected last year after overwhelmingly defeating a representative who'd been in Congress for 20 years, Cindy Wight is new blood in the House, though she'd been an activist leader for a decade before running for office. On day one of her tenure as an elected official, she led a coalition marching to the White House to demand the administration "reverse the war on drugs."

She's the one my team told me would be toughest to convince. A firebrand and idealist. If I can sway her, it means six votes that will make a difference to passing the bill. And a coalition built with the progressive wing of the party. I'm good at that balance: Avoiding waves but getting the credit. That's why the president sent me into this particular battle.

The edge of her skirt is flipping, making it hard not to notice she has beautiful legs. Her long, dark hair is floating around her in the wind from Marine Two. "The female Obama," according to a magazine profile. That comparison is thrown around this town too often; an op-ed last week called me "Obama's wishy-washy heir apparent." It seems everyone is ignoring the fact Cindy and I are both white.

But Cindy Wight is young, passionate, unproven—too fearless to be wishy-washy. I've been looking forward to seeing her in action in person. I need her help on this legislation to shore up the youth and minority voters, as my chief of staff puts it. This business can be so crass.

She's standing by the media pen, away from the rest of the group, the star of the cast. The White House reporters are clustered around her like moths to a flame, looking to catch the viral soundbites she's known for giving, and ignoring the ostentatious display I just made landing on the White House lawn. What a pain. I'd had to get all sorts of permissions for that.

I do my job and I do it well, no matter how I feel about it. This day is no different.

I wave at the press. Of course *they* didn't forget it was Valentine's Day and now ask me the usual prying questions about my love life, or lack of it.

Without stopping to talk to the group from Capitol Hill, I lead the way into the White House. It's another power move, designed to make them like supplicants rather than equal parties at the table. So is using the White House for this meeting rather than the Eisenhower Executive Office Building, where the vice president has a ceremonial office. My job is to make it appear as though the White House is open to demands we will never actually consider.

And to come out looking like the man who gets deals done, a few short years from the end of the president's last term.

Cindy

WHEN I'D PREPARED for this meeting with my chief of staff and communications director, we braced for the dynamics across the table. We planned for the face-off with the vice president and the members of party leadership, and expected I'd be isolated on my side of the table, alone without any others from the activist coalition.

None of the other fledgling group of six members who have joined in demanding more than the establishment wants to give were invited to this meeting. I'm the *de facto* leader—a sore subject among some of the group. I have to speak for all of us to be taken seriously by them *and* the White House.

"Speak up. Don't let them interrupt. Take credit," I'd repeated to myself this morning as I readied for battle.

Unfortunately, I didn't prepare for how arctic the physical temperature would be in the Cabinet Room, where we're meeting. I wave off the offered ice water. I'm shaking in my heels, I'm so cold. Definitely should have worn the pants. Or at least hosiery. Colorado-born, I'd turned up my nose at the relatively mild Washington, D.C., winters. Mistake. The air in the White House is as poorly regulated as in the halls of Congress. Well, I'll know better next time.

Because there *will* be a next time. I didn't come all this way to Washington not to get in the rooms where decisions are made.

"Thank you all for coming," Vice President Drake says, taking control of the meeting from the start. "We've got a few concerns to raise with this proposal, but I'm certain that in the spirit of party unity, we can reach a compromise."

First shot fired. *Party unity* is supposed to make us all toe the line. But there is no party unity on cannabis; the issue is still too fraught in many districts.

One of my senior colleagues, who positioned himself on the vice president's side of the table, opens his mouth but I jump in before he can speak. "As excited as we are to work with you, Mr. Vice President, let's just be clear from the start that *our* goal is nationwide decriminalization, record expungement and reformed banking rules within the year. Polling shows an astonishingly high level of national support for this bill and, *in the spirit of party unity*, we are of course happy to let the White House get on board with legislation. I, for one, have been advocating for this for my entire career."

Vice President Drake gazes at me silently for a moment, blue eyes meeting blue. Acknowledging the fact I'm not going to be steamrolled here. Everyone else turns to me as well. I keep my expression neutral. Then he says, "Polling shows high support for this *concept*, not this bill. What we do with the bill itself is the subject of this conversation."

He might as well have slapped me, the vice president of the United States patronizing me in front of a dozen other people.

I need a moment to recover without becoming defensive. Perhaps I can direct their eyes to the folders on the table. "Mr.

Vice President, I believe we sent your people the current draft of the bill in advance, if you'd care to go over it with us."

"I've looked at your draft and have a revision of my own to suggest." No reprieve. He signals to one of his aides, who pulls out a folder from the leather binder clutched to his chest and starts passing out sheets of paper. Of course the White House is surprising us with new text without any notice. I hold back a groan. I'd expected a marathon discussion and this feels like a sprint on an obstacle course I've never seen before.

As I read the heavily edited revision, I try to subtly build some friction from rubbing my calves together under the table for warmth without making the leather chair squeak.

Every man in this room is wearing a suit jacket over two shirts. The vice president is casually elegant, as on the cover of *Time* Magazine last month, not shivering in his leather shoes. Deep lines bracket his mouth that make him look thoughtful and not a hair is out of place.

But *my* dress sleeves are silk and my coat is somewhere in another room, collected by a staff member. I take a quick peek down my front to make sure I'm not showing nipples through this dress and lightly padded bra. Thank God. I ease off one shoe and rub my feet on the red and gold-starred carpet because even my toes are frozen.

"Mr. Vice President, I don't see a problem passing this language through my committee." My colleague, the chairman of the Judiciary Committee, speaks up first. Of course he doesn't see a problem; the White House's version of the bill has been stripped of anything controversial.

The vice president's gaze flickers to me, as if inviting my reaction. Surprised, I don't turn down the opportunity. "But it would not have support from the progressive wing, and you need those votes for it to pass the full Floor vote," I say.

"Why not?" The vice president leans back in his chair, like

we're discussing dinner and not the lives of thousands of people wrongfully imprisoned on what should have been minor charges. It could be the two of us alone in this room, facing each other across the table. "This bill, my revision, could pass the Senate as-is and the president would sign it," he says. "You'd get your decriminalization. That's your flagship issue, the one you were elected on, and it's huge progress from where we're at now."

"It doesn't address the wrong that's been done in the past or the need for reform going forward," I say, some welcome heat building as we volley back and forth.

"Polls show high levels of national support for decriminalization."

It's like he's serving me softballs. "Polls also show high levels of national support for expunging the records of people convicted of marijuana possession and allowing banks to be able to work with money in states where cannabis is already legal."

"Among 18- to 29-year-olds, and not across all demographics." He responds easily, his tone free of the scolding tone I can hear creeping into my own voice.

Even knowing I'm leaving myself open to criticism, I can't help blurting out, "It's the right thing to do." My staff had repeatedly warned me not to come across sounding like a white savior high on the importance of an issue that disproportionately affects minorities. But the people most impacted weren't invited to this room to speak out, so I will.

"Politics are about what can be done, not what should be." He glances down at the paper in his hand, as though giving me a chance to collect myself after teaching the newbie a lesson. I *know* he's right, and I ran for office because I wanted the hands-on experience that could lead to real change, but it still stings to feel called out as an impractical idealist.

He turns his level gaze back to me. "Representative Wight,

this legislation would please every member of our party, some on the other side, and the majority of voters. Why can't you just take the win?" His light blue eyes are like a laser beam, putting me in the spotlight. He doesn't fidget. The two busts on either side of the fireplace behind him stare me down along with him.

A clock ticks as everyone waits for me to answer. He's maneuvered me into a corner where it appears I'm only concerned about power—holding ground for the sake of saying I went toe-to-toe with the White House and got them to bend.

But I've been in office a year and an invitation into this room today is my biggest win so far. I haven't made any difference for the voters who sent me here based on big promises to change things in Washington. I'd promised to take on "the Swamp" and make lives better not just for my constituents but for people around the country who donated to my campaign. Who believed in me. I glance around the room at the men, from the vice president to the jowly senior members, all of them happy with the way things are. So many people who aren't here are counting on me now.

"I think we're in agreement that *this*," and I push the paper back toward the vice president. "Is a non-starter. My voters—*our* voters, members of this party—want more. They want justice."

The chairman of the House Financial Services Committee snorts. "Let's not get hyperbolic here. You would stall a bill you want over a provision that will never pass the Senate?" Great, already repeating the vice president's lines after telling me this morning he was here to negotiate. Because, he'd said to me, "your election is a clear mandate for our party." Talking out of both sides of his mouth. Typical.

The vice president gazes back at me. The words clog in my throat, but I try to say with my eyes that I'm not backing down. And I can see it in his eyes: he *hears* me. A moment of empathy passes between us, a zap downward from the powers that be to the woman trying to make a difference.

He closes the folder in front of him and hands it to an aide, breaking eye contact with me and setting me adrift from the moment we'd shared, while he smooths his red tie. "Well, I think this meeting is over. Let's allow the press in for their pool spray before you head back up the Hill." He stands.

Did I just screw this whole negotiation by speaking up rather than letting the men feel like they're in charge? *No.* The roaring in my ears won't accept this.

"I would stall this bill because it's toothless," I say, finally responding to the chairman and now speaking over the members shuffling papers and aides beginning to open the doors. "It doesn't expunge criminal records retroactively. It doesn't make allowances for an industry that brings in millions of tax dollars to the states where it's legal. It merely de-prioritizes an offense that, in most places, is already a low priority for law enforcement."

The vice president doesn't even glance at me as he continues straightening his cuffs with long fingers. He pauses, though. Then he drops his hands to his sides, and scans me and the other members of the party already standing up from the table. I hope the others remember why they should do more on this issue, but I suspect they're all caving in the face of the vice president's confidence.

"By decriminalizing at a national level, we address an inconsistent system," he says coolly. He returns his eyes to mine. "The party is in agreement on decriminalization. Are you sure you-" his wave encompasses me, but also everyone I represent, as though dismissing all of us. "Want to be left behind?"

I almost admire the flair with which he's threatening my cause. But I know, beyond all the window dressing of the setting we're in, that I'm right.

I dig the toes of one bare foot into the carpet beneath the table and decide to say what I'm thinking. "Well, we certainly appreciate the drama, Mr. Vice President. But you'll find that the compromise you insist the party wants exists a little further to the left of the status quo. I can show you fundraising totals to that effect. My group—including the members of Congress who weren't included here today—is much larger than you think. We may be new to this negotiation, but we represent millions of people who want to address the historic injustice in the laws of this country."

His eyes are not angry. A traitorous, fluttery feeling strikes over my sternum when I realize that what I'm seeing is the vice president's respect.

"Alright," he says, and signals to an aide at the door. "Let's keep talking."

Holding back a grin at this small victory, I nod.

"I suggest we take your revised proposal back to the Speaker and discuss it among our conference," the Judiciary chairman says. "Then we'll get back to you."

Immediately plummeting back from the high of winning a concession from the vice president, I sense I'm losing the tenuous control I'd gained. The senior members of the party are going to undercut me no matter what.

"It's pointless to take two copies of this bill that are so far apart to the Speaker," I say quickly. "But I agree that a smaller group should work on the language before we present it. I can take the lead on that. As the lead sponsor of the original bill."

The chairman grumbles, but is abruptly cut off by the vice president raising his hand. He nods. "We're happy to work with you. I plan on overseeing this process myself, with the full support of the president."

What the vice president is offering might appear meaningless, but it's still a step forward. If I don't take it, I have no path forward at all. I'd expected negotiations to continue with members of House leadership. For the White House to be involved in the nuances of writing legislation is unusual and suggests this process is going to become even more of a political minefield than I'd expected. But knowing the vice president cares about it passing gives me leverage. Now I know something he wants.

Trying not to shiver, I lift my chin in the vice president's direction. "I look forward to working with you, sir."

three

Alex

I HAVE three sisters and a mother who are always cold, which is why I recognize the signs: the subtle shift of legs rubbing, the arm-brushing, and, while I'd pretended to not notice, Congresswoman Wight's furtive glances at the front of her dress. Beneath the precise lines of her bright red lipstick, her lips are practically turning blue.

That's why I end up suggesting we pop into the briefing room to talk to the press rather than inviting the media into the Cabinet Room as planned. I can tell from the way one of my communications aides reacts that I'm creating a nightmare PR scenario, but I've spent my whole political career listening to my gut and I'm not going to stop now. My instincts say Rep. Cindy Wight and I can help each other. Might as well start now.

I pause at the Cabinet Room door, allowing the lawmakers to proceed before me and giving my own people time to put their heads together for a last-minute strategy. As I do, I catch the congresswoman folding herself in half to reach under the table for her shoes. Her skirt is riding up her thigh and one long, shapely leg is sticking out at an angle, her toes pointed on a bare foot with red toenail polish. It's not a typical sight in a meeting with Congress, nor is the stirring it ignites in my stomach. I smile involuntarily, but suspect the lawmaker would not appreciate being witnessed in this moment, so I step outside the room with the others.

"OK, brief statement to the effect of 'we're working toward a compromise; this is important to everybody,' but no questions, period," says Kaylee, the White House press secretary, hurrying alongside me toward the west terrace. Her two clearance badges are bouncing around her chest in the rush and she's talking while typing away on her government phone, a secured BlackBerry.

"The congresswoman can take two questions, on topic, from the wire services," Cindy Wight's chief of staff says, keeping step with me and my people.

"Just because your member has never been behind the White House podium before doesn't mean she gets to take over the bully pulpit," Kaylee hisses back, without missing a step.

My mouth curves as I recognize that I've frazzled the staff.

"We don't need the bully pulpit. We're the ones writing the legislation your White House wants to pass, remember?" Wight's aide snaps. She glances at me, remembering they're bickering across the vice president. "Sir."

"They can take a couple questions, I think, Kaylee," I offer, giving her a weighted look. I don't want to be the face of this particular issue. It's too easy to turn me into an one-issue candidate.

As we're walking, I turn back to Cindy Wight. Her arms are folded around her body and she's obviously still freezing. Her expression makes it clear she wouldn't appreciate me offering her my jacket, however. It would be controlling in this context.

I get it. Power is a precious commodity in Washington and no one can afford to appear weak. My job isn't immune from that. In fact, I'm not entirely sure my use of the briefing room is authorized, but I'm not going to stop now and ask for permission. I'll tell the president I was trying to impress a woman. Tim will understand. Cindy Wight is unexpectedly compelling. Something about her unapproachability makes me want to climb past her barriers.

We walk in through the side doors and I see my team did their jobs even at short notice and rounded up the press already, likely creating a scramble in the basement. Even now, correspondents on campus are rushing to inform their editors, colleagues and followers of the addition to the daily White House schedule as they are racing to their seats in the room.

The blue stadium seats in the small briefing room are filled with reporters, all with badges on lanyards around their necks, all typing away on their phones. Most likely ginning up buzz for the unusual briefing on social media. The broadcast cameras in the back row are all manned and likely ready to livestream.

"No news for you all today, just an update," Kaylee tells the room immediately upon taking the podium, setting the tone for the briefing. "The vice president and representatives from Capitol Hill had a productive meeting. They are moving forward toward a compromise on cannabis legislation," she continues. "The vice president has the president's full support to reach a deal that would best benefit the American people." She gestures for me and the others to step up to the podium. "We're going to take a couple questions."

Glancing down at the seating chart that's on the podium, I point at the first person I recognize on the front row.

"What is the sticking point for the bill, Mr. Vice President?"

I smile a smile that gives nothing to Josh from the Associated Press. "It will surprise no one to hear that this White House wants to take meaningful action on this issue. But we are committed to listening to all ideas, whether more conservative ones from members of the opposite party or more progressive ones from within our own. And I'm sure we'll achieve a deal that addresses the wrongs of the past as well as the promise of the future."

The reporters in front of me all raise their hands for another question, but I don't want to offer them more specifics or veer into the wrong territory. So I turn to Cindy, gesturing her toward the podium. "Congresswoman Wight has agreed to be an important partner in this process."

She steps toward me and catches her heel on the fraying carpet. The James S. Brady Press Room, unchanged for years, is nearing hazardous conditions. She's barely started to stumble before I grab her by the elbow and draw her up to the podium in one motion, releasing her once she's regained her footing. She smells like vanilla.

She pauses. I meet her blue eyes and try hard not to smile. We are, after all, surrounded by cameras. But there's a hint in her eyes that she *wants* to smile back.

"This White House has pledged to compromise," she says, her eyes still on mine. She turns away, before it starts to become obvious we're having some kind of moment. "We plan to hold them to that. I want to bring this bill to the Floor in two months, on 4/20. I plan on making sure we have a deal by that time."

Damn, this woman plays hard ball. Walking into *my* house as a freshman representative and throwing her weight around. Tim's popularity as president is a rising tide that lifts all boats in the party. But in the House, this woman fragmented an otherwise comfortable majority, splitting the conference between the senior establishment and a younger, more progressive freshman class. Her group wants to push the party to change laws—more laws, and faster. The leader of that movement is taking no prisoners right now from a podium marked with a White House seal. My staff must want to kill me for putting her up here.

As someone whose position on issues is endlessly polled and vetted, watching Cindy take a fearless stand is like breathing fresh air.

Kaylee steps up to the podium, neatly cutting off the shouted questions from the other side of the room. "One more question, please. Emily?"

"Mr. Vice President, do you have a date for Valentine's Day?"

Of course. They couldn't possibly stay focused on my job when I'm the first single VP since 1933. Wonder if anyone also speculated Charles Curtis was closeted, despite his dead wife.

Smiling my most friendly grin, the one that shows all my teeth, I say, "I have about 300 dates, Emily. I'm hosting a private fundraiser this evening."

Then I escape the raised hands as quickly as I can.

* * *

Cindy

I've had many conversations with mentors on gaining control of my short-fuse temper. In the few seconds after the briefing ends, I realize I failed in the briefing room. The rush of gratitude for the vice president conferring authority with that "partner" comment and smoothing over my stumble came with worry that he saw me as soft and needy. And so I snapped—*how dare he think I needed his help?*—and set a deadline we can only hit if everything goes smoothly from here on with the bill. Which it won't. This is a historically fraught issue with a significant party split.

But I can't admit to anyone else that I got carried away.

"You set a completely arbitrary deadline that means nothing to the rest of the party," the Judiciary chairman says the moment we are out of earshot of the press. But not out of range from the rest of our colleagues or the vice president. "We won't stand by it."

I seek to ground myself by looking around where we're standing in the back of the press building. There's a sliding door leading into the briefing room and the offices of the deputy press secretaries in this end of the communications wing. Everything is rundown in here, especially compared to the rest of the west wing of the White House. The media is treated a little like I am: Mostly irrelevant but loud at inopportune moments.

"The deadline I set is not unreasonable. This is a priority for the conference," I raise my voice to continue before the chairman does. "I want to *introduce* it by 4/20, not get it through the committee and to a Floor vote."

"The White House is willing to make some accommodations within that time frame," the vice president says, which is hardly a commitment but comes at the right moment to halt this public scolding.

Because I resent that I need the assistance at all, I can't quite feel grateful. I spent 12 years as a community organizer before ultimately realizing I needed an elected office to get the legislation I'd been working for my entire career into law. As a female, freshman lawmaker with ideas that are more ambitious than the rest of my party, my opinion is always less respected than my majority-male colleagues, most of whom have been in office for years. My priorities, and those of the diverse freshman group I've assembled who have similar views, are easy to dismiss. But I can fight my own battles and don't need the vice president to step in.

The vice president waves me toward him. "Congresswoman, a sidebar?"

Kaylee opens the door of a nearby office and we step inside. There are newspapers on the floor stacked as high as the desk and the desktop is covered in sticky notes and a pile of granola bars. But it smells like sandalwood, a scent I realize must be coming from the vice president. My gaze flickers to his wrists, wondering if he puts a little scent there in the mornings on the pulse points. I have a brief vision of the vice president getting ready for work, putting on that gold watch and buttoning up his shirt over some dark hair on his chest. I'd already noticed his long fingers and I can see delicate veins in his wrist as he raises it to run those fingers through his short hair. His presence, so close to me in this little room, is suddenly very physical. He's more than his office, he's...a man.

"Let me give you my personal phone number," he says. "Or about as personal as it gets for me. I can't text and rarely answer my own phone, but whoever answers, you can tell them to put me on the line."

I'm very aware that Kaylee is standing within earshot and the office door is open. Everything is moving so fast, but I need to keep this man on my side, if that's where he is. I still can't quite believe he wants to help me. "Thank you, Mr. Vice President. I appreciate the access. And the time. Your schedule must be tight."

"I have a fundraiser this evening that I need to get to, unfortunately." He swipes his hand through his hair again. I bet it's a habit when he's—what is he? Irritated? Tired? Frustrated?—something. I don't know him well enough to guess. "I hope your plans are more fun."

"I'll just be looking over the revised bill at home with my heels off over a glass of wine." The words are out before I think about them, too caught up in evaluating whether the whirlwind of the last few hours made real progress.

He pauses with his hand in his hair and his chin on his chest, his eyes turned up at me beneath dense eyelashes. I try to backpedal from the accidental intimacy. "Working, I mean. I'll be working. Like you. But from home."

"Well, I sincerely hope my ideas improve your evening," he says with a smile. "And that you do your reading some place warm. That room was chilly."

I run a quick visual check down my front again to make sure my body is behaving. "It was cold," I admit. "Don't worry, I have lots of blankets at home. Even a fuzzy onesie."

My mouth is like a snowball rolling downhill. I clench my jaw to remind myself to *shut up*.

He smiles briefly without looking up. "Sounds like a nice evening."

Then he nods once and his gaze shifts away, toward the door. Our meeting is over and I've accomplished nothing concrete with the time. I had a private, face-to-face with the vice president and used it to reveal a fondness for barefooted wine consumption and the mortifying ownership of something furry. I try to summon parting words to remind him I'm his counterpart in this process, not his secretary.

"Happy Valentine's Day," he adds, as he steps toward the door. The words throw me off and my mind goes blank. I cannot come up with anything to say that would assure the vice president I'm a competent professional who doesn't only think about getting out of uncomfortable clothes.

"Same to you, Mr. Vice President," I murmur. Then he's gone and I'm no longer cold. My entire body is flushed, a cross between embarrassment and adrenaline.

four

Alex

I HAND out what must be hundreds of roses, creating a lot of smiles from women of every age group at the fundraiser. I keep recycling the joke about having 300 dates for the evening to everyone who asks, the people who tease about my bachelor status and how I could be the bachelor on a reality TV show with these flowers. Better than joking that another man's wife is my date.

One of my sisters texted me—Sasha, the one who argues "this made-up Hallmark holiday should at least be equal opportunity torture"—and so did my mother, both telling me "happy Valentine's Day" and sending love. The texts were filtered through staff members to the point that they became generic well-wishes, even though I know my family meant well. None of it is quite the same as having someone of my own to give flowers to today.

Marguerite Clayton, wife of Dan, mother of Chelsea, is hovering nearby. She has fulfilled her duty to hang on my arm every moment I had one free tonight. She's the perfect hostess.

But her attitude is so possessive that it can't help but rub me the wrong way.

"Alex, dear, the ladies will understand if you don't hand out all the flowers yourself," she says, resting one bejeweled hand on my back. "As sweet as it is of you."

"Wanted to offer the personal touch," I say with a friendly smile, not wanting to admit I have ulterior motives for hiding behind the flowers during the reception part of the event. I step forward so that her hand falls off my back.

Dan Clayton swoops in. "I bet Alex's flowers open pocketbooks at least 10 percent wider tonight, if you know what I mean," he says, jostling me with an elbow to the side. I do know what he means and he's probably right. If nothing else, the Claytons definitely know money. "Could open up something else, too, not that you need any help in that area, eh, Alex?"

I offer a painful grimace that might pass for a smile. When I'm president—and I *will* be president—I'll have to deal with many more of these inane, mildly offensive conversations for the sake of raising money. Something to look forward to. My stomach churns.

"Oh, Dan," Marguerite says, her jewelry clacking as she gathers her arms across her chest. "You know we want Alex to save himself for Chelsea. Good heavens."

Fortunately, Chelsea, who is busy getting her MBA, can't hear her parents transparently scheming about her romantic prospects. Not that she and I haven't heard it all before to our faces. I keep grimace-smiling.

"Can't expect the most eligible man in the world to be a monk, Marguerite," Dan says, hooking both fingers in his belt loops like he's settling in for a conversation on the subject.

Since I'm not enjoying having my love life mapped out nearby, I decide the flowers are no longer working as a hideout. But first for some diplomacy. "Dan, Marguerite, both of you know Chelsea and I are just friends," I say, sliding in the hard truth before cushioning it with a compliment. "Your house makes such a wonderful event site. We couldn't have had such a successful evening without you. Now we'd all better stop ignoring our guests or we won't do your home justice." I give them both a friendly tap on the back with an open palm and move away, giving a subtle signal that draws an aide rushing to my side. I'm not proud of it, but when the situation warrants, yes, I'll use my staff as a distraction.

"Have we heard anything from Cindy Wight yet?" I ask in an undertone. I don't really need to know, but I want to. I'm curious whether she's at home, reading legislation with a glass of wine and thinking of me. Well, of my input. And if she's donned that oddly intriguing fuzzy onesie. I'd had an aide Google them before the event. Now I can't stop imagining her in one.

Most likely, she's cursing my name under her breath over what is, I'll admit inside my own head, a genuinely "toothless" bill draft. But I have more constituents to please than Cindy Wight does.

The aide fumbles in one of their pockets for my phone. "No, sir, I don't believe so."

"OK, thanks," I nod and move on. No distraction there, either, which means it must be time to face the crowd of tinkling silverware on hors d'oeuvres plates and crystal cocktail glasses.

Marguerite catches up with me, taking her place at my side. I smile at her, because I can't help but appreciate how seriously she takes her job even if she's in no way who I'd choose for the permanent position.

"Well, here we go," I say, and step forward to do my duty.

* * *

Cindy

I don't get out much. And when I do, I prefer dive bars or breweries where I'm rarely recognized out of my Capitol Hill power suits. Tonight, sitting at the circle-shaped bar at the Willard InterContinental hotel, I'm still wearing my outfit from the White House and my feet are killing me. So I order a stiff drink and prop them up against the metal bar running around the bottom of this bar stool so my weight is off my toes.

A short clip taken outside the White House that morning is playing on a loop on my phone, where I opened it after a member of my staff sent me the link. The captured moment is the one I pledged not to vote for the president's ticket if he doesn't move my direction. The video is embedded in a news piece discussing whether I can "radicalize" my party. My staff has warned me to never read the comments, but I take a peek—just a quick one, like looking for 10 seconds doesn't count.

The first comment calls me a "mouthy bitch who should go back to her hippie commune." Unsurprised, I close the browser window.

Kari doesn't make me wait long. She's a journalist, but she doesn't cover my beat, and she's only in the District every once in a while between assignments. She covers campaigns and events, not regular old politicking. But I try to surround myself with other women who are in the arena, Doing Things, no matter what the arena is. I trust Kari. She doesn't talk bullshit, unlike 99% of this town.

"Hi," she says, unwrapping her scarf. She's wearing jeans and boots, and I envy her intensely for a moment. Not only is she in comfortable clothes, she's the only person in this place not wearing a suit. She attracts eyes like a magnet, and then there are second glances when I'm recognized. I sit up straighter on the backless stool.

"You look tired," Kari says. See? No bullshit.

"I *am* tired," I reply. "That's my natural state these days."

A man in a cheap suit holding his cell phone in one hand is approaching us with an intent expression that makes me even more exhausted. I don't recognize him, but he has the vibe of a never-off-duty reporter. Kari gives him a little wave with the back of one hand and says, "Buzz off, Dennis. Girls only." She hoists herself up on the stool to my right. "I'm serious," she adds, when Dennis only pauses, gaze darting between me and my bodyguard. Then she turns her back to him.

I keep my eyes on Kari as she gestures for the bartender, but can see out of the corner of my eye that Dennis takes a picture of our backs with his cell phone before he turns away. "You know there will be a 'Spotted' column tomorrow implying we were on a date," I say, making a mental note to warn my staff.

"We both know you only care if it implies you were sleeping with me to gain power," Kari replies. She orders a "very dirty, very dry, very cold gin martini."

"Fair enough." Like most cishet women, I'd wished once or twice that I could be attracted elsewhere. Or at least interested in someone outside the industry. Male politicians and activists tend to be the worst at listening. But who else am I going to meet —a constituent?

"How did it go today?" she asks.

"Better than expected in some ways, worse in others." I lower my voice. "My party hates me."

Kari shrugs. "Better to be hated than forgotten."

Laughing, I raise my glass at her just in time for the bartender to put a stemmed glass in her hand. She clinks with me. "To never being comforting," I say.

"What do you want to hear, that the people who voted for you love you? Voters are fickle. I bet you get so much hate mail from people who loved you last year."

That's true, unfortunately. I don't read it, but I get the

reports. "If I can make progress in the next year, they'll come around again."

Kari nods. "That's true, but watch out," she says, taking a sip of the hazy liquid in her glass. "The vice president throws a big shadow. Be careful not to disappear."

The headlines from earlier are everywhere, and they all lead with the vice president. "VP to work with..." and "VP makes an ally." The only two stories to highlight *my* work today were the one making me out to be a radical and another piece headlined, "Ms. Wight Goes to the White House," that analyzed my outfit.

But it isn't Alexander Drake's shadow that flashes through my head when I think of our meeting. It's the way his eyes were steady on me when I spoke. And how he smelled spicy and sweet standing so close to me in that nook behind the White House briefing room. His presence much more real, much more masculine than a shadow.

"The only thing that matters is passing this bill," I say, talking to myself as much as Kari. Even if I'm voted out of office next year, I want to have used my time on Capitol Hill well. "I don't need the credit."

"It's ok to want something for yourself." Kari raises her eyebrows at me. "It's easy to get caught up in the work in this town. But you're a person, too."

Rejecting that instinctively, I shake my head. "It feels better to crusade for someone else." I don't say it, but it's also easier to ask for help on someone else's behalf. "But don't worry, I'm not about to end up in a campaign ad for the vice president."

Kari shrugs. "Famous last words."

Firmly, I shake my head. "I'm not here to be a stepping stone for some male politician with a generic platform. I'm here to do real work that changes life for everyday Americans."

She nods. "I know." Kari has known me since before I took

office. If she thought I'd caved—become establishment, something less than the activist who ran for office—she'd tell me.

"But," she continues, and I brace myself. "What if your work changes you? What if that's *part* of the work?"

I like being challenged, but usually, I'm the one posing philosophical questions that stump the listener. I frown at Kari.

"That's a rhetorical question," she adds with a smile. "Just remember, you're not only one thing, Cindy. You're an activist *and* you're new to the job. Sure, you came to shake things up, but maybe you still have a few things to learn. Stay open to different ways of doing things."

Taking the last sip of my Old Fashioned, I consider this. It sounds like the kind of advice I'd give someone else. Someone whose entire identity and life goals aren't wrapped up in achieving this one thing: Justice at the federal level. There is already too much compromise in politics. I won't be another weak link, another person who came to Congress promising one thing only to discover it's too hard to accomplish once I'm here. One achievement won't be enough for me.

And one man, even one of the most powerful ones in the country, won't stand in my way.

five

Cindy

I MIGHT HAVE to fit in with the boys at the White House, but in my own office, I make sure my majority-female staff know they're allowed to be as much women as they are professionals.

There's an emergency kit of tampons, Tide sticks and makeup wipes by the office door for easy use by anyone running to the bathroom down the hall. I gifted my staff—both people with me on the campaign and new hires after I was elected—with a sweatshirt, since the old Cannon office building is drafty. The temperature, I found once I'd moved in, is largely out of my control. And I have a generous telecommute policy that tends to most benefit the mothers working for me.

Every time I walk through my office suite, I'm pleased to see the photos of children on almost all the desks. And, of course, I'm not at all bothered by the lack of them on my own. I content myself—mostly—with always being the adopted auntie or with "momming" my staff when they need advice or to hear "go home, you're working too hard."

I'm only thinking a bit more about the missing pictures on

my desk this Wednesday morning because I'm about to turn 45, have been so far stalled on the lofty goals that got me elected, and have no personal life.

In lieu of dwelling yet again on those problems, I decide to take a muffin and coffee into my office after greeting my two front desk staffers and gift myself 15 minutes of my guilty pleasure: Reading gossip sites.

My favorite time-suck is no secret. I have *People, Entertainment Weekly* and *InStyle* magazines sent to my House office along with *Politico, Roll Call* and *The Hill.* If my brain needs a break once in a while—and it does—so do those of my staff. It also gives us all something common to talk about when we're sick of politics and policy. Nothing bonds a group of women quite like dissecting the inherent sexism of a "Who Wore it Better?" layout.

My chief of staff, Lizzie, wanders into my office while I'm reading and asks if I'd ever wear a cashmere bra, like the one being worn as a top layer on the front of this magazine.

"Sure," I say gamely, meaning it not at all. "Right on the House Floor. It would go with my American flag pin."

Lizzie grins. She's a Capitol Hill veteran I'd hired last year at the recommendation of my campaign manager, even though she's from Hawaii—about as different from Colorado as possible. "I know, I know. Washington is more sweater set buttoned all the way up than decolletage."

"You can't talk," I say. Lizzie, a petite round woman with stick-straight black hair, is wearing a light blue sweater set that matches her heels. I don't have to double check before I tease her; it's Lizzie's standard outfit.

"When in Rome," Lizzie shrugs. "I'd never dress like this when we go back to the home district. By the way, I noticed you were very matchy-matchy yesterday at the White House."

"What do you mean?" I close the browser window where I'd

been reading about one of the Hemsworths and open my schedule for the day. Back to business.

"Your red dress; the vice president's red tie? You looked nice together, almost like you planned it."

"We definitely didn't."

"Oh, I'm 100 percent sure I would be aware of that level of coordination between our office and the White House. I'm just saying, if the D.C. gossip were anything like the Hollywood gossip, the two of you would be on the cover of *US Weekly* by now."

Rolling my eyes at Lizzie, I scan for any empty places on my calendar. "Well then, good thing it isn't. The last thing I need is some kind of rumor starting about me sleeping my way to the top." I pause, uncertain I want to pursue this line of conversation about the vice president and romance. Lizzie raises her eyebrows, waiting. "Isn't he supposed to be dating the daughter of that lobbyist, anyway?"

"Chelsea Clayton. Unconfirmed. He's only ever been seen with both her and her father, so unless they have some kind of retro courtship going on, I think he's still very, very eligible."

"Alright, alright." I wave her off. We could go down the rabbit hole of the vice president's love life all morning, probably, and I might not hate it. He'd been...different from what I was expecting. More like a *man* than a political robot. But I don't need to share that observation with Lizzie. "Enough with the speculation, let's talk facts. The White House proposal is obviously a no-go. It's barely more progressive than no bill at all. But I have no idea how hard he's willing to fight to give us the bare minimum of what we want."

My chief of staff smiles. "I am pretty impressed you got him to agree to work with you directly. Maybe the VP will turn out to be your white knight."

I scrunch up my face at that vision. "The vice president is

hardly some Fabio sweeping in from a novel. More like the villain threatening our legislation with a fate worse than death."

"But it's likely to be a party-line vote and they can't pass it without your six votes. Unless they strike a bipartisan deal."

"Right, but the easiest route to bipartisan support is for the White House to promise to convert our bill into something milquetoast that would appeal to the other side. I need to figure out what the vice president *really* wants and whether I can give it to him. Don't say it!" I hold up a finger at Lizzie, who is grinning. I left myself wide open for a joke about giving Alex Drake *what he wants*. "You're quite unprofessional this morning."

"I'm sorry," Lizzie says, pressing her lips together to hide a smile. "I'll pull their past attempts at this type of legislation and have our team start analyzing it. The rest of the six also left you messages. And Representative Wilson gave an interview you're going to want to read. I emailed you."

Grimacing, I open my email. My tiny group of freshman colleagues—given the derivative name Freshman Six by the press—will be less than thrilled with my progress at the White House. At least two of them—Steven Wilson included—were seething with jealousy that I'd been the one invited to the White House to represent them. Unfairly chosen, they thought.

The article is essentially Wilson attempting to retake control. "We're happy to have a media darling on our side, but the real work of passing this legislation won't happen in front of the press or even at the White House," he told the *Post*, referring to *me* as the "darling" and implying *figurehead*.

But *I'm* the one with all the contacts and the political action committee set up specifically to support my campaign because of this issue. I'm the one who has been working on this issue for more than a decade. No one could have done better in that negotiation. I tell myself that in my moments of self-doubt.

The *Post* article describes our bill as one "that would finally piece together federally the patchwork of laws that have legalized marijuana at the state level" but fails to dig into the provisions within the bill: the two clauses under debate that would allow banks to handle money made by cannabis retail businesses, or wipe out the convictions of nonviolent offenders charged with nothing more than possession over the past decades of the so-called War on Drugs.

Even the other party has stopped putting up a fight against decriminalization due to its massive popularity. But the provisions contain the language that would move this country forward and help millions of people who fell victim to archaic laws. And Wilson didn't bother bringing them up.

I close my browser window. *More work to be done.*

"Thank you, I'll call them back. But let's reach out to the *Post* ourselves. And please have a call set up between me and the vice president." I dig in my purse, an oversize leather satchel that is perfect for access to thick stacks of files but easy to lose small items in. I pull out the business card the vice president's aide gave me. "This is supposed to be his private line, but I'm sure a secretary will pick up."

* * *

Alex

The president always tells me that I shouldn't have a favorite Secret Service agent—"it's about competence, not personality" —so, officially, I don't. But my dog's favorite agent is Ted, and it's hard to disagree with my dog's judgment.

It's Ted who hands me my ringing phone on Thursday night while we're at the park after sunset. "The call you expected," he says, his breath a puff of white in the air.

"Thank you." I hand Ted the ball I'm holding and take the phone. "This is Alex," I answer.

"Oh. Hi. Hi. Mr. Vice President?" The voice on the other end sounds young and nervous.

"Yes, this is me." I keep my voice neutral, reassuring. Like I'm fundraising.

"Sorry. I didn't expect you to answer."

I'm smiling, watching my dog's little legs churning as he runs after the ball Ted tossed for him. "But you called me."

"Yes, but..." Cindy pauses and I can hear her gather herself because her register is deeper, more formal, when she continues. "I apologize for the confusion. I expected an assistant."

"That's alright. I'm allowed to answer if the Secret Service expects the call. My assistants are, hopefully, all home eating or watching Netflix. Please excuse any noise on my end, though. I'm at the park with Thor."

There's a pause.

"My dog," I add.

"Yes," she says. "I, uh, follow Thor on Instagram."

I laugh. "You and 30 million other fans. Thor has more followers than I do."

"Well, Thor is pretty adorable."

"Unlike me?"

There's another pause and I wince, realizing I made it awkward. "I'm sorry, that was a joke."

"Of course. No. I mean. Yes. Your choodle is more adorable than you are, yes. I'm sorry, it's just a fact and I want you to know from the start that I'm an honest negotiator."

I laugh again, surprised and delighted at being teased; it happens so rarely. "Well, I appreciate that, congresswoman. Thank you."

"You're welcome."

She clears her throat and there's a hint of discomfort in it. I wonder if she's at home, perhaps curled up on a sofa with her shoes off. Perhaps in that onesie. It's a cold night. "I wanted to continue the conversation we started at the White House," she says. "I wondered if your end goal was bipartisan support."

"Hmm," I say. I can predict where she's going with this, but I'll let it play out. "Why would I need bipartisan support when I have the majority?"

"Because you're trying to bypass the progressives I represent."

It's a legitimate question about an option I've discussed with my staff. It's almost *too* perceptive from such a new lawmaker. Letting the pause grow, I kneel to pet Thor, who waits for me to toss the retrieved ball with the infinite patience of canines. I decide to pivot, trying to gain more information than I'm giving out.

"Are you saying you no longer want to work with me?" I don't expect her to say yes. Cindy Wight is new to having to balance more than one cause at a time, but this is her first piece of legislation and her pet project. I'm relying on her giving it everything she has.

"Absolutely not," she says. "We're still going to have to find a way to meet in the middle. I'm trying to feel out where that middle is."

"Interesting." I stand and throw the ball again.

"Interesting?" she repeats, her voice sharp.

"Interesting," I repeat, keeping my voice calm. Her anger is justified; I've been playing my cards close to the chest.

Maybe it's time to take a chance on her. It's quiet and my breath puffs in the air as I consider my options. It doesn't take long. "Listen, here's what I can do for you. I can have a series of conversations with the leadership in the Senate about what language I took out of the bill they think could gain support if we put it back in. Meanwhile, you poll your coalition in the House, and your outside supporters, on which provisions they want the most. Make sure they understand they can't have all of them. Then we can compare notes and start to find that middle ground you're talking about. So long as we're both honest about what we find."

"Honest?" She sounds skeptical. "A rarity in Washington."

"I'm willing to try if you are." I realize I'm asking for more than mere honesty; I'm asking for trust. It's a gamble, and one I'm not certain that I should be taking. But I have a good sense about Cindy Wight.

Besides, I have other options if Cindy doesn't come through on this.

The phone line remains silent for a long moment. "I wish you could meet my dog," I add suddenly, wondering if Thor would confirm my read on her. I've often wished I had Thor's innate sense of people in negotiations. "Thor usually wins people over much better than I can."

Cindy laughs gently in my ear. I imagine her, barefoot and bare-legged like she was in the conference room, drinking that glass of red wine she mentioned the other day. "I'd like that, but you're doing an OK job of it, Mr. Vice President."

I like the way she says my title. I'd told myself, when Tim and I were first elected, that I'd never get used to it. But I hear it so many times a day that it's hard to avoid taking for granted. It sounds fresh in her voice. For a moment, I stand surrounded by agents in a small patch of grass in the dark and remember what it was like to just be Alex Drake. And I remember how important it is to do this job for the few years I have it. It's a good reminder.

"Great, we agree, then," I say. "Shall we plan on checking in regularly over the next couple weeks?"

"I'd like that," she says. And as much as I want to do this job for the millions of people who chose our ticket, right then I also want to do it for her.

And I bet she didn't even vote for me.

six

Cindy

I CATCH up with the House Judiciary Chair, who for some reason willingly goes by Randy, in the tunnels between the House office building and the Capitol on the way to votes.

"Better take the subway, in those heels," he grunts at me instead of a greeting. He gestures at the little trolley running alongside us that the Capitol refers to as a subway.

"That's OK, I like to walk," I reply, smiling aggressively. "I wanted to chat with you about cannabis."

"Not in the middle of the day," Randy replies, and his entourage laughs with him.

I keep smiling, keeping pace in the musty corridor. The flags of all 50 states hang over us. When I'm frustrated, I like to watch for mine and imagine being in sunny, dry Colorado wearing hiking boots instead of in this humid swamp wearing heels. I search for it now.

"I'm meeting with various members to see which provision there's most interest in: Bank access or expungement of past records." The vice president told me to talk to my own coalition

—the other five votes I can promise in the House and the outside groups that support us. But what *I* want to know is how much support I have from House leadership.

He scowls. "I don't think you'll get either."

"Surely you, in your work, recognize the benefit of allowing banks to work with money from state-legal marijuana businesses." My heels click, click, click along on the concrete walkway as I hurry to keep up with his longer strides. Damn tight sheath dress shortening my stride. There's just no winning with women's business clothing.

He shakes his head. "Don't have the votes for it. Not with the midterms coming up."

Familiar anger rises within me. The midterms are almost a year away and already all I hear about. This is why politicians suck: They're constantly preoccupied with preserving their own positions. "Well, that's why I'm doing an informal poll. Party wisdom says we don't have the votes but I think more members are open to..."

"Can't pass the Senate. You should drop it," he advises me, not bothering to address me head-on.

I persist. "The banking provision would support the booming economy around the legal cannabis businesses. The White House might even support it if we can prove we have the votes here. Their support could push it through the Senate." I need the tiniest bit of leverage to show the vice president. Something that says House leadership understands how much voters want bold action and are willing to push further if he offers White House support.

"Pipe dream," Randy snaps, still walking. He's breathing heavily from the mild exertion. "Just because you young guns want the world to be some ideal place is no reason to destroy a bill the rest of us can get behind. This might be your first rodeo, young lady, but it's not mine. Take my word for it: The bill you wrote wants too much."

This is not the first time a man told me I *want too much* or called me *young lady*. Not *my* first rodeo, in other words. "Then how about expunging records? There are thousands of individuals in some states suffering from a criminal record for minor possession..."

He sighs and pauses in the hallway to focus on me for the first time. "The White House has too many legislative priorities of its own to back an unrealistic bill from some young upstart. You're deluding yourself if you think you can win their support for either of these provisions. Try aiming lower."

I chew on my back molars but don't lose my pleasant smile. Randy is reminding me he doesn't think I'm qualified for my job, as if it matters to me that I'm not doing it to *his* satisfaction. I'm here because I won a landslide election and I won based on my support for change. Letting my voters down is not an option, especially not because a Capitol Hill squatter decides I'm too green to understand the job.

No shame in requesting rescue, I decide, throwing a glance over my shoulder. If I stand here with Randy any longer, I may tear into his jowls with my neatly-trimmed nails.

Taking my cue, one of my aides rushes up to me from her trailing position and says quietly, "Ma'am. We need you."

"Thank you," I say. And thank God, I have an exit plan to keep from walking with this man one more second. "Excuse me, Randy."

Talking to Vice President Drake about what needed to be done, I'd almost forgotten how thankless it would be. His own process probably involves a lot of phone calls, scheduled for him by his staff, that members of his party would drop everything else to take. Lucky him. I don't have that kind of sway.

After voting, while members are milling around in the lower

chamber waiting for the count to close, I manage to spot the House Financial Services Chair, Adam. I weave through the wooden chairs and members clustered around chatting—including my five freshman allies, who I've been avoiding—to reach him. He holds up a hand to me before I open my mouth.

"Drop it right now, Madam Wight. I'm a no-go on the banking provision, and I speak for a number of members, as well."

An actual list would be helpful, but I hesitate before asking for one. "How did you know?" I ask, smiling like this is not bad news.

"I spoke to Randy. And I spoke to David."

Earlier, I worked on convincing David, the No. 2 in seniority from our party on his committee. After an hour, he'd agreed that banking seemed easier to spin than expunging millions of records nationwide.

"David is a no, as well," Adam says, tidying up papers in a folder and tucking it in a briefcase. Casually destroying my work without bothering to turn his head.

Instead of throwing a fit over being undermined like this, I say, "Adam, I'm doing my job. Voters overwhelmingly want action on this issue."

Adam smirks. "And the party wants to stay in power. What do you think takes priority?"

I wish I had a witness to this ridiculousness. He's like a parody of a congressman. "I'd like to think that serving our constituents takes precedence over winning the next election."

He snaps the briefcase closed. "Then you're even more naive than I thought." He smiles and walks away from me.

My nails dig into my palm from my clenched fist, but I try not to change expression because there are C-SPAN cameras in here.

I wander over to Steven Wilson and Jesus Pérez, members of

the Freshman Six, who will at least understand how infuriating that conversation was.

"Any updates?" asks Steven, the most nervous of our group, before I can fill them in.

"Looks like it's banking or expunging records right now," I say wearily.

Steven and Jesus exchange glances and waft judgment. "That's not good enough," Steven says. He means, *you're not doing good enough.* I'd like to watch *him* do better.

"I need help calling members to see which provision the majority would support," I tell him. Smart strategy says to keep them on my side by drafting them to do the work.

"You're literally calling everyone up and asking if they would vote for one or the other?" Jesus frowns.

"It shouldn't be a question of one or the other," Steven interrupts. "We need both."

I try to stay patient. We are not children, able to throw ourselves down on the floor of the chamber and scream until Congress gives us what we want. That would be so much easier. "I'd like both, too, but I'd rather have one than neither and I can't craft an argument until I know where we have support."

But neither of them agree to help. I'm playing a game from a losing position. Time for a new strategy. More firepower. Leverage.

I'm in a race with the vice president and I'm not going to be the one who can't deliver.

* * *

Alex

My sister, Sasha, is making baby-talk sounds at Thor while

holding his front legs off the ground and goo-gooing at his fluffy face.

"He hates that," I say mildly, from where I'm sitting on the loveseat trying to focus on marking up a working draft of the president's State of the Union speech. "He's a grown dog, not a little baby."

"But he looks like a little baby, doesn't he, yes he does, yes he does," Sasha says, and picks up the long-suffering Thor to walk over to me.

"I've got a PR plan for you to consider," she says, surveying my slump.

I raise one eyebrow at her, afraid to encourage this. My sister rarely visits, despite living closer than the rest of the family. When she does visit, she's a whirlwind blend of late-night New York City energy and youngest-daughter recklessness. She is *not* the Secret Service's favorite.

"You should unveil your wife-to-be at the State of the Union. When the president wants to slide in something controversial about greenhouse gas emissions, he can drop a line about your surprise honored guest and no one will ever notice." Sasha cocks a hip, scratching Thor's floppy ears.

"What wife-to-be would that be?"

"*Hypothetically*," she handily dismisses reality by waving her free hand. "Although I'm sure mom has one or two picked out for you. If you'd just get married already, you'd cement your place as the golden child of the family."

"I'm hoping to do that by becoming president, Sasha," I say drily. "Of course, pleasing our parents is the whole goal of my political career."

"Har har har," Sasha says. "You think you're joking, but I know it's true. You're as scared of Mom and Dad's opinion as the rest of us."

I close the folder, giving up on working while Sasha is here. I expect she'll go out tonight but she'll want me to feed her first. Standing and walking to the kitchen, I ask mildly, "You? Scared?"

It's a transparent attempt to avoid acknowledging her accusation that I'm still cowed by our parents' expectations for me. My parents groomed me to go into politics from the time I was old enough to read a biography of Franklin D. Roosevelt. I'd done my duty, and then some. And where our corporate-attorney father couldn't open doors, our socialite mother could. The sole obligation I have left to our parents is financial, for the extraordinary amount they have put into my many campaigns.

"Why do you think I live across the country from them?" Sasha retorts, following me. "Anyway, we're getting off track. This is about *you* pleasing the parents, not me."

"I think I'm doing all right," I reply. The fridge is full of pre-made food with printed labels. I push aside the guilt that I don't have time to cook for my little sister. I suspect she subsists on a lot of ramen, and not the good kind.

"Bet being that close to perfection and not quite there is killing you," Sasha teases.

Grimacing into the fridge, I let the cold air chill my irritation. She's right, is the problem. My life checks off every box our parents set for me except one. Why has that *one* box—marriage —been so hard?

"I don't want to marry just anybody," I say. I straighten up with a pre-made box of stir fry in one hand. "Even Mom and Dad understand that."

She laughs and finally releases Thor to scamper off to find a toy to comfort himself with after the humiliating baby talk. "Come on, what's the real issue." She sits down at the bar and frames her face with her hands, giving me an exaggerated listening expression.

The issue is that I have a very different idea of who I want to marry from our parents or my advisors, and trying to find a happy medium never works out. I don't want a "helpmate," as my mother would put it. Not someone who will cater to, rather than check, the innate arrogance and naked ambition that come with reaching this level of political power.

I want...the image of a woman who would tell me off while wearing a fuzzy onesie pops into my head.

"Let's talk about something else," I suggest, dismissing that image. "*Your* love life, for instance."

She waves me off. "Alex, I can give you all the dating app tips you want but I don't think they will help. I'm trying to imagine the vice president's profile." She pulls out her phone and pretends to swipe. "'Two truths and a lie: I'm vice president, I own a dog and I have a sense of humor.'" She grins.

"Har har har," I say, mimicking her tone from earlier. I pull out a wok. I wonder if Cindy Wight uses dating apps and what that's like for her. Dating as a congresswoman can't be much better than dating as vice president. "I can get a date if I want to, thank you."

"But would it be a date *you want*?"

I sigh the sigh of a big brother being tormented yet again. Time to turn the tables. "I'm surprised at you conforming to the heterosexual norm." I raise an eyebrow at my sister. "Who says I *want* to get married."

She smirks. "I do, because I know you. But OK, hypothetically, say it's only our parents and the political system putting pressure on you to conform. Aren't you lonely?"

"When do I have time to be lonely?" I reply, turning away to grab more oil. It's true that I have no spare time. I have a pile of books on my bedside table *and* in the bathroom that I'm never going to read and a very full schedule every day this week, including Sunday. It's also not even a little bit true that I can't fit in time to feel alone.

"I'm not going to dignify that with a response, but it's

obvious how much you want to escape this conversation, so I'm going to cut you a break. I hope you're talking to *somebody* about this. Or talking to anyone who doesn't work for you, period."

I open my mouth to say: *Sure, I talk to the president and the Secret Service*. But I close it again rather than keep deflecting. After all, she has a point.

"I appreciate your concern," I say, then hesitate. Perhaps I should give my sister a tidbit of something real in exchange for her real concern. "And if it helps...I have been talking to someone who doesn't work for me. Lately."

Her eyes widen. "Alex! Holding out on me!"

I shouldn't be turning some light banter with Cindy Wight into something worth talking about. Filled with regret, I hurriedly add, "It's nothing serious."

"I'll take something over nothing," Sasha says, a little smugly. "I knew there was hope for you yet, big brother."

I shake my head as I swirl the oil around the pan. But I hope my sister is right and that at least my conversations with Cindy Wight mean *something*.

seven

Cindy

THE FIRST THING I do every night when I arrive home to my tiny garden-level D.C. apartment is take off my shoes and work clothes. Tonight, I slam the front door and throw my shoes across the front room.

Lizzie forwarded me the email from the patronizing little twerp who works for the Speaker's office and who's acting as gatekeeper for bringing the bill to the Floor.

Maybe if I golfed, I'd be able to approach the Speaker directly. But no, I have to get in line with everybody else not in the Speaker's little cabal of favorites. And since her entire office knows it, they treat my staff like crap.

It infuriates me.

"Yes," I answer my work phone when it rings, expecting it to be Lizzie following up on the email.

"Hi, is this a bad time?"

I pause as I'm rolling the panty hose I've learned to wear down one leg. I know that deep voice. "Hi. Mr. Vice President. Hello."

How is he this good at catching me off guard? I pride myself on my poise and yet here I stand, balancing on one leg with my underwear showing while I talk to the second most powerful man in the world.

"Hello. I wanted to call and check in. But I didn't schedule in advance, so if you're busy…"

"No, no. Please." I sit on the end of my bed. "This is fine. Your time is valuable."

I'd swear I can hear him smile, one of those toothy ones he gives in campaign ads. "Hardly. You're actually writing laws over there. Everything on my schedule today consisted of important things the president was doing and 'the vice president will also attend.' I'm a human asterisk."

I smile back, biting my lip and absently rubbing the sole of my foot, which is slightly swollen. Chasing down men in tunnels today got to me. "It's tough being the understudy. You have to be just as prepared with less credit."

"Tell me about it." His voice is warm on the other end of the phone, self-deprecating but not bitter.

Standing and holding the cell phone between my shoulder and ear, I unhook my skirt and let it drop to the floor. "I was an understudy multiple times in college."

"Oh? Did you study theater?"

"PoliSci major, theater minor, believe it or not. I was very dramatic."

"*Was?*"

It's a surprisingly insightful comment. I laugh. "OK, Mr. Vice President, I don't think you know me well enough to tease."

"I'm sorry, congresswoman." Ironed free of any humor, his voice says he takes me seriously.

In the mirror on the back of my closet door, I'm flushed and half naked. This conversation is unfocused, but I'm tired. "No,

I'm sorry. I'm just...I'm frankly tired of talking about politics after a long week and I've distracted us."

"We don't have to talk about politics," he says immediately. Then we both pause a beat while I realize I *want* that—a conversation about something other than the bill we should be talking about—and he adds, "As hard as that is to imagine in Washington. Or, we can also reschedule this conversation."

I hang up my silk shirt and stand in bra and panties. The air sliding across my skin might be his eyes, like he's in the room with me. "Perhaps we can do both," I suggest. "You can tell me about your dog for now and we can reschedule the political part for later."

His chuckle brushes intimately against my ear. "You're only interested in Thor, I knew it."

I can't help smiling wider. Bantering with this man is my biggest win today.

"I'm hoping for some exclusive content." I unhook my bra, trying not to sigh in relief at dropping the underwire. I keep talking while I shimmy out of my thong and put on briefs and a t-shirt, balancing the phone on one shoulder. "But I guess you can't text me any pics."

"No, but if you play your cards right, my assistant can."

"Just tell me what I've got to do, Mr. Vice President." I stop, eyes widening at my own reflection. Why am I implying some kind of pay-for-play relationship?

He's laughing. "Work a mention of Thor's Instagram into your next media interview. He loves the free publicity."

Thank God, he's going to keep it light. I pull on my fuzzy robe. "I've always wondered if his name was Thor when you got him or you picked it."

"Well, my mother gave him to me when I was still in the Senate. She said I needed company but I think she hoped he would get me a date. My dad called him a sissy dog and I wanted to defend his honor. Or defend my mother's choice, one or the other."

I'm trying not to be judgy, but his dad sounds like someone I wouldn't like. This anecdote alone reminds me of my own dad, who always had his own way of putting my mom in what he thought of as *her place*. "Alexander Hamilton Drake, defender of women," I say, walking out to the kitchen. "I think we've found your next campaign slogan."

"As president, I pledge to provide as many cute puppy pics as possible..." he drawls, slipping into a lazy voice.

"As president?" I cut in. "Very revealing, sir."

"I can neither confirm nor deny," he recites, his voice dry. It's the answer he gives when the press asks him if he plans to run in three years. "I am focused on the issues of the current administration," he repeats by rote. I'm smiling, again, into the phone. It's almost like we're friends—the type of connection I haven't made with anyone so far in Washington. Unless you count my staff, but I'm paying them.

I pour myself a large glass of Malbec. I have a lot of questions about Alex Drake's plans, but I don't want to put him back on guard. Backstabbing is too common in Washington for me to raise suspicions for the sake of my curiosity.

"Are you drinking wine?" he asks, as I'm raising the glass to my lips.

"I am," I say. "Are you?"

"No, I'm out in the park again."

"Do you always call me while you're alone and walking your dog?" It doesn't sound right the minute I say it. Why am I suddenly thinking about his penis? I'm as bad as Lizzie.

Putting my wine down, I sit on my lone kitchen stool, the one I use to eat alone when I'm not at some networking event. I pinch the bridge of my nose between my fingers as the line between us goes quiet again.

"Well," he says. *Is he going to tease me again?* I hold my breath and cross my legs because of an unexpected tingle there. "I don't *always* anything with you. Walking Thor is how I try to relax, which means I don't usually have a lot of calls scheduled."

"I should let you go then." I tap my fingers on the bottom of my wine glass. I'm embarrassed I'm taking up this man's time for a conversation with no real point to it. Again. But. I don't *want* to let him go. This conversation makes me feel like myself again after a long day.

"No," he says quickly. "No, I just meant to say...I *can* always call you while I'm walking Thor. If this time is convenient for you."

I shut my open mouth. My fingers tremble as I pick up my glass. I take a sip of my wine and try to decide how to answer. The answer that doesn't even cross my mind is *no.*

"To talk about the legislation," he adds, his voice a little more stiff. "As we progress."

"That'd be quite helpful," I say. I hear how formal it sounds and slap my own forehead with my free hand. I can't stop. "This is a priority for me, as you know. I appreciate you giving me precedence. *It,*" I amend. "Giving it precedence."

"Of course," he says softly. "Well, I should let you go. My dog is impatient for my attention. But we'll talk soon."

"Thank you. Goodnight, Mr. Vice President."

"Goodnight, Congresswoman Wight." His tone is warm. My fingers tingle and I rush to hang up before I drop the phone.

I take another long sip of wine. I'm not sure what the vice president had on his mind during that conversation, but I know where I *thought* he was going, because my instincts—thanks to a long history of disappointed hopes—freaked out. I have to trust Alexander Drake to some extent to work with him. But just because I like him doesn't mean he's not plotting to stab me in the back. Trusting him on a personal level isn't going to happen.

Not in this town. Not when we represent starkly different agendas.

And not when I know better than anyone not to trust a politician.

* * *

Alex

I keep waving at the applauding crowd until the signal from an aide that I can step off stage. I'm exhausted. It's 9 p.m. in Los Angeles but it's midnight on the East Coast and I still have to fly back tonight.

"Great job," my aide Dan tells me as we hurry through the back of the hotel to the limo, following Secret Service's direction to cut through a quiet back hallway. The deep carpet silences the passage of a dozen men, me at their center.

"Lacking some energy tonight." I can't help critiquing my performance.

It took a while as a politician for me to believe nobody noticed when I gave the same stump speech at every appearance. For many people, these events are their sole in-person exposure to me and my message. Often, these days, my aides fill in the blanks for my location and the group I'm speaking to, and the rest I deliver on autopilot.

It worries me that I'm so worn out in the middle of a non-campaign year. I've got around a decade of robust campaigning ahead of me if I want to be president. And I *do* want to be president. My well of ambition and motivation used to run a lot deeper.

These days, I long for some sameness in my day. Hitting the gym. Walking Thor at night. Flirting with Cindy Wight.

There was no chance to call her today. I check my watch as

the streets of LA pass by outside the reinforced SUV window. *What time did she go to bed? Did she wonder about me while she drank her evening glass of wine?*

Probably not.

"You have an email from your mother," Dan says, holding up my phone.

"Does it say I look tired?" I ask, leaning my head back against the seat.

"It says..." Dan pauses. "I'm sorry, sir, it says your father went to see the doctor last week and didn't want to tell you, but it's nothing too serious. She says he was having stomach pain and it's an ulcer."

I close my eyes, resting on the headrest. My father is a named partner at his law firm and could have retired long ago. "He works too much."

"Must run in the family," Dan suggests.

Nodding, I don't bother opening my eyes. "Oh, it does." Growing up, I heard nothing but "you have to work hard to provide for your family like a man" and, worse, "your wife shouldn't have to work a day of her life after she marries you." It's hard to break free.

"Did Mom say anything else?" I ask Dan.

"She asks if you are dating anyone. There's a girl she wants you to meet next time you come home to visit?"

She must not be *too* worried about Dad, then. "If only my mother would accept that I'm an old maid." I hold up my hand to halt any response. "And I don't want to talk about my low chances of becoming president as a bachelor. Not tonight."

"Of course, sir. Why don't you go ahead and sleep. We have some State of the Union matters to go over but we can always talk on Air Force Two."

I tip my head forward from the chin, with effort, to meet Dan's eyes. "Unless there's a nuclear emergency, I don't want to talk about anything that requires decisions until morning, Dan. Consider yourself off duty."

"Yes, sir. Good night, sir." Dan returns his gaze to his phone and I shrug and put my head back on the seat. I can't convince my people to rest but I can at least set an example.

I drift off thinking it'd be nice to have someone who doesn't work for me to tell good night.

eight

Cindy

I'VE NEVER BEEN to the White House gym, located in the residence on the third floor, but it is a lot like any other gym except clean and empty. A Secret Service agent and one of the vice president's aides stand by the outside door. It's a little claustrophobic but not isolated.

"Thank you so much for multitasking. I hope we have everything you need." Alexander Drake gestures around the room.

It's awkward talking to the vice president face-to-face again after days of phone calls. It could be because we're both wearing exercise clothes and I miss my business armor.

He'd asked if I wanted to join him for a workout while we talked, citing how slammed his schedule was ahead of the State of the Union, and it seemed like a good idea at the time. Endorphins can only improve politics, he'd said, and suggested we lift weights. I'd guessed the gym at the White House would be a lot nicer than the gym in Rayburn.

But then I'd spent an hour before coming trying on combinations of yoga pants and sports bras and shorts and tank tops. Out of desperation and at the last minute, I ended up wearing a pair of sleek capris and a slouchy t-shirt that showed just a hint of my strappy bra. Going informal was the right call, because when I arrived this morning, I found the vice president wearing basketball shorts and an "ACLI Capital Challenge" T-shirt.

Somehow, even a casual vice president can't put me at ease while in the White House.

"This is great," I say, hearing myself sound a little too peppy to be normal. This man brings out my insecurities. "I usually work out in the House gym, where it's me and a bunch of male freshmen representatives. Do you work out here often?"

"No, it's much more the president's domain," he says. "Sometimes I go work out with old colleagues in the Senate gym in the Russell building. But fortunately I'm pretty friendly with the boss here, too. Unlike the last administration, I hear."

"Really?" My gossip-loving ears perk up. "That wasn't all public perception?"

He shrugs. "The president-VP relationship seems like a marriage. Sometimes the reasons you get together end up being the reasons you can't stand each other. Not that I'd know anything about marriage," he adds, and starts fiddling with his sports watch. "Do you want to warm up on the bikes?" He hops on one and I start adjusting the seat on the one next to it.

"So what habits do you have that bug the president, now that you've been together five years?" I ask, once I start pedaling. It should be a safe enough question; I'm not asking for any privileged information. My appetite is for information on what this man is like behind the scenes.

He smiles wryly. "Don't tell anyone, but I made him wait overnight to accept his VP offer."

"So you don't commit easily?" I take my hands off the handlebars to tighten my ponytail.

He starts pedaling harder. "Well, he told me he appreciated

that I had a measured response. But you'd have to ask him if he still feels that way."

I notice he slid out of admitting to any personal fault, but let it go. After a few minutes of silence aside from our breath, I decide that even if I'm the guest, I need to take some control of the situation. "I keep my warm up to a few minutes if I'm lifting," I say.

He smiles, fiddling with his monitor. "Lead the way."

Refusing a challenge is not in my repertoire. He probably assumes I don't know my way around a weight room, but I've been lifting since I was 16 and my dad told me it would help my downhill skiing. Over the last year, I've been on the road a lot for work, and free weights at hotel gyms or bodyweight exercises in my room are often the one workout I can wedge into my schedule. As I age, the benefits have changed.

"This is the nicest-smelling gym I've ever been in," I say, as he follows me over to the squat rack. A tingly sensation tells me he's looking at my butt in these tight pants, but I must be paranoid. The vice president wouldn't—would he?

"You sure you don't want to use the Smith machine?" he asks.

I give him a sharp glance, because the Smith machine is like a crutch for squats. He's smirking. "Cute," I say, because it is. I like that we have jokes between us. His expression is good-natured. My fingers tingle with the impulse to reach out and poke his flat abdomen. *Inappropriate. Even between friends. Are we friends?*

He interrupts my racing and far-too-friendly thoughts. "Well, I've seen you bluff before and you're good at it. I just wanted to assure you, you don't have to injure yourself to impress me."

I start the process of lowering the bar on the machine, which is obviously used by taller men. "Got it. And no problem, I only worry about impressing you when you're wearing a suit." A blatant lie.

He laughs, brushing off his T-shirt. "I outpaced multiple members of Congress and several very fit members of the press in this race, thank you. It deserves some respect even if it is about to be soaked with sweat."

"Don't worry, I'm used to being surrounded by sweaty men." I pause to wince at myself. Again with the foot-in-mouth disease around this man.

"You're sort of the majority leader of unintended innuendo, aren't you," the vice president says, turning on a floor fan that feels good against the heat in my face. I can't help but smile a little at his teasing.

"Around you, I am, yes," I admit, concentrating on putting the bar back on the rack. Turning around, I position myself to do some warm-up squats with the unweighted bar behind my neck.

He walks over to the free weights and starts warming up his rotator cuff on both shoulders. "Every time I see you, you are surrounded by men."

"That's politics for you," I say. I would *love* to enter a room on Capitol Hill, just once, to find it full of women. It's never happened.

"You're good at playing the game, but it must be tough sometimes when all the rules are against you."

He's not wrong, but there's so much more to it. For some reason, I want to vent to him. I want to tell him about the casual sexism, the undermining, the dismissal of my expertise. About the members of my own party undermining my mission to pass this bill. About my dreams of changing things by bringing in more, new, diverse blood.

He's concentrating on positioning for seated arm curls now, so he doesn't notice my gazing at him. He could be any attractive guy at the gym right now and not one of the most important men in the world.

"It is tough. Sometimes," I agree, deciding to err on the side of safety by not opening up. I put the bar back and start clamping disc weights on it. "How about for you?"

He glances up, but I've turned back to my squats so he doesn't catch me looking. "Sometimes," he agrees. "I get tired."

I exhale hard on the way up from a back squat. "Thor helps you relax?"

"He does," he says. "I highly recommend a pet. Of course, I have a lot of help taking care of mine when I can't make it home during the day."

His biceps flex as he curls them. His muscles are not huge—they don't look like he spends hours every day in this gym—but they look like they can pick up what they need to. They could pick me up, for instance. Not that I'm thinking about that. Much.

Trying to stay concentrated on the squats as I respond to him, I make sure to keep breathing. "That does help. I'm sure my schedule is no more dependable than yours."

"Yours might be worse than mine. All those late-night votes that you have to do in person." He flashes a smile. Clearly having an easier time than me at being friendly.

I nod, pausing to regain my breath between sets, my chest heaving. "Not my favorite part of the job. My least favorite part of *your* job would be not having my own phone."

He huffs and drops the 35-lb. dumbbell he's using. "I also can't drive or go anywhere on my own. But technically, I have my own phone, it's just a 'dumb' phone. No SMS, no Internet. I can basically call my mom and that's it."

"How old-fashioned," I murmur, watching him stand to his 6-foot-plus height and shake out his arms. I'm just hormonal or something, possibly from not having any sex in...well, I stopped counting after a year. This isn't flirting; it's a work meeting. The vice president probably does meetings like this all the time with members of Congress. We aren't alone; his aide and security detail are keeping us under watchful eyes from the door.

"At least I'm an old-fashioned kind of guy, so I guess it works." He shrugs. "I don't have anything like your star power online, anyway. Don't you have more followers on social media than the White House?"

I make a face. An entire staffer is now dedicated to running my social media accounts. It became too much for my press secretary and interns.

"Only because of the rally I led to the White House last year. Liberation from the war on drugs resonates with a wide range of people, from those affected by cancer to those involved with the criminal justice system. But I'm pretty sure I'm too old to be a true social media influencer." I smile back, and then the discomfort eases in. It's uncomfortable getting swept up in this man's smiles and banter. It could mean losing track of my goals, the whole reason those people on social media follow me and my voters sent me to Washington. I can't do that. I won't let myself.

"Not that I'm not enjoying this workout but didn't I come over to talk about the bill?" I ask, turning away from him.

"Back to business, huh," he says, and there's a note of disappointment in his voice. I side-eye him, but he's already moving on. He picks up the next heaviest set of dumbbells.

"Everybody I've talked to thinks the time is right for progressive action," I say, lying through my teeth. The vice president previously admired my ability to bluff, so I shove aside the guilt.

"But would they accept a small step toward the ideal?" He looks up at me over the weight he's curling. It's such an establishment answer and makes him sound like those men on Capitol Hill who care more about keeping their power than using it.

"I think you know the answer to that." My voice sounds stiff.

He watches me. He might admire *my* poker face, but his is masterful. "Did you ask them? Did you ask them if they'd rather have some progress than none at all?"

I've avoided my freshmen allies all week, only acknowledging their questions by email with lines like "too soon to tell."

I haven't tried talking to my contacts in Cannabis Now or the Reverse the War on Drugs PAC, the outside groups who helped me fundraise as a candidate well beyond my district and throughout the country based on this one issue. They're composed of people with lives negatively impacted by the "War on Drugs." Due to harsh felony laws lingering in parts of the country, some of them could no longer vote, but they were activists by proxy and by their support of me. I knew they would want the whole bill, the one I'd written with their input, not some watered-down version.

It's a valid question. I'm speaking for people I *haven't* asked. Frustrated, I start doing my last set of squats too quickly and feel my knee tweak a bit. Paying attention, I slow down and reposition myself.

"Do you need a spot for that?" he asks, watching.

"I'm fine." I never use a spotter. I don't lift as heavy as I could because I refuse to ask for help. Why depend on somebody when they're not going to be there next time?

"They're not interested in only taking a bite when it's going to look like they caved," I continue, pivoting back to business, forcing it out between breaths.

He nods, still watching me rather than continuing his curls. "That's what I expected," he admits.

I finish my set and re-rack the bar. Grabbing my small towel, I use it to wipe the sweat off my forehead. "Look, I get it. I've been pushing decriminalization for years and it's barely becoming nationally popular enough to force the establishment to accept it without fearing they're going to get primaried next cycle. But the Senate is full of conservatives, no matter what party they're in. They're not going to go all the way unless you tell them to."

"Let's not throw the baby out with the bathwater," he says, standing and putting his weights back. It's an evasion, not a real answer. "I am confident we can come up with a compromise."

"Save it for the cameras." I put the towel over my face, hearing how harsh that came out. I'm his *guest*. "I'm sorry. I didn't mean that."

"I strongly suspect what you say when you're mad is your uninhibited brain talking." His words could be a jab—they would be from my mother, chiding me for ever making a decision based on emotion—so I lower my towel to see. He's smiling at me.

"Well, maybe," I say. "But it's not you. It's the politico-speak. I hate it. I pledged to never be that politician and yet here I am, a year in and I hear it creeping into my speech. Don't you get tired of never saying anything real?"

He nods, his eyes not leaving mine. "I do."

I sense he's going to say something next, something real. I'm both glued to his mouth and terrified to keep staring, which is why I'm relieved when someone else enters the room, someone tall with short, black hair.

The vice president stands immediately. "Madam First Lady. I'm sorry, we-"

"Oh, don't worry, I knew you were in here." Anita Meyer waves him off, walking toward us. "I should apologize for interrupting *you*."

"Ma'am, this is Congresswoman Cindy Wight." The vice president stands near enough that I can feel his body heat, heightened from working out.

I have an odd urge to curtsy to the woman in front of me that

I firmly reject. I hold out my hand. "Sorry, First Lady Meyer. I may be a little sweaty."

"If you're not, you're doing it wrong." The first lady smiles and shakes my hand, slightly flexing her famously toned biceps. She's taller up close than I'd thought—a tall woman cursed to never wear high heels next to her shorter husband—and her angled bob looks sharper in person, but even this close she could be 10 years younger than her husband. "When I heard Alex had a woman in here, I came to see for myself." She raises her eyebrows.

The vice president shifts, looking at his feet. "Just a convenient business meeting, Anita. We're working on the cannabis bill together."

"Very convenient," the first lady agrees. "...location," she adds with a straight face.

I'm hot all over. I'm not sure if I should deny the insinuation flat-out or be flattered. What I absolutely, positively cannot do is get angry with *the first lady*, even for thinking the only reason for me to have face-time with the vice president is to sleep with him. It's my own fault for agreeing to an informal meeting.

"Anita," the vice president says, gently but with an edge of warning in it. Confronting the innuendo before I have to. "The congresswoman is doing me a favor by multitasking."

The first lady's smile shifts and then when she turns to me, the insinuation has drained from her face. "Of course, congresswoman. Forgive me for teasing Alex. The president and I are always trying to convince him to get out more."

The vice president coughs. "Alex is *busy*," he says, and coughs again, pointedly.

He's saved me again, from a joke that could become a rumor or someone dismissing me as something less than I am. It's becoming a habit of his. I smile at him, losing the edge of anger, and if my expression feels a little too close to fondness, I'll let it go this once. The first lady keeps her attention on me as I shrug. "I'm sure it's a hazard of the job."

"Well, I'd hate to tell you how little *I* get out for fun, and I'm not even the one who got elected." The first lady smiles. "Are the two of you just starting? I can come back later. I don't want to interrupt your negotiations."

The vice president defers to me, like he often does at opportune moments.

"We're at a bit of a stalemate," I say. "You're not interrupting."

"Actually, I think Cindy needs a spotter and she won't let me do it," Alex says, picking up 45 lb. weights and sitting back down on his bench with his back to both of us.

I blink and find myself staring back at Anita Meyer, who is waiting expectantly. There's no polite way to demure. And so I cave and let the first lady of the United States spot me on the bench press.

* * *

Alex

The president greets me with, "So I heard you had a girl in the White House."

"I did not *have* a *girl*." I grimace, imagining how Cindy Wight would react to that phrase. "The girl is a congress*woman* and nothing involving *having* went on. It wasn't a date."

"Anita seems to think you wanted it to be one." President Tim Meyer sits down and picks up his glass of water. He's an ex-footballer whose current paunch serves to make him more imposing. "But no need for quibbling over the definition of a word, this isn't an impeachment trial."

I grin and sit down across from the president. "Not yet."

Tim raises his glass at me. "Don't even joke."

We're in the small private dining room off the Oval Office for our weekly lunch, which serves as our project check-in and information download. Anita Meyer teasingly calls it our "coffee klatsch."

The menu today involves something with tenderloin. I always eat well when I'm with the president.

"Besides, you're the last person I would expect to be impeached over a sexual scandal, Alex." Tim unfolds his napkin and nods at the White House staff waiting to begin service.

"I'm offended, Mr. President. Are you referring to my complete lack of sexual activity?"

My familial relationship with the president is rare. I've heard plenty of stories about friction at the top of the presidential ticket, and *Veep* dramatized how easy it is to sideline a VP who falls out of favor with POTUS. The fact that Tim and I are friends is rare in Washington, a town where the major industry is power, not politics.

"I would never refer to your sex life, not even in my White House Correspondents' Dinner speech—which is one of the items on our agenda today."

"Fancy that." I glance at the paper agenda on the table between us. Tim is good at never getting completely off track. His day is planned in 15-minute increments. Aimless small talk doesn't fit. But somehow he always reserves enough time to tease me.

"There's a joke in the latest draft of my speech at your expense and I wanted to run it by you first. It's tame, but I don't know what your polling is telling you about your image."

"I appreciate that. And my polling is telling me I need a wife."

Tim smiles. He thanks the staffer who put down our salads and asks for an iced tea. "There's more reasons than image to get you a wife, friend."

"We can't all find Anitas."

"You know..." Tim leans back. He's about to dish out some annoyingly wise advice. "The reason I don't think you'll ever end up in a sex scandal is because of how careful you are to never be alone with a woman. Maybe too careful, considering I would never have ended up with Anita with that kind of rulebook."

"Well...you weren't president when you ended up with Anita." I give Tim a long gaze, waiting for him to take in our surroundings—the heavy wood, the oil paintings, the center-piece on the table for an ostensibly casual lunch—and remember how *not* casual the White House is.

"True. It must be hard to date while in this office."

"Try impossible," I mumble, picking up a cucumber between two of my fingers.

"What about that woman you took to the State Dinner with the French?"

"She took her insight from that dinner straight to Podesta or one of those other lobbying firms, I can't remember which one. She did the Washington thing, in other words." I shrug. "She wasn't interested in me."

"That's right." Tim scowls. "I can blacklist her if you want."

"You already offered and I still say no. If we blacklisted every date I ever had...well."

"It would be a short list?" Tim grins. He pushes his uneaten salad away. Tim is more of a meat-and-potatoes guy, to Anita's chagrin. "Alright, I suppose we should talk shop. What's going on with that marijuana legislation?"

"The congresswoman and I..."

"You still call her congresswoman?" Tim interrupts. He moves his hands off the table as the staff clear our salad plates and bring in steak sandwiches.

"Of course."

Tim shakes his head. "No wonder you're still single. OK, go on."

I grimace but continue. "I doubt we're going to hit her deadline. The 4/20 thing."

"Wait, did she really say 4/20?" Tim laughs. "I always appreciate a woman with a sense of humor."

That makes me roll my eyes. The connection between cannabis and 4/20 has always seemed like 13-year-old humor to me, but maybe I need to partake of the substance more and learn how to chill. As a teenager in California where it was omnipresent, I'd passed on weed more often than accepting. It wasn't worth the risk.

Focused on my parents' plans for my future, I never spent much time with the people Cindy talks about supporting her campaign. Maybe that was a mistake, now that I'm in a position to speak for them and don't know what they have to say.

"You're trying to get under my skin and it won't work," I tell Tim. "This is a professional relationship."

"Alex, not everything you do has to have a whole plan to back it up." Tim starts cutting into his large sandwich with a knife and fork.

I pause with my hands on my own silverware, because I'm literally the "backup plan" for this office. "Easy for you to say, Mr. *President of the United States*."

An aide is hovering by the Secret Service agent at the door, holding a file folder. It's surprising that we haven't been interrupted until now. Must be a slow day. Tim gestures her over as he's wiping his hands on his napkin.

Tim reads the document as I keep eating my fries. He shovels a final bite into his mouth and stands up. "OK, I've got to go. We'll continue this later. Oh-" He pauses. "Think about whether we want to add a mention of the marijuana legislation to the

State of the Union." He holds up his hands. "It's still your project. But that might build some momentum. We can talk about it."

Tim exits back into the Oval. I'm content to be briefed later on whatever called him away.

As I finish my lunch alone, I wonder if it's true I need to learn to compromise in my personal life the way I do when I'm making a deal. The marijuana legislation isn't "my" project, for example. It's a win I'm going to take with me to my next campaign, but only if it sits on a longer list of them. Cannabis can't be my only thing. That's one reason I need Cindy to remain the face of the issue. Coalition-building is what I need to be known for, not drugs.

If Cindy knew my thoughts, she'd get that snap in her eyes and tell me something like, "People in prison for minor drug possession didn't want that to be the only thing they were known for, either." But I can't let my goals be clouded by emotion.

All of politics is leverage and bargaining and making promises you might or might not keep. There's Tim's suggestion about using the State of the Union to goose the cannabis legislation. It might mean hitting the April 20 deadline, but there are risks. Mainly, it's likely to solidify opposition and characterize Cindy as a traitor to her coalition for relying on our support. But it's also bad for me, because this is supposed to be *my* big legislative win, not the president's. I'm going to need this for my future campaign ads.

I walk back across the short driveway to the Eisenhower executive office building. I have offices in the west wing of the White House, but I do most of my work at EEOB because I prefer my own space and the chance to walk back and forth on campus. It's a chilly February day but I like the fresh air.

Watching my parents operate, growing up, I identified the assumption that my mother would always support my dad's work outside the home and Dad would support Mom with money. As if the heiress to an almond fortune needed it. That traditional relationship dynamic never appealed to me. But I struggled to find a counter-example.

I'd tried a few times, gotten close with a few women, but then suddenly I was 40, unmarried, about to become the first bachelor vice president of the United States, and still hadn't figured out relationships.

Over the last few years, I've tried to reverse engineer one like Anita and Tim's but still can't quite figure out how they make it work. I recognize what I want when I see it, but I don't quite understand how to get there.

"Deena," I say, catching one of my aides as I walk into the office suite. "Can you send Representative Cindy Wight an invitation to the Correspondents' Dinner? And if there's a spot at my table, see about giving it to her."

"Sure, Mr. Vice President," Deena says, taking a note. "You know that's April 15th?"

Sighing, I nod. "Consolation prize for not making her deadline on the 20th."

I run a hand through my hair. Either because it's Washington or because I'm cursed, there's no avoiding transactions in any of my relationships.

Cindy

SO THIS IS 45.

This number is different, somehow making it impossible to deny that my life is half over. The "set up" part of a lifetime is behind me. At this point, my life is established. It's what it's going to be.

If I'm effective enough to win reelection, I'll be splitting my time 50/50 between campaigning and governing, even if I run for another office. I'll have security people following me around forever, whether event-based like it is now or full-time. I'll get hate mail forever.

Considering how impossible it is to date under those circumstances, I'll be single forever.

OK, 45 is a little morose and fatalistic so far.

At least I'm home. Unlike some members of Congress who would live in Washington full-time if they could, I love going back to Colorado. The sun comes out more often than in Washington, the mountains are arguably more beautiful than monuments, and some of my favorite members of my team are based here.

My parents live on the western slope, so I drive the hour and a half from Denver to go see them on Saturday, making work calls whenever I have reception. I don't mind the drive; the scenery is beautiful and the roads are manageable since I only rent vehicles with big engines and all-wheel drive when I'm in my home state.

My parents don't come down to Denver to see me when I'm in town unless my visits coincide with a supply run to Costco.

Huge rifts of snow are piled up along the highway but the roads are clear, the snow-capped mountains are ahead of me, and I give up on work and start listening to an NPR podcast.

Mom and Dad are loading the car when I arrive. My mom, a wiry woman with the same build as me and the same dark hair but streaked with gray, walks out the front door of their two-story house with an extra snow jacket as I park on the street and walk up. We hug.

"Your father wants to go snowshoeing," Mom says, like she had no say in the adventure. She's already trying to force me into the heavier coat. "Do you want to come?"

I appreciate that my parents are fit and stay active, but I wish that just for once they scheduled around me, rather than scheduling me around their busy retired life. I have no choice but to join them now if I want to see them at all. "Sure," I say.

"John, she's coming, make a little room," my mom calls, turning to the vehicle. Dad, also wiry and gray but with a gut from too much Colorado craft beer, waves.

My mom looks back at me. "Dear," she says. A comment about my appearance is coming. She puts one hand to my forehead and pushes her fingers into the roots of my hair. "You need a little touch up here. More than a bit of gray showing."

I will never be too old for my mother's "constructive

comments" or my dad's misinformed judgment. Visiting is exactly like traveling back in time, every time.

"How's the politics?" my dad asks as he's driving us to a trailhead. I'm sitting in back, bundled up in the extra clothes my mom keeps for me at the house.

"They're...the same as usual," I reply. "Lots of bickering."

"Don't know how you do it," he says, shaking his head and glancing at me in the rear-view mirror. "Especially with those people you hang around with," he adds. "Bet that trip to the White House was something else, though."

His use of "those people" makes me cringe. My parents are very white and middle class, and voted blindly for the current president just because he's from the right party—in sharp contrast to me, the upstart who ousted a more established candidate from doing a job my parents considered "pretty good."

"I try to work with anyone open-minded, Dad."

"You ought to do a little more listening," he replies, shaking his head as though disappointed with me. "You're new there, shouldn't come in acting like you know everything already."

"Now, John," my mother says, but she doesn't disagree with Dad because she never disagrees with him. She doesn't like disagreement, period. "Let's not talk politics all day. Cindy needs this fresh air to clear her head! Don't you, dear?"

It isn't worth it to explain that I've come to believe, despite my upbringing, that compromising *isn't* always worth the peace. "Sure, Mom. Fresh air always helps."

"You don't get enough in that Washington," she says. "I can tell."

Watching the trees begin to close around the car as we wind toward the trailhead, I can't disagree with them. Washington has nothing on Summit County, which sits at around 9,000 feet above sea level. The air is thin and clear, the reservoir is shining from the nearness of the sun, and the trailhead we arrive at is relatively quiet compared to the ones that Denverites regularly crowd.

I strap on the backpack that my mom gives me, which is packed with water, food and emergency supplies. When I buckle on my snowshoes, I fumble a little more than my parents, who do this nearly every day during the half-year of winter up here.

As I follow them on a single track running up a steep hill, I wish for poles like my parents have. When we reach a clearing, I catch up to my mom while Dad keeps pushing ahead. He's marching like he's late for an appointment.

"How are you and Dad?" I ask. Despite the evidence that my parents are in better shape than I am, I still worry about them living alone up here in the mountains. Whenever the pass closes due to snow or landslides, they're shut off from the rest of the world. They moved here from Denver when they retired, so they aren't that integrated with the mountain community yet.

"We're good, sweetheart," my mom says. "We worry about you, alone in that awful place."

"It's not that bad," I reply, but it's a weak answer. Sometimes, Washington *is* awful. And sometimes I do feel very alone. I listen to the crunch of snow with every step. The air is the kind of cold that's crisp against my skin. The District never smells this clean.

"You have no time for a personal life," my mother says, watching where she's going. Her cheeks are rosy and her breath comes in regular clouds of air. "Are you dating anyone?"

"No, Mom," I reply, like I always do, whether I am or not.

Before I took office, I'd been in a vicious cycle: go on an awkward date filled with silences around things we don't want to talk about, like party politics, or filled with incredibly dry policy talk that might as well happen across a desk in an office. Then stop dating for a while because it doesn't seem worth it. That's where I'm at in the cycle now. Give me another few months and I'll get lonely and try again. But I don't have time or energy to date, and there aren't a ton of prospects who aren't a security risk or part of my chain of authority now.

"You need to take your future husband into consideration. Is there space in your life for a man?"

This sounds like it comes straight from some self-help book my mom's been reading. "Mom," I groan.

"You think worrying about a hypothetical is a waste of time, but if you don't plan, you might never get married, dear," she says, navigating a large root in the path.

I open my mouth, but my mom continues, "I just want you to have what we have, Cindy. What would I do without your father? At this time of life, can you imagine me living alone? I'd have to be in one of those *communities*." She shivers as she says this, and not from the cold.

"I'm glad you have Dad," I agree, hoping that's the end of the admonishment. It's true, I can't imagine my parents without each other. I'm lucky to have grown up with happily married parents, even if their happiness relied on my mother's agreement with everything my dad demanded.

"Oh, I can't cry in this weather," my mother says impatiently, pausing to push the strap of her pole around her wrist and flick a gloved hand at her face. I pause, because I can't ignore how strongly my mom feels about this.

"Mom...you don't *need* Dad. To be happy. You could be happy in one of those communities, if you needed to try one," I say, tentative because I'm not at all sure that pushing back on this is worth my energy. Is it ever possible, as a child, to convince your parents there's another valid way to live?

From my mother's expression, I might as well be turning blue. "Cindy, don't even suggest such a thing." She turns and pushes forward, following my dad, who is extending his lead without checking on us behind him.

I sigh and follow, which has always been my role when it

comes to my parents. At least visiting them keeps me feeling young.

* * *

Alex

When people line up with matching awestruck expressions on their faces, it's hard to take them in as individuals. I often find myself going into subway mode, staring straight ahead and turning the crowd around me into visual white noise.

But retail politics is all about connecting with a crowd as individuals. It triggers anxiety, sometimes. If I can focus on one person at a time, I find some enjoyment in shaking hands and kissing babies. It's all about touching lives who will then, hopefully, go on to share their personal experience with friends, family or social media.

Thor makes the whole process easier. Thor loves strangers and being the center of attention, and he gets plenty of both when we make "unplanned" stops at local small businesses in the District. My little dog slurps a puppuccino from the coffee bar and the people at tables and lining the walls around them all document his whipped cream-covered muzzle.

"Have you ever seen such a spoiled dog?" I grin at the owners, a married couple who have been serving a sandwich named after me for the past year. The Drakewich. It's a mouthful, both to eat and to say.

My staff put the little bookstore/cafe on the list of places to visit once the sandwich started appearing on lists of "must eats" in the area. It's an overstuffed reuben pierogi. "Meaty with a touch of vinegar, just like me," I'd joked when I took a bite.

Amanda and T.J. have a display set up at the front of the store of local authors and I pull a few off the shelf that the two women point out. I have cash on me specifically for this purpose.

"Got anything along the lines of 'How to survive your fifth State of the Union'?" I ask, prompting an easy laugh from everyone within earshot. The reporters on duty for the press pool that day are busily typing up every word I say on their phones.

"How about a coloring book?" Amanda asks.

I laugh. "If I got caught coloring during the State of the Union, the president might never speak to me again."

"We wouldn't want to cause an international incident." T.J. smiles, hugging her wife. They're nervous, but they're doing a great job demonstrating why their bookstore/cafe is so successful. The whole point of my visit is to shine a brighter spotlight on entrepreneurs doing well.

"Not international," I say, dragging out the joke. "But definitely domestic."

"Maybe the president is the one who needs the coloring book?" Amanda suggests.

Appreciating how easy the banter is with them, I laugh. "Good idea, show me what you've got and I'll see what he thinks."

Of the two of us, Tim dislikes retail politics more. He'll do it, but he'd prefer to wave from the car and stay on stage during events.

Part of what I brought to the ticket was my facility with "regular people" that balanced out what focus groups described as Tim's East Coast elitism. I'm accessible and quirky. Tim is predictable and soothing. Together, we are the perfect parents to this country.

Amanda and T.J. bring over two coloring books: one for kids with cars, and one for adults with swear words.

"Oh, this is a tough choice; I'd better take both of them," I say, again projecting my voice for the press and the crowd in the cafe. After all this practice, my pitch is perfect. Loud, but not forced. The people around me feel included, but not marketed to.

"The president might need the one with cussing, but the one with cars is staying with me," I continue with a grin. "This is as close as I get to driving anymore."

As I exit the bookstore, I wave at the people lined up outside, held back by a row of police and Secret Service. I'm holding Thor in one arm and pause to wave a doggy paw, prompting a collective "awww."

My short walk to the black SUV is covered by an awning and the vehicle takes off immediately after I'm inside, all seamless protective measures I barely give a thought anymore.

Dan is sitting in the backseat with me, tapping away at two phones. "Effective trip, sir," he says. "Lots of pictures and video already on social media."

I nod, loosening my tie, and then pick up one of the books I bought that an aide tucked into the SUV. Another book I won't have time to read.

"By the way, sir," Dan adds. "It's Cindy Wight's birthday. Deena found something on her official feed."

"Is it?" I'm oddly pleased that my staff knew I'd want to know this. "Can we send her a tweet or something?"

Dan's face tells me it's a bad idea. "Um," he says. "We haven't done that before...from the official feed?"

I nod. "Right, right." It would be odd to call her and wish her a happy birthday. She would assume it a work call, interrupting, while perhaps she's out celebrating. I sift through the pile of books again and pull out the swear word coloring book. "Send her this, will you?"

Dan takes it, his face impressively neutral. "Of course, sir."

I'm pleased with the idea because it toes the line between personal and professional. Retail politics means more than kissing babies, after all, doesn't it? Sometimes work partnerships require a personal touch.

* * *

Cindy

"Happy birthday," says Max, my press secretary on the campaign side, as I join her at the table. We're grabbing a beer at a little craft brewery near my district office. I've never been here before, because I'm not in Denver enough to identify the best places anymore.

I sigh a little as I slump onto the high-top table. I trust Max with some honesty. "Let's not talk about it."

"You are the most badass 45-year-old I know, with no ceiling for the future," Max says seriously. "There's no way I will have accomplished as much as you by the time I turn 45, congresswoman."

I've seen Max go through her own turmoil, but now she lives where she wants to live, with a dog and a boyfriend, and does her job without breaking a sweat. She doesn't have any reason to be jealous. She doesn't sound jealous, either. She sounds content. The real problem is I'm *not*.

"Cindy, please," I say instead of dwelling. "Nobody needs titles at happy hour."

"Except in D.C., where happy hour is an extension of work," Max says mildly. "Don't get me started on some of the dates I went on that turned out to be networking."

I grimace, but I feel better already. My conversations are rarely this apolitical these days. "I'm glad I don't have much experience in that."

Max raises her eyebrows but says nothing until she comes back with our beers from the bar. "So, no juicy flirtations with middle-aged white men in the Capitol?"

80

It's a joke but the vice president floats—very inappropriately—through my mind. "No, I don't have much time for that kind of fun," I say.

"You hesitated!" eagle-eyed Max declares, astonished. "What's been happening back in the District?"

I shake my head, looking anywhere but at Max, who knows me too well. "Nothing, nothing. A tiny flirtation. It's not going anywhere. That's all."

Max is wide-eyed, already half-way through her IPA. "Maybe you shouldn't deny the possibility?"

"I don't think I want to have any expectations in this case," I say, cautiously. Even in a friendly environment, I don't want to say too much. I've probably been in Washington too long, but I've learned to be careful. "It's cliched, but well...we work together and it's complicated. And," I add quickly. "I'm not sure I like him like that. I just find him...interesting."

"Interesting is a better start than most things," Max says. "Is there chemistry?"

My gym date with Alexander Drake comes to mind, and how I wanted to lean into him and touch that soft-looking t-shirt.

"There is," Max answers for me. Her eyes soften, the expression of someone whose romance worked out. "Honestly, Cindy, I think you should go for it," she says. Her tone is the one she uses to give me talking points before an event when she says, *Repeat this as many times as you can in as many ways as possible. Make sure this is what people take away.* "You need something besides work in your life. I mean, do an asshole check, of course. But you have good judgment. I vote for a one-night-stand, at least. Or tell yourself it's a one-night-stand if that helps you psychologically. Then...see what happens."

Unconvinced by the advice, I only give her a neutral smile. "Usually the person who gives up power in a one-night-stand is the woman."

"Ugh," Max says. "You're giving me flashbacks to D.C. and how everything is a power struggle. You want another beer?"

I hesitate.

"I've never seen you drink more than one, but come on, it's your birthday." Max grins. So I nod and she brings me another.

"Ask this guy to agree, when you're together, to set aside politics," she says, as she's sliding back into her seat. "If you can trust him, you should be able to trust that he's not going to use sex against you."

My entire body cringes at the idea I could trust Alex Drake— or any man—not to use my vulnerability against me. Experience tells me that's impossible. For example, the man I was dating when I decided to run for Congress. He'd called me "too hot to make it in Washington." He'd thought it a compliment, I think.

"Try a drink to relax next time you see him?" Max suggests. "Or some weed?"

"Still a federal employee," I remind her. "So is he."

"OK, first fix these ancient prohibition laws and *then* cele- brate with this guy," Max says, waving her half-full glass around to make me laugh.

By the time I finish my next drink, I have almost forgotten about my birthday and politics. But I can't quite push the vice president—or that vision of him in his sweaty t-shirt—off my mind. So I'm thinking of him when my phone rings and the caller ID says Unknown. I can't *not* pick it up with a chance it's him, so I hold up a finger to Max and answer. "Hello, this is Cindy Wight."

"Hello, Cindy Wight. It sounds like I've caught you at another inopportune moment."

"Ah, hello..." I trail off, not wanting to identify him out loud. I smile at Max as I slide off my tall chair and look for a quiet corner.

"Is it *him*?" she mouths at me. I make a face and don't confirm, but she widens her eyes and mouths, "Ask him!"

"Not inopportune. I forgot to mention I was going back to my district." I wince as I say it. Why would I tell the vice president my schedule, like he's going to mark it down on his personal calendar?

"Are you visiting old haunts?"

"No, new ones. Enjoying a drink with a colleague." I step outside, where the patio is filled with people playing cornhole under the waning winter daylight.

"I'm sorry to interrupt."

"No, no, I'm happy to hear from you. I mean, I'm happy to talk about the bill anytime." I end up pacing between Subarus in the parking lot, where at least I can hear the way his voice expands to fill the space between us. Is that voice the mark of a seasoned politician or just this man?

"I got a request from a couple of chairmen to set up a meeting. The House Judiciary Chair-"

"The fucker," I interrupt, the words hissing out of my mouth without thinking. "Never trust a man named *Randy*."

The vice president's laughter curls up in my ear. There's so little laughter in most of my relationships in D.C. It's unusual. Not *special*, just *different*.

"Your next piece of legislation?" he asks. "Outlawing Randys?"

"I wish." I pause, in the darkness between two vehicles blocking out the overhead outdoor lights. This is not a call with a girlfriend. *Sober up, Cindy.* "What did you tell him?"

"I told him I'd be happy to meet at the convenience of the entire coalition."

"Oh," I say. Grateful, horrifying tears pop into my eyes.

"I'm not about to meet with them without you...congresswoman." His pause suggests he wanted to say my name, and suddenly I want to hear it in his voice. Badly.

"That's really nice of you," I murmur.

"You're right," he says. "And I don't know why. I hear you didn't vote for me."

His voice is good-humored, but it embarrasses me that I've gone around characterizing him and the president as mere figureheads for an old-fashioned system. He's much more *real* to me now.

"There's always next time," I say.

"You think I can win you over?" I can tell from his voice that he likes a challenge as much as I do.

"I do," I say simply. "If you try."

"Oh, I'm trying," he replies. I stand in the parking lot smiling and somehow I know that 1,600 miles away, he's smiling too.

ten

Alex

I HAVE to know the policy points of the speech like the back of my hand, but my job tonight is to clap.

It's similar to my mom's role at my younger sister's wedding a few years ago. It was her job to lead the rest of the crowd in standing when the bride came down the aisle and show everyone when to take the floor after the first dance. The vice president is basically the mother of the bride at the State of the Union. I show everyone when it's time to clap, and lead the crowd when it's time to give a standing ovation.

I also have to attend a lot of events surrounding the big one on Tuesday night. And every time I walk into a reception—at the Library of Congress or the House Speaker's office—I wonder if I'll run into Cindy Wight.

Cindy and I haven't talked on the phone all week, due to the intense pace of my schedule leading up to the president's speech. So far I haven't bumped into her, though she's left a trail of irritated representatives as evidence of her presence. I can't help but find it amusing she's got a bunch of grown men in suits ruffled over the threat of change.

It doesn't surprise me that she would try to sway votes even while telling me she was polling the votes already on her side. But there's little evidence of headway.

Few things ever really change in Congress, an institution that prides itself on tradition. I see small ones in the House Chamber since the last time I was here, this time last year, like the chairs refinished in a slightly darker shade. Little difference.

I'm in the Senate Chamber more often, especially last session when I needed to break ties fairly often because of the 50/50 split. I miss the structure of working in that chamber sometimes, despite the dress code and temptation of the Candy Desk.

There's plenty of time to scan the room during the endless clapping as the president enters the chamber, shakes hands and exchanges a few words with members lining the aisle. The Speaker and I stand side-by-side watching the doorway as we abuse our palms.

I'd joked with Tim beforehand that he needs to start sprinting for the rostrum to save everyone the extended hand-bruising before his speech. Tim, who hates the performative parts of politics in the first place, bet me $5 he would do it this time. Looks like I'm winning a small coffee from the president tonight.

An endless four and a half minutes later, the president reaches us. Tim reaches out to shake hands with me, and then the Speaker.

"I tried to get here sooner," he tells me with a grin. I shake my head without answering, both because my face is on camera and because it's such a lie.

Tim reaches behind him and picks up copies of his speech in manila envelopes already placed on the rostrum and hands one to each of us—another bit of theater, since we could easily pull up the pre-released text on our phones.

The room is still clapping. I gaze up into the gallery, which runs around the top of the room, and spot Anita standing in the first lady's box. She would ordinarily be seated with the vice president's wife as well as her guests. I wonder if Anita ever misses the built-in companionship she would have had if I married. The vice president's spouse must be the one person who comes close to understanding what it's like to be married to a president.

Finally, the Speaker raises her gavel. "I have the high privilege and distinct honor of presenting the president of the United States," she says, once the room quiets.

Everyone starts clapping again, myself included. My palms already hurt and I've got another hour to ask of them.

"Thank you," Tim says after a long moment of applause. "Please, everybody take your seats."

I sit down, making sure my back is against the tall frame of the chair. Experience has taught me to get comfortable immediately, so I'm not shifting around while on camera the rest of the speech. I put one hand on the padded armrest and start tracing the carvings on the wood underneath. This is my trick for retaining a focused expression for the next hour.

"Madame Speaker, Mr. Vice President, members of Congress," Tim begins, speaking with his back to me.

Tim is delivering his list of legislative priorities for the coming year. I picture myself, briefly, as the one up here giving the speech. But in my head, the possibility sits far away on the horizon, not somewhere in the next few years.

I scan the room without moving my head. It is packed with members from both chambers of Congress. Senate and House leadership is up front, along with the Supreme Court justices.

Seating for the rest of the House members is first-come, first-served. Most of the members who shook the president's hand as he walked down the aisle likely camped out to save their chairs.

If Cindy's here, I can't quite see her around the rostrum and Tim's back. Unfortunately, as vice president I really can't shift around in my chair in an attempt to lay eyes on my crush.

And that's what she is. *Of course.* Because I don't casually think about any other members of Congress at least once a day.

Of all the times and places to have an epiphany. Fortunately, the president is talking about Russia when I frown.

* * *

Cindy

I can see the vice president's shoulder and left arm.

It's a nice shoulder, as I know from joining him to lift weights. Strong and rounded in all the right ways. But that's not the point. I'm annoyed that my prime seating cuts off the best view. I hadn't wanted to be on the aisle, where I'd be pressed from all sides to shake the president's hand, but had ended up too close to observe more than the president at the front of the room.

Some of the other members of the Freshman Six had suggested skipping the State of the Union entirely, as a statement of misalignment with the president's positions. I'd reminded them that I need the White House's support for our current top priority legislation, which somehow led to Steven offering to camp out in the chamber to save us six seats up front. My young allies vacillate wildly between fed up with Washington and awed by it.

I'm nervous. I'm 99 percent certain Alex or someone would

have warned me if the president planned to mention cannabis in his speech. He'd probably only do so if he planned on cutting my goals out of the bill. My jaw feels sore from how tightly I'm gritting my teeth. *Just let me take it one step at a time, Alex.*

Oh. I called him by his first name in my head for the first time.

It's usually not hot on the House Floor, but I'm sweating under my blazer. Around me, everyone is standing from both parties, so the president must have mentioned the troops or people beating poverty: the only causes that earn bipartisan ovations. I follow the crowd. I can see Alex's—the vice president's—face as he stands, as well. It is excruciatingly neutral, even as he claps emphatically. The politician expression. I miss the openness of his face when we were in the gym, out of these dress clothes and talking about things other than politics.

He's scanning the crowd, eyes lightly dusting over everyone. But then he finds my eyes. I miss a beat and have to catch up with the rhythm of the clapping. *Is he looking at me on purpose?*

I sit back down with everyone else and miss the physical sense of his gaze. I'm back on my feet a few minutes later to clap for the strong economy, smoothing my skirt as I stand, my eyes drawn like a magnet to the back of the rostrum.

Standing framed in front of the giant American flag, the blue eyes of the vice president are on me in the middle of this crowded room, airing live on every network TV station and C-SPAN. His expression doesn't change, but he's definitely staring at me. Suddenly, the clapping is happening in my heart.

It's a good thing when I can sit back down. My legs are about to give out. I swallow several times, still feeling caught in the gaze I can no longer see.

The next time my party all stands to give the president a standing ovation, I rise dutifully with everyone else. But I'm eager to regain my view of Alex's face. His eyes are right there, steady on me, despite the room filled with people and the cameras and lights. I'm flooded with warmth under his gaze. I almost collapse back in my seat this time.

Alex sits as well, disappearing from my view, and I realize when I re-cross my legs that I'm more than flushed, I'm aroused. Based on nothing but the vice president giving me a look in public, I'm imagining being stretched out over the blue carpet in front of these chairs, pencil skirt hiked up over my hips, taken from behind while I'm bowed over the rostrum. The thong I'm wearing shoved to the side, the need too urgent to wait...

Swallowing and forcing the images out of my mind, I tell myself to tune into the president. I'm going to have to read this speech again later for all I'm hearing now.

I must have let the conversation at my birthday happy hour go to my head. I have a working relationship with the vice president and nothing more. We disagree on so many things. He's cautious and measured where I'm bold and impulsive. He tries to please the crowd; I care about the underdog. He's a career politician; I'm only here as long as it serves my activism.

The president must mention the military again, because the whole chamber is starting to stand. I follow, a little unsteady on my heels. The vice president catches my eyes again. His expression does not change and heat trickles down my back imagining him plowing into me with that same dispassionate gaze hiding, I hope, uncontrollable intensity.

This time, there might be a tiny smirk on his face. *He knows.* But no. We shared a moment but it's impossible his thoughts shared the same vivid mental image.

I swallow and re-take my seat with everyone else. I need to escape and put a cold washcloth on the back of my neck. But I'm trapped until the end of this speech, and then there's the rebuttal to watch and I have a scheduled interview from the rotunda with a broadcast network. I'm supposed to talk about where the president didn't go far enough in his speech and I've barely heard a word of it so far.

Push Alex Drake out of your head, Cindy, and concentrate on the job.

eleven

Alex

IT'S LATE.

It's late and I shouldn't call but I want to.

I can always poll Cindy on the State of the Union next time I talk to her, during daylight when I have a good reason to discuss business. Right now, I'm sprawled on my bed, still wearing my suit pants but with jacket and tie off and the top of my shirt unbuttoned. I was too tired when I finally walked in the door to do more than scoop up Thor, who a staffer walked earlier in the evening, and flop. I'm holding my cell phone, which Ted reluctantly handed over after a final sweep of the house.

"Don't do anything I wouldn't do," Ted warned me.

But Ted is married. He must have gotten that way somehow.

Cindy had gotten me through the speech earlier. Every time I stood, I sought her out in the crowd, staring at her so hard that if I'd had a magnifying glass I could have set her on fire. I hope she felt the warmth in my gaze, as I fought to keep my expression dispassionate. I want to know if she felt the heat building the same as me.

I wish I could text her. What would I say, though, "R U up?" I smile to myself at the ludicrous idea and turn on the phone's screen so I can see the time. 1:13 a.m.

She's probably still up. I open her number and stare at it. Even as I press the green phone button, I'm uncertain I should do this.

She answers after the first ring, while I'm still considering hanging up. "This is Cindy Wight."

"Hi," I say. "It's...the vice president."

There's a pause in which I cringe at myself. "Hi," she says. "Good morning," she adds.

Relieved at her welcoming tone, I smile. "Good morning. I hope I didn't wake you."

"No, I just got in. I was taking off my..." She stops herself, and I fill in the blank: *My heels. My dress. My...* I stop there.

"I just got in," she repeats. "Good speech tonight."

"Yes, I agree."

"From a delivery perspective, obviously. Not policy."

I smile again. "Of course." She went on TV and criticized the president of her own party tonight, accusing him of being "soft" when "the American people want boldness." She's the bane of existence for a lot of people in the White House comms shop who want to achieve party unity so they only have to counter the other side.

We both pause. I need to explain why I called but I don't have a good explanation.

"I saw you in the chamber," I say, but then run out of things I can tell her, my mind filled with ones I can't. *You looked good? That blue shirt brought out your eyes? I wished I was sitting next to you? I wanted to hold your hand?*

"Yes, I...saw you too," she says slowly. She must think I'm insane. She'll start dreaming up ways to pass her cannabis legislation that don't involve negotiating with a crazy person. "I wondered," she begins, her voice cautious.

"Yes?" I say quickly. Ideas jump into my head: *I wondered if we could see each other. Right now. Come over.*

Not that I could. The Secret Service would *strongly* object.

"I wondered if the president would bring up the cannabis legislation in his speech," she continues. "I'm glad he didn't."

"Oh," I say, trying not to sound like I expected anything else from her. I clear my throat, emptying it of foolish responses. "Right. I would have discussed it with you. We didn't think it would help, with so much still up in the air." I don't mention that it wouldn't have helped my legacy, either.

"Right. But if he made it a presidential priority, you would probably have a bill you could pass sooner and without my support," she says. I hear a tapping sound on her end, like glass against glass. "Part of me wanted that. For my bill to become so important it would come up in the State of the Union. But I had a birthday and I guess it made me kind of impatient about things."

"Happy birthday," I say. "Belatedly."

She hesitates. "Thank you. I didn't mean to suggest you should have known."

The book I sent her way must have been misplaced. I wonder what happened to it. Better not to tell her my staff stalks her on the internet.

"I wish I did know, though," I say quietly, wishing I knew so many more things about her. It's a weak comment. It implies something I'm still not willing to say outright and puts the pressure on her to either ask or assume.

Or ignore, which she does. "What are you doing right now?" she asks, matching my quietness.

I tip my head away from Thor, who is trying to lick my face. "Laying on my bed. Trying to avoid Thor kisses."

Her breath stutters. It might be a sneeze or a cough, or it might have been a gasp. "What are you doing?" I ask, because it's only fair. And I want to know.

"Drinking a glass of wine," she says. "Seems like that's what I'm always doing when you call. You must think I have a problem."

I laugh. "It's not like I'm calling you every day at 9 a.m."

"Maybe if I had a dog or someone, I would relax differently," she says, speaking in that poorly filtered way I love. We both pause again, as I form a dirty mental picture involving relaxing Cindy Wight. I've seen her out of that uniform of dresses and pantsuits. I want to see her with nothing on. I want to follow those long legs all the way up her thighs.

Clearing my throat to dissipate that image and what it's doing to my body, I say, "Yeah, dogs are great."

"I got the invitation, by the way," she says, jumping to a new subject. "To your table at the Correspondents' Dinner. Thank you."

"Can you come?" I pause, a new idea coming to me. "Did they give you a plus one? I'm sorry, I didn't think to ask." I rub a hand across my face. If Cindy Wight sits across from me with another man, my staff will suffer for it.

"No. I got the impression it would throw off the table."

"That's because you're balancing me out," I say, relief rushing through my entire prone body. "You're doing us a favor. No one ever knows what to do with me."

"Oh, I'm sure someone knows," she says, and her register sounds deeper, like she meant the innuendo this time.

I smile up at the ceiling, because for what may be the very first time, I'm not the only one flirting. On purpose, anyway. My stomach loosens. "I'm glad you can come."

She hesitates to follow my laden words farther down the innuendo rabbit hole. It might be a secure line but everything is still insecure between us, with me unable to promise too much and Cindy...perhaps afraid to ask?

"My schedule is a little unwieldy in March," I add, the

colorful blocks on my calendar piling up in my head. My stomach roils again. "So I might not be as available as I'd like."

"Of course," she says, like this doesn't matter to her. "I'll be busy, too, with the meetings we discussed. But I can always update someone else on your team, if necessary."

I make a sound of regret, although it *is* necessary. "I'll send you detailed updates on my progress, as well. Our people can try to schedule a few meetings or phone calls. I want to stay in the loop. I don't want you to think I'm not devoted to this project. I just have…"

"About 30 other projects? I understand." But she still sounds disappointed. "Are we still in agreement on the 4/20 deadline?"

The question I hoped she wouldn't ask. "I'm concerned about it," I admit, quietly. "But I think it depends on what kind of movement you can get."

"Don't put it all on me," she says, her voice snapping from tentative to brisk so fast it gives me whiplash. "If we have the chance to pass something more significant, we should."

"Even my version would still be some of the most significant drug legislation to pass in decades, and that would be thanks to you introducing it," I interrupt, because she sounds like she's growing angry. She crystalizes, somehow, when she does, all the anger making her glow like her skin is transparent and the fire shows through. I like to witness it. But she's also prone to making impromptu declarations when she's angry, and I'm not sure I want to be on the wrong end of an improvisation tonight. "But you have to get it through the Senate. That's why you need me."

"I definitely need you," she says, the anger dropping out of her voice without warning.

The words hit me with physical weight in the middle of my chest. So many people need me every day—to ask informed questions, to sign off on something, to smile and wave and give someone else a reason to vote for me—but I've never wanted to be needed by one person this badly.

I take a beat to breathe through it. "You and I could agree on this tomorrow. Unfortunately, *we* can't get it to the president's desk by ourselves. I don't want to create some kind of arbitrary line that we both have to pull our sides toward. The date might have to change depending on the temperature of the conference. That's all I'm trying to say."

"So you don't have a line in mind already," she says. Her voice isn't angry, but she still sounds suspicious.

"No, I promise," I say. But I wonder if that's true. She's got to get her people on board with dropping at least one provision or there's no way to push this bill across the finish line with any kind of fanfare. While she's still trying to preserve her whole version of the bill, talking to members who have no intention of voting for it as-is, I need her to shift her focus back to the votes *I* need. "OK," I continue, rushing my words because I'm afraid I'm about to piss her off. I'm springing this conversation on her so late at night. "We've got to drop at least one thing—expungement or banks—and then I can convince everyone else to line up to vote for it."

"We can at least have one? *Either* one?" Her voice sharpens, and I worry I've made her a promise I won't be able to keep. I *need* this win. The bill has to pass, even if it means stripping it of everything extra she wants in it. "Everyone will vote for one or the other?"

This win is about more than my legacy now. Now it's about *her*.

"I'll talk to the Whip about it. Hell, I'll come to a party lunch and talk about it. I'll give speeches about it. I can get you the votes," I say. I'm carried away with the desire to impress her, but I can't stop. "As long as you can guarantee me the progressive votes."

"OK," she says. "OK. I'll see what I can do."

"I know you will," I say. "And I'll see what I can do to meet your deadline."

No need to tell her about my doubts.

* * *

Cindy

I don't like my legislative director. He's one of the few men in a senior position on my staff, and I hired him because everyone told me he gets results, not because I got a good vibe from him. But sometimes I wonder if I should have kept interviewing until I found someone good at the job who I also got along with better.

"So it's either? The banking lobby will help us on that provision if we come to them hat-in-hand. They'd love to make working with cannabis money legal." He's pacing in my office. Martin makes me tense, and I also sometimes find him triggering. I already spend the majority of my time surrounded by men who dismiss my thoughts and undermine my work here in Congress only to invite another one onto my payroll. "Weed brings in millions of taxable income in the states where it's legal. We can talk about getting that money flowing through the country."

"Cannabis," I correct him. "Cannabis is the most neutral term."

"Weed, MJ, cannabis, whatever. Some of these old school guys aren't going to appreciate dressing up the words. Ma'am."

I sigh. He's particularly frustrating because he's not wrong. "I think both issues are worthwhile."

"Yes, but what we *feel* about the legislation isn't going to pass it."

"Be careful," I warn him. "You're coming dangerously close to telling me I'm too emotional about the bill."

His brow furrows, like he has no idea what I'm talking about, then his expression clears. "Oh, that's a female thing. Got it. No disrespect."

Martin told me in his job interview that he lacks social awareness and responds well to directness. Not inaccurate. But it's tiresome to work with someone who isn't working on himself. Every time I warn him about something like this, he's forgotten it by our next meeting.

"I meant that the rest of Congress is going to look at it in black and white terms," he goes on. "It's not about people behind bars who don't belong there. It's about what benefits them."

"I'm well aware of that," I say. "I keep reminding myself this bill is going to do a lot of good, even watered down."

Martin sits down, perching on the edge of one chair in front of my massive mahogany desk. It's not my taste, but choices were limited. "Personally, I don't care what's in the bill. I just want them to pass it. That's why I think we should stop calling the members who don't care and start convincing the ones who do. The rest of the Freshman Six, the blue staters."

"I'm aware of how you feel, Martin," I say, emphasizing "feel" out of pettiness. "I told the vice president I would do just that. Start calling our coalition. I need you to help find me a compromise that *can* pass."

He pops back to his feet. "On it."

My stomach sinks like I just lost a battle as he leaves. *This is the right thing to do, isn't it?* I need to live in reality. But I worry I'm letting Washington chip away at my ideals.

Lizzie walks in as Martin walks out. I start to pull up my calendar to check if I have another meeting immediately, but I don't need to. Lizzie knows my schedule better than I do and wouldn't distract me if she couldn't.

"You got a special delivery." Lizzie is holding a wrapped package in her hands.

"Where from?"

Lizzie sets the rectangular box on my desk, making a dramatic flourish at it with her hands. "The White House. Or EEOB, whatever, same thing. Delivered by a courier, not by mail."

"The vice president sent me..." I pause, staring at the red wrapping paper. I'm sure an aide wrapped it, but for a moment I picture Alexander Drake carefully cutting paper and folding crisp corners. For me.

"Open it!" Lizzie urges me. "Do I get to see?"

"I don't think it's anything *private*." I imagine pulling a set of lacy lingerie out of the box, like a sketch on an anti-sexual harassment video. Neither of us has crossed a line in our tentative flirting so far. We're nowhere close to panty presents, and realistically never will be.

Lizzie raises her eyebrows into her bangs, like she's realized something shocking. "*Could* it be anything private?"

"No. No," I repeat, emphatically, and start pulling at the edges of the package. I don't want to give my chief of staff ideas. Lizzie is discreet, but a little bit mercenary. She would want to use the relationship. "Of course not."

Pulling off the wrapping paper reveals a cardboard box. Inside is a framed photo wrapped in tissue paper. I hold it up and smile. It's me and Alex Drake standing at the briefing room podium, the White House seal and American flag behind us.

"I told you you were very matchy-matchy!" Lizzie declares. She's right: My red dress and the vice president's red tie look like they were meant to be together.

"The red balances out all the blue in the room," I agree,

trying to stay neutral. The vice president sends photos to a lot of people. Just standing next to him is an honor that people want to remember. "It's a great photo."

"What a thoughtful gift," Lizzie says. "It's not every day you brief reporters at the White House with the vice president."

There's a small card in the bottom of the box. It's printed, not handwritten, and reads, "Happy belated birthday." The letterhead declares: "From the Office of the Vice President." There is no signature.

"I mentioned it the other day," I murmur.

"Do you want me to hang it in here?" Lizzie asks, leaning over the desk to admire the picture.

I scan my office, which is furnished not in my style but from a catalog of items approved by the Committee on House Administration. I have a number of framed photos of myself on the walls —being sworn in, speaking on the House floor—but I'm not sure this one belongs with my list of accomplishments.

"No, I think I'll take it home," I say slowly.

Lizzie pulls back across the desk with a hint of surprise, but she says, "OK." She goes on, "You have another meeting in 15 minutes, so I'll let you have your break."

Lizzie leaves, closing the door behind her, and I pick up the photo for a moment. Alexander Drake and I do look good side-by-side...but in a town as artificial as Washington, is it anything more than appearances?

The fact that he didn't sign the card says maybe not.

twelve

Alex

ONE WEEK in April brings out all the decadence Washington, D.C., can offer. The hair salons in Georgetown are booked, the luxury fashion at stores like Rent the Runway is all spoken for, limo companies are scrambling, the very small membership of the local paparazzi fends off an influx from the other coast, and hotels and restaurants around Adams Morgan hire extra help. It's White House Correspondents' Dinner week.

Ostensibly a charity fundraiser, it's also a time for media companies to demonstrate influence and for TV and movie stars to seek connections in a different system of celebrity from that in Hollywood. It's a time for politicians to feel glamorous as they walk down red carpets and for an old-fashioned and practical town to pretend it's trendy.

I find it tedious. Tim, that lucky bastard, only attends the dinner itself at the Washington Hilton. I've been anointed the top socialite on the Meyer ticket. The White House likes to trot me out to appear involved without taking up the president's time.

I wear what my team tells me to wear and go to the events they determine have the best ROI. I have an aide at my side at all times to identify people and whisper conversational tips like "pilots his own plane" in my ear.

The whole scene reminds me that I'm disconnected from pop culture, even if I *do* listen to a lot of podcasts. I have no time to watch television and no idea who the three people in front of me from the latest hit TV show are. Usually, I'm safe asking people where they film.

"We're in Vancouver. Tax credits," says the blonde woman, almost apologetically.

I nod. "Wish we could solve that one. There are some good state programs that must not have worked for your production."

"Incentivizing the movie business would keep more productions in America," the younger woman says, her voice a little wobbly from nerves. She's holding a champagne flute but I'm skeptical that she's even legal to drink. "The economic impact is huge for the local community. I mean, I'm always going out to town to drink and stuff."

I can count on one hand the celebrities who come to Washington to advocate for some cause and know the details of what they're advocating. I've talked to maybe two who could answer questions on basic details of their supposed plans. I call it celebrisplaining: When a famous person thinks their celebrity is all it takes to convince someone. Of course, I always smile and talk pleasantly to all of them and promise to look into their project.

"The revenue studies on economic impact are inconclusive in most states," I offer gently, trying not to embarrass her. "But it's worth additional research."

She opens her mouth again and Deena, who is staffing me tonight, interrupts. "Excuse us."

Gratefully, I walk away. Arguing with someone ignorant

while trying to keep from looking like I'm arguing is my least favorite kind of diplomacy.

I'm mingling with the throng at the British Ambassador's residence the night before the main event on the slim hope that some celebrity here will want to host a fundraiser or a journalist will write something favorable because I'm present. It's hell on my security detail, so at least I have an excuse not to stay very long.

"Mr. Vice President, can I get a picture of you and Zack Ryder?" a female photographer stands a few feet away, wearing a stunning red dress but clutching a Nikon and a large bag that makes it obvious she's working tonight. She points at a man at the center of a nearby pod of people who even I recognize as a movie star. "He played you in the movie *Attack on the White House,*" she offers.

I nod. "Sure..."

Deena whispers, "I think it's Madeline."

"Madeline, is it?" I add.

The photographer brightens. Knowing people's names is a real superpower. "It is. Thank you, Mr. Vice President. I'll set it up." She wades into the herd in front of us, using her bag as a phalanx and elbowing random people out of her way. I appreciate the work ethic.

I decide I'll wait for her, even as two lobbyists approach me while I'm standing there defenseless.

I greet them. Jimmy is familiar from way back and he introduces me to his colleague. "We've been working on the marijuana issue," he says. "A lot of the big companies are interested in getting behind Cindy Wight's bill. If it's ever introduced."

"Representative Wight," I correct. "...Is working hard on that legislation. Have you met with her?"

"We were wondering about the White House's position. Do

you *have* a position?" Jimmy smiles, friendly. Anything I say will eventually get blown up in the press.

"We can't take a position on a bill that doesn't exist yet. But we might be as interested in the process as you are," I reply, deflecting. I tuck my chin, the "rescue me" signal to my aides.

"Excuse us, we promised to take a picture," Deena interrupts, swooping in from some other task without hesitation. My staff is full of heroes.

"Feel free to reach out to my people," I tell Jimmy, shaking his hand again briefly before I follow Deena's sweeping gesture.

The crowd the photographer disappeared into grew more raucous in the last few minutes spent waiting for her to reappear.

"Can't blame them for wondering."

I pause and turn around at that voice. It prompts an immediate stirring in me that is inappropriate for the middle of a party.

Cindy Wight is standing there, wearing a shiny blue dress with no sleeves that shows off her toned arms and more cleavage than I've ever seen on her. Her dark hair is down, flowing around her shoulders. She is breath-taking.

"Congresswoman," I say, barely able to manage speech. I tell myself to keep my eyes on her face.

She gathers up the hem of her dress in one hand and smiles as she walks toward me. The dress is tight enough that she sways as she walks, every move of her hips clear through the fabric. "Mr. Vice President. Long time no see."

"I'm sorry about that." I wince. March was excruciatingly long and not only because I jetlagged my way through Europe for 10 days *and* had to attend the Easter Egg Roll, a massive event that takes over the White House lawn and involves posing with a full-grown man in an Easter Bunny costume. I had people like

Dan and Deena giving Cindy's office regular updates, but I missed talking to her myself.

She shrugs, the movement raising her breasts a little. If this is what she wears the day before the dinner, I wonder what she'll be wearing tomorrow night. I need to be prepared for a heart attack. "You look lovely tonight," I add quickly, realizing I haven't complimented her aloud. This is a woman who should be complimented regularly.

She smiles. "You do, as well."

"Ah, I can't take credit," I say, touching my lapel. "Somebody picks everything out for me."

"But you're the one wearing it," she replies, with a small quirk of her lips that makes me want to adjust my trousers a little. My fingers flex. Her eyes follow the movement, and her lips quirk as if she understands.

She stops a foot away from me. I want her closer and us alone. But we aren't and Deena is wearing her *we're-late-but-I'm-trying-to-be-respectful* face.

"I've got to do this picture," I say.

Zack Ryder walks up to us both and Cindy's eyes flare with interest. Just for a second. But it sparks a small flame of jealousy that her attention transferred away from me after I'd been basking in its sweet spotlight.

Ryder is tall, sculpted in both muscles and cheekbones, with a presence to him that bumps up against my own. I've never met him before, but perhaps this party isn't big enough for the two of us.

"Hi, I'm Zack," the movie star says, holding out his hand. A peculiar habit of the ultra-famous people I meet is they always pretend no one recognizes them. And they never recognize anyone else, either.

"Hi, I'm Alex," I reply, dryly. Two can play that game.

We shake hands. A camera flashes.

Zack turns away from me to Cindy. He pauses, one foot forward, to put his hand to his chin. Pose: Movie Star Contemplates Beautiful Woman.

"I'm Cindy," she offers. She glances at me. "And since I'm the least famous person here: I am a member of Congress."

"A woman that looks like you needs no title," Zack says, without sarcasm. He takes her hand and raises it to his lips. I catch Cindy and Deena exchanging a wide-eyed glance while Zack's eyes are downturned to her hand. Betrayed by my supposedly loyal staff.

"I played you in my last movie," Zack says to me as we rearrange for a less candid photo.

"I thought you were playing *a* vice president, not necessarily me," I say. I remember the press tour came to Washington and that's how the White House press secretary spun it when asked about the movie.

Zack laughs toward the camera and not at me, as the shutter clicks. "Sure, but it was clearly you we based it on. The socks. And you love old cars. Did we get that right?"

"I only wish I had as many Corvettes as you did in that movie," I say, trying to keep my smile wide to prevent people speculating about my attitude in the pictures later. But I'm offended by the "old cars" comment. I have a *classic* 1967 Corvette Stingray sitting in the garage back home at my parents' house in California.

"Let's do one with the thumbs," Zack says, and gives the camera a thumbs up, like his character did in the movie. *Ugh.*

I play along, feeling like an idiot with my thumb in the air. Finally, Deena rescues me, telling the others that we need to go. As we walk away from the movie star and the photographer, Cindy stays put. She gives me a little smile and a wave. "See you tomorrow."

As if in slow motion, Zack looks over at Cindy, like he's about to steal her attention again. "Are you staying here or do you have another party to go to? We could drop you," I offer, a little desperately.

"Oh," she says. "I planned to hit the W Hotel next but you don't have to…"

"Not a problem, it's practically on our way," I interrupt. It isn't; the W is by the White House and I'm headed home to Northwest Washington. But Deena and Ted won't give away the truth.

Cindy shrugs. She smiles and nods. "OK," she agrees. We sweep away from Zack, who has already been drawn into another crowd and won't be left unadmired.

I wave at the crowd around the door as we make our way to the limo, carefully not making eye contact with anyone. I don't want my exit to be delayed.

Belatedly, I realize I appear to be leaving for the night with a woman, which could lead to some talk even if Cindy is spotted later at the W. Too late now, though. I decide, for tonight, I'm living on the edge.

"Did you want me to…" Deena hesitates at the door of the car, asking if she should ride with Cindy and me.

"No," I decide. "Let's just leave the slider open, thank you."

Cindy doesn't ask until we've slowly rolled out of the gates of the embassy compound and are driving through the absurd mix of curving and diagonal streets around Dupont Circle. "What was that about?"

I glance up at the front of the car, at the back of Ted's head. The modified SUV is longer than average, so we have some privacy, but I very rarely close off the back seat and never when I have someone with me. "Uh, I don't," I pause. "I typically am not alone with…"

"Oh my god," she says. "The rumors are true. You won't be alone with a woman."

"You make it sound like I'm afraid of women. That's not it."

"Then what is it?" she starts to cross her legs and can't in her tight dress. She crosses her ankles and curls her legs to one side, leaning toward me slightly as she does. I can see—by accident—directly down the shadow between the mounds of her breasts. Smooth skin disappearing into her dress.

I swallow and stare hard at the shape of Ted's head. "It prevents any hint of impropriety if there's always a witness."

"You realize that puts the burden on the woman, don't you," she says, frowning at me. "Women already struggle to get access and you're creating a higher barrier to entry."

"No one gets turned down to find a witness. I'm almost always surrounded as it is."

"Have you always had this rule? Before you were vice president? I bet you turned down meetings with women then, before you had a constant security detail and aides always guiding you." She crosses her arms—I can't help noticing it's pushing her breasts up—and turns her head away from me. "Maybe you're trying to protect women, but we're the ones who suffer from fears of false accusations."

I squirm uncomfortably. I've heard this criticism before, but it's never been worth the risk to reassess my system. It worked for my dad; it works for me. My father always warned me that powerful men are held to a higher standard. And a lower one, when it comes to innocence.

"The rule is relatively new," I say quietly. "It's just since I've been in the White House." I run my hand through my hair, catch myself, then do it anyway because it's the end of the night and it doesn't matter if my hair is a mess. "Look, it's the office I'm trying to protect," I insist. "It's not really even a rule. I mean, we're basically alone right now. It's not like the Secret Service can testify on my behalf." I nod at the front of the car.

Cindy turns to me again, and she's not smiling. She wears

this firm expression during Floor speeches, usually in less revealing clothing than now. I've disappointed her. It hurts to realize. I don't deny her point, but can't she try to see it my way?

Without warning, she unfolds her arms and one hand snags my tie and yanks me toward her.

Off balance, my lips collide with hers. When I bring my hand down to catch myself on the seat, I brush the side of her breast and she makes a soft sound into my mouth like "hmm."

I open my mouth to say...something. My brain and body can't communicate. My lips catch on hers and I taste the satiny underside of her top lip. Her tongue touches my lips and I open my mouth to her, body taking over my brain. She tastes like gin and lime and I want to get drunk on her.

When the seat squeaks beneath us, I come back to myself, realizing I've yanked Cindy to my chest. One hand is on her bare back and the other on her arm, my thumb resting on the upper curve of her breast.

"Um," I say, releasing her and darting a quick glance at the front of the car, where Ted hasn't turned around. "What?" I'm known for my oratory skills.

She brushes her hair off her face. Her lipstick is smudged.

"Is that what you were afraid would happen?" she asks.

It takes me a moment to remember what we were talking about in the pre-kiss times. "I *wish* that was a danger I faced regularly," I reply. "If you were trying to make a point, I'm not sure you made the one you wanted to." I'd like to build on this argument by sliding one hand up her dress.

She rolls her eyes. Trying to redirect my thoughts, I pull my handkerchief out of my front jacket pocket and start wiping lipstick off her cheek. She visibly softens and smiles up at me from under her eyelashes.

"I wanted to know what it's like to kiss the second most powerful man in the world," she says. I can tell she's teasing because of the way she bites her lip after. I stop wiping at her mouth, trapped by her eyes.

"How was it?" I ask softly. *My* whole body may have elevated a few inches off this car seat. I don't have complete control over what I'm doing. She meets my eyes for a long moment, her gaze clouded and her lips parted. We're both hazy, together inside a bubble of our own making.

"Seemed about the same," she whispers, popping the bubble. "Maybe I better go try the president." She smiles.

I bark out laughter and flop back onto the seat, resting my head against the backrest. "Ouch," I say.

We're pulling up outside the W Hotel, the street lights dimmed through the tinted windows. Her expression changes, flickering from teasing to concerned in a moment as we drive in and out of the shadows.

She turns to me and touches my chest before I can say anything to pull her out of her thoughts. "I'm sorry if I got carried away. I do that sometimes."

I'm not certain what she's apologizing for. Surprising me? Kissing me? Joking about it?

She picks up her purse and starts to gather up her dress. "I just wondered what would happen, I guess."

She's going to walk away. I grab her wrist. "And?"

She meets my eyes, and whatever is in mine changes things between us. Like a switch flipped, the electricity between us reignites.

"And," she pauses, as Ted opens the car door. "I might have to try again."

She smiles at me and takes Ted's hand as she climbs out of the car. I remain slumped in the back seat, still aroused and not sure what to do about it, as we drive away.

* * *

Cindy

As a general rule, I don't shame myself over speaking my mind or acting on my wants, even when it's impromptu. It's something I've worked on in therapy, after blaming myself for years for not being able to control my quick temper and snap reactions. I try to give myself grace if my actions were in the pursuit of a personal value.

But kissing the vice president of the United States in the back of his limo seems like a *massive* exception to my rules.

He'd made me angry. And instead of channeling that anger into a logical argument, I'd gotten physical. I'd acted on a fantasy of putting my hands on him that I thought I'd locked down tight, compartmentalized into nonexistence. My desire for him bounded out at the least opportune moment. Now he knows I want him.

The want is dangerous. I can't be with the vice president. My career would never be the same. And who is he, really? The late-night conversations might not tell me enough about him. He might use the wanting against me.

After a sleepless night thinking about my inappropriate move—and dreaming, when I fell asleep, of what I wanted to happen next in the backseat of that bulletproof SUV—I almost skipped the garden brunch on the morning of the week's main event. But I'm trying to be a more visible presence. It might add pressure to my legislative campaign. So I get up, put on a cute sundress, and go to hang out with celebrities.

The long-standing garden brunch at the Beall-Washington House is a surreal experience, like most WHCD week events, because I recognize almost everybody but don't *know* all of them. The garden brunch has been the pre-party to hit since the '90s for everyone from Jay Leno to Lindsay Lohan. Zack Ryder is here this year, somehow looking both disheveled and dressy.

"Ah, my favorite member of Congress," he says when he sees me, surprising me by recognizing me. Even though we're in the lobby inside, he's wearing sunglasses.

"I'm flattered you remember me," I respond, pausing in my beeline toward some other congresswomen in the corner. I take a sip of my too-sweet drink. There's not a whole lot of eating or drinking at the garden "brunch," in my experience; the sustenance is mainly in the form of shaking hands and giving long-winded responses to reporters. I picked up my own coffee on the way and am drinking it now from a tall reusable cup.

"Of course, I remember you," he replies, and the sincerity in his voice is like the uncanny valley of responses. "You look like you should be cast in my next movie."

I laugh. I'm trying not to be taken in by his flattery, but it's hard not to feel its impact. I can't quite decide if Zack is charming but harmless or charming and malicious. It's always harder to tell with people who are famous for non-political reasons. I assume the worst of the political ones.

Me and the female anchor standing next to Zack exchange an incredulous glance over his charm. She's a blonde woman wearing makeup intended for high-def screens. Her face must exist behind it somewhere.

"Congresswoman, when can we expect to see your marijuana legislation? Or should I say, the vice president's marijuana legislation?" the woman asks, fluttering her hand as if we're discussing the spring weather.

I force a light laugh. *Is that what people are calling it?*

"You'll be the first to know, Anne," I say. "But don't let Mr. Ryder here think law-making is all that we're capable of talking about in Washington."

"Zack, please," he smiles, tipping down his sunglasses. His eyes are red-rimmed. I wonder if he's even been to sleep since last night. "We saw the V-POTUS last night," he adds in a low voice to Anne, spelling out "vee" and then pronouncing the acronym "poe-tuss."

"Oh?" Anne's gaze on me sharpens, her journalistic spidey sense clearly tingling.

"The vice president stopped at the British ambassador's party, I believe," I say, going for casual. "I saw the two of you take a picture," I add to Zack, trying to redirect Anne's attention and the conversation. "You played him, didn't you, in that movie."

"Yes," Zack agrees, pushing his sunglasses back up. "Two years old and it's all anyone can talk about in this town."

"We're all a little obsessed with *this town* in Washington," I say, sympathizing with him on this at least. "Which is particularly funny, considering how hard it is to film in D.C."

Zack's voice suddenly sharpens. "It really is! I've been trying to get a permit for the National Mall for months." His voice lowers, "It's for my directorial debut."

"The security and the jurisdiction issues are complex here. Why don't you have your people call my office. We might be able to help?" I dig into my small, party-sized purse and hand him my card. I'm still not sure about him, but I'm leaning toward "harmless." "It doesn't really fall under my purview, but I'm a movie fan."

Zack smiles as he takes it, and it's still a movie star's smile but this time might be genuine.

"Aren't we all," Anne murmurs, watching. I hope I've sufficiently thrown her off whatever speculation she'd been mulling over a moment ago. I excuse myself and head toward the safe corner I'd spotted earlier. But my colleagues are gone.

I pause to pull my vibrating phone out of my purse and have a text from one of my mentors.

Sara: Just finished your chapter and think it
needs more of the REAL YOU in it. Let's talk!

Despite dreading the work implied, I smile at Sara's directness.

Sara is a former PoliSci college professor who is now tenured and loving a life buried in original-sources research. She's been reading the latest draft of the memoir I've been struggling at writing, re-writing and revising for far too long. I'd been approached, immediately after taking office, to write about my "shocking election," and what a background in activism meant to politicking. While I'd hesitated over writing a book so soon into my political career, I'd thought it would be a chance to talk about my goals for change. To build momentum. But then I'd gotten bogged down in the complete lack of change since I'd taken office. I should take a cue from Barack Obama and call it *The Arrogance of Hope.*

Cindy: This afternoon? I'll be beautifying
for WHCD

Sara: Call me! I'll be editing

I pause before I tuck my phone away and open my contacts. The number saved as "VP" is at the top of my screen. If I called and asked whoever answered to put him on the phone, he probably would talk to me. Unless he's in the Oval Office or the Situation

Room or doing any one of the many more important things he does that aren't dwelling on that kiss.

I put my phone away. I have no idea what I want to say to him. *Sorry I'm not sorry? Want to try again?* No matter how old I get, romantic feelings still turn me immature. It's so much easier to talk policy than emotions.

Scanning the room, I decide to set myself a goal of three more conversations before I can escape. I head toward the cameras, where it's a decent bet that people will be networking.

An hour and a half later, I arrive back at my apartment in Capitol Hill, take a shower and change into sweats and a t-shirt. I have a hairstylist and makeup artist coming over this afternoon to redo my look. I call Sara over Bluetooth as I'm shaking out my rented dress for the evening and using a handheld steamer on it.

"So you hated it?" I begin, a blatant request for reassurance that I should never attempt. My long-time mentor never bothers with niceties.

"Nobody wants to read this book any more than you want to write it. It's boring," Sara declares. There it is.

I spread and fluff the layers of my dress to get the wrinkles out, trying not to take this feedback too personally.

"And *you're* not boring at all," Sara continues, thankfully. "So you're hiding in this."

"It's supposed to be a *partial* memoir," I defend the manuscript. "It's about running for office as a woman. It's meant to be a new metaphor for success, beyond *leaning in* or *climbing the ladder*. It's about stomping as you climb."

"There's not much stomping in what you sent me."

"Did you read the whole thing?" I wrote about getting into politics because I cared too much, about running into walls and learning how to build coalitions by accident. I wrote about discovering that pursuing the things that made me passionate worked better than following the proscribed steps to success.

"I did."

I'm not sure why I'm being defensive. I knew something wasn't right with the manuscript when I sent it to her. "OK, you're right," I sigh. "How do I fix it?"

"The first thing people want to know is *why* and you never talk about that for you. You get into politics spontaneously because you're mad, but that's not a real reason."

"Why? Isn't the *why* obvious? Because the system is broken."

"But how is it broken *for you*. You make it sound like your life is easy. As far as anyone can tell from this, you didn't have any real problems to overcome on your way to where you are. No bills or babies or deadbeat boyfriends or crippling self-doubt to worry about."

"Well, I had a couple of those things. Definitely the crippling self-doubt at times. And parents who discouraged me and people who called me *too pretty, too rich, too smart,* too something to climb the ladder on my way to getting anything done."

"Humble brag," Sara says. "That doesn't sound compelling to me. Not unique enough."

I pause, experiencing the crippling doubt we were just talking about. Is my story not compelling enough for a book? The things I've faced—the tiny, cutting comments, the piles of hate mail, the talking-head who called me "Lawmaker Barbie" and analyzed my proportions on live television—are no more than what any woman in the modern, western world faces.

But maybe that's the power of my story, too.

The moment Sara became my mentor was the same: Harsh but accurate. Still a student, in the middle of an equal pay campaign for student employees, I'd invited Sara out for coffee to "pick her brain." She'd asked me, "Be honest: Do you really want equality for all or do you just want enough money to buy a latte once in a while?"

I'd protested, of course. I'd accused Sara of missing the point.

But Sara had said, "A compelling argument starts with what it means to you."

So I'd changed the campaign to "everyone should have enough money to buy a latte," and earned enough support to enact a small student wage change on campus. I still use that advice, and try to get close enough to every argument I make for a constituent that it means something personal to *me*. Cannabis as a cause sat in the back of my mind since my teen years, getting high with friends who were punished for it more severely than me. I didn't have personal experience with the criminal justice system, but I did with Malik and Jodi and Hugo. I spoke for *them* because a white woman holding a blunt could be symbolic instead of a Most Wanted poster.

"I know the book needs to be more personal to be good," I admit finally, pulling the steamer cord out of the wall. "But I'm not sure I want to write *that* book."

I put the steamer down to respond to a knock at the front door. I let in my beauty team, asking Sara to wait a minute while I show them where they're going to set up. A mirror is propped up in the larger living room, where it can get more natural light. I can't afford a nicer place on my budget, not while I have to keep a residence in Colorado too, but I like my little basement apartment and its quirky character.

"Sorry," I tell Sara. "Fancy dinner tonight."

"I've heard of it," Sara says, sounding unimpressed. She's not part of the minority of people who lose their minds over this dinner. "So think about what is your biggest personal challenge right now and then work backward. And include the journey in your book. That's what it needs."

I meet my eyes in the mirror as I settle into the chair in front of it. No matter how I consider it, my biggest personal struggle right now involves the vice president. "Right," I say.

"You're thinking of something right now, aren't you? Go with that," Sara advises. "That's compelling. Drama!"

"It's drama, alright," I agree. "But I can't write about it."

"Well, you can put this book out as-is if you want. It's not going to advance you or your interests in any meaningful way, though. Listen, I've got to go. I have a coffee with a student and I'm still wearing my sweats."

"Heaven forbid. Thanks for reading it, Sara. I'll keep you posted." I end the call and apologize to my style team. I already went over the aesthetic I wanted for tonight with my stylist, but I hate being a person who acts like the people they're paying are nothing more than tools.

And I need their best effort. I want to appear museum-good tonight, like someone people long to touch. Never mind who "people" is in this scenario.

I don't want to think too hard about my book, either, but I'd promised to have a draft to my editor in two months.

The real problem with my book is I'm afraid of releasing a retrospective. I'm terrified of looking back because I don't want *this* to be the pinnacle of my success. Elected on a landslide but unable to achieve anything I promised. A so-called firebrand without an actual brand. I want a book that ends at the precipice of something more.

I just don't have a cliffhanger in mind yet.

thirteen

Alex

THE BALLROOM of the Washington Hilton is like a Costco crossed with Bloomingdale's, in that it's filled with people in fancy clothes scanning for what they want. I get a lot of second takes from the more than 2,000 greedy eyes surrounding me, as if I'm a good deal on GoGurt or something. Fortunately, the Secret Service keeps most people from approaching my round table.

There are 10 place settings at the table, all already occupied by the time my entourage sweeps into the room. Cindy is far across the table from me—I should have been more specific about her seat—but I suppose it's for the best that no one will mistake her for my date. The last time I brought a date to an event, it was a ball for the second inauguration and her name is *still* linked to mine in every magazine or feature piece about me. I haven't talked to Chelsea since she gave an interview in which she called me "a little stiff."

At least if Cindy gave that quote, she'd be blushing while she said it.

Smiling at everyone as I sit down, I give her a nod of polite acknowledgement. She's wearing black, her hair is up and she's wearing bright red lipstick again. Her dress has long sleeves and a deep V in the back. She's crisp and collected and delicious, like an elegant apple. I want to rub her against my shirt before I bite into her. *Great, now who's blushing.*

I turn my attention to the raised platform at the front of the room, where Tim and Anita are both sitting. Tim is required to give a speech before the actual entertainer of the evening, and his sense of comedic timing is not his best quality. The presidential campaign staff worried so much about him bombing the year of the last election, they managed to get him out of giving the speech by "donating" the time to charity.

Tim can let the dad jokes fly for the rest of his presidency, though. I'm not sure whether I'm looking forward to it or bracing myself not to cringe in front of the cameras.

I wish I could tell Cindy the full context. Lean in and whisper it into her neck. She meets my eyes over the rim of her glass, her head tilted toward that damn movie star, Ryder, on her right. *Doesn't that guy live in California?* He keeps popping up at everything this weekend.

Keeping her gaze, I lean over to the governor of Florida, who is seated next to me. "Didn't you bring the sunshine with you, Melody? It's chilly tonight."

She smiles. "Tell me about it, Mr. Vice President. I'm freezing." She shivers and pulls her silk shawl thing closer around her neck.

"You let me know if you need my jacket," I tell her, earning a smile from the women within earshot. I need to remember to thank my sisters for teaching me this amazing shortcut to every woman's heart: Warmth.

"Ever the charmer," murmurs the senior White House correspondent on my left side.

"I should have brought a case of slippers," I whisper back. "Could've won some votes for life."

"Hell, *I'd* swoon if I could wear something besides these new shoes," the man replies.

I laugh and clap him on the back like we're friends. The last time this guy caught up to me walking down the White House driveway toward EEOB, he'd asked if I thought the party should invest more in other leadership options. "Your poll numbers indicate only half the country knows who you are," he'd said. I hate how two-faced this job is, sometimes.

Tim gives his speech, getting mostly polite laughs until he makes his crack at my expense about how "unlike my VP, I'm not literally married to this country."

The whole room bursts into laughter and some light applause. Heads swivel toward me as I try to keep a mildly self-deprecating expression on my face. Can't appear too surprised; don't want to start any rumors about friction between me and the president.

"Bet that doesn't keep you warm at night," is the hearty response from the asshole on my left, getting a few more chuckles from our table.

Sipping my water, I don't respond. My lips are curved, like I don't mind being the butt of everyone's joke. Cindy gazes back at me, pressing her lips together. At least *she* didn't laugh. The lights in the ballroom catch in her eyes, obscuring her expression, but I can tell she wants to say something. I wish, again, we were next to each other. Maybe she'd even rest her knee against mine.

I straighten to ensure I'm not touching either of the people who are next to me in reality. She smiles, like she knows what I'm thinking, and turns back to the front of the room. I want to trace my fingers down the spine of her bare back. From this angle, she could be naked, sitting in a sea of silks and sequins. I want to rest my chin in the crook of her neck and whisper into her ear, watch the shiver travel across her skin.

This is worse than sitting at the United Nations, pretending to understand anything that's said before the translation catches up in my ear. Watching Cindy Wight and acting like I don't want to touch her is torture.

* * *

Cindy

Oh my god, we're going to have to have the Sex Talk.

While the president mercifully finishes his speech, I remain tense. As though people can see that I'm inappropriately fantasizing. The tension between me and the vice president is already thick enough that I'm worried the whole table can read it in the air between us. I didn't expect this. I planned to focus on my goals, my career, on being a powerful, independent woman who doesn't need any VP dick. Then I saw him in his suit.

Now I'm imagining sex with him and the terms under which I'd have it. He might not feel the same, but I have to know. *Immediately*. The urgency sings in my overheated veins.

Powerful, independent women can have sex on their terms, right? Of course, we can. A man invented the idea of abstinence granting power.

The comedian giving the keynote speech launches with a joke about all the "nerds" in the room, which is an easy laugh in this crowd. He keeps going, keeping it uncontroversial: "Have you ever noticed there's no such thing as a *wonk* anywhere outside Washington. There are no Hollywood wonks. You don't say 'I'm a huge Marvel wonk.'"

The crowd laughs more.

I'm not sure I'm going to make it another minute of this

inane speech, with the vice president's eyes on my bare back and the need starting to build between my legs. But I know leaving the vice president's table during the program would cause a fuss, so I grit my teeth and try to look like I'm completely focused on the front of the room.

It's was before I ran for office, the last time I had sex. It's a huge risk given my job and the rampant sexism that would make me notorious if certain facts became public. That means any potential relationship requires a level of fierce trust early on, something that seems nearly impossible to find.

For that reason, I've chosen my reputation over sex—not such a huge loss, when most of the sex in my life has been unfulfilling. I was in my late 30s by the time I allowed myself to admit that I'd never directed my negotiation skills toward what I wanted in bed. I'd spent the last few years beating myself up for not speaking up, not following my own values, when it comes to intimacy.

Now I *have* to speak up, and I have to do it with the vice president. Because it feels like if I don't at least try to sleep with him, I might regret it for the rest of my life.

And now that I've determined to raise the subject, it's all I can do not to stand up in the middle of this crowded ballroom and start shouting: *Sex! Now! Yes?*

Almost on cue, the comedian takes a shot at Alex: "The safest person in the United States to handle the nuclear codes is Vice President Drake, who we all know is the model of abstinence." The room laughs again, too heartily.

Alex's reputation can't be true. I've never heard more than a whisper about the vice president's sex life—and then it was that he doesn't have one. In a town like Washington, where those kind of secrets are usually open, he may have less sex than I do. Which is honestly a travesty against the United States, considering the tabloid shot I once saw of him back home in California with his shirt off. I suspect plenty of voters have that photo saved, even printed out and taped somewhere near their beds.

Zack leans over to me and murmurs, "Now we know why no one trusts *me* with the nuclear codes."

I offer a single, soft laugh in response. I'm not sure if he's flirting *with* me or flirting in general. The only people more obsessed with image than politicians are movie stars, so I doubt his interest is real. But I'm starting to like Zack and he's a good distraction. I smile at him.

My bare back tingles. I've felt the vice president's eyes on me all night, but now his gaze burns. I resist the desire to check over my shoulder again. Someone is going to notice the hunger in my eyes when they're on the vice president.

The rest of the speech is excruciating, and not just because jokes about Washington by an outsider are hard to get right.

I imagine launching the conversation I want to have. Do I call him and bring it up while any member of his staff or security might be listening? Can I ask for a private meeting? Not if he won't be alone with me. The aloneness is something else we have to negotiate, a clear issue of trust on his end. He must trust me a little; why else would he have let me into the backseat of his SUV last night? We'd gotten lucky—the rumor mill was too busy with other gossip for anyone to notice I'd left with him. But he'd taken a risk, and Alex doesn't seem like a risk-taker.

I'm forming quite a lengthy mental list of obstacles, each one increasing the yawning hole in my stomach. My dinner is swirling around with everything else and I'm off-balance. Borderline nauseated.

The comedian finally ends with "and that's why, next year, I've decided to register to vote." The crowd claps, and a few people stand for an ovation, prompting others to rise. I admire the complete lack of reaction on Tim and Anita Meyer's faces, standing on the platform, clapping for the man who roasted them.

When I turn back to the table—reluctantly, given that I'm afraid my own expression is easier to read—the vice president is getting up.

"Leaving so soon?" Zack asks.

"I need a quick break before the next round of hand-shakes," he says without looking directly at Zack. I'm getting the impression the vice president is not a fan. "Please excuse me," he says to the table. He nods at me and leaves, his security team with him.

After a count of 10, I murmur: "Excuse me, I need to run to the restroom myself."

I walk away from the table in another direction, but circle the room to follow the vice president's detail. This is a risk and I'm being an insane person, but at the moment I don't care. I'm obsessed. I *need* him, or at least to know if I can't have him.

We head toward the back of the hotel, away from the crowds, to a bathroom that's guarded. The vice president goes in as I hesitantly keep walking toward his entourage, afraid of being tackled from behind, until at almost the last second a Secret Service agent comes out of nowhere to block my way.

I'm not sure if I'm about to be arrested or possibly face-planted into the floor—this was *such* a bad idea—but the Secret Service agent nods at me politely and says, "One moment, congresswoman." Like he expected me.

We stand in silence for a full minute, waiting for a signal invisible to me. Then he nods and turns to the side to let me keep walking. I slowly approach the closed door and one agent opens it for me, so I go into the bathroom. I catch sight of the vice president in the full-length mirrors across from the door as I enter. He's fixing a cuff on his sleeve. The gold cufflink flashes in the light.

He stands between the wide counter with a gold sink and the wood-slatted privacy stall. Waiting for me.

"I'm so sorry, this is such a bad idea," I blurt out, hesitating as the door closes behind me.

The vice president smiles as he walks toward me. "I like when you're impulsive," he says. Then he pushes me up against the mirrors and kisses me.

I gasp, because the glass is cold against my bare back. His tongue meets mine. He tastes like the amazing chocolate cake served for dessert. My nipples go hard and my panties are instantly wet. It doesn't last long enough before he yanks back and looks down at me with concern. "This is what you wanted, isn't it?"

"Yes, of course. Always. Yes." I'm having trouble regaining the thoughts that were circling in my head a few minutes ago. "I just thought there'd be more talking."

"Oh." He lets me go, brushing the fabric of my dress back down my sides. "I'm sorry. Of course, we should talk."

"No, don't be sorry," I say quickly. My lips feel chapped. Still spread for him, my thighs pull at the sides of my dress. My skin cools without his touch and calls out for more. "I want this." I scramble to find my words again. "Um. Did you know I was following you?"

"Not until they told me." He flicks his head at the door, which is opening.

"Did you want us to stay outside?" the agent who stopped me in the hall asks, poking his head through the doorway.

"Yes," the vice president says. "Thank you. We're fine."

I vaguely acknowledge that he's willing to be alone with me —a good sign for getting what I want. But my brain is on holiday after that kiss.

"They didn't stop me," I say.

He smiles. "I told them you have access. Obviously, there are times and places you can't go, but in general," he pauses. A line creases his forehead—*this is serious*—as he finishes, "You have access to me."

I'm glad I'm still propped up against the wall when he says that, because it makes me a little wobbly. "Are you sure you want to be alone with me?" I manage.

He laughs. "I want nothing more than to be alone with you, but believe me, we're *not* really alone. Is that what you wanted to talk about?"

"Yes. That and, well, a few other things." I straighten up and put my arms around myself, holding my elbows.

"Cold?" he asks, and slides off his jacket without waiting for me to answer. He puts it around my shoulders, a move that never fails to make me want a man. Not that I need another reason with this one.

Holding the jacket around my chest, I smile. His gesture creates a small space where I can think again. "Thank you." I step toward him to touch my lips to his, very gently, then step back. *Do this right, Cindy.* "I wondered if you wanted to do this sometime when it's planned and not in between engagements."

He nods. "I'd love that." He eyes me as I'm struggling to find the next words. "What do you mean by 'this'?"

I internally go over the appropriate options to say—kissing, talking—but all my mind keeps whispering is *sex, sex, sex.*

"You don't have to know exactly," he adds. "But I want to make sure we're on the same page here."

Looking down at my hands clutching the lapels of the jacket to try to hide my smile, I tease, "Maybe we could draw up a draft proposal."

"If you want," he says, evenly.

I turn my head up and meet his eyes. He's serious. I like that. "A verbal agreement is fine." I can't stop smiling.

"OK," he nods. He runs a hand through his hair, then pauses

to grimace and pulls his hand away. "I'm not supposed to do that when there are so many cameras around."

Stepping forward, I reach up to put his hair back into place, combing through strands he's disturbed. "Perfect," I say, and start to step back, but he grabs the lapels of his jacket around me and keeps me close to his chest.

"I'll go first," he says. "I want an exclusive arrangement. For as long as we have one."

My nipples brush his chest as I nod and it sends a zing up the space between my bare back and his jacket. I have to hold my breath for a moment. "I agree with that."

He lets go of the jacket and rests his hands on my hips beneath it, his fingers skimming the curve of my breasts as he drops them to my sides. I'm not sure if it's an accident or on purpose, but my body wants more. But I need to think straight for this conversation, for at least long enough to get to the good part.

"I don't want this, whatever this is, to be public," I say. Any hint of a conflict of interest between me and the vice president would sink the cannabis legislation. Who wants to vote for something produced secretly by two scheming lovers?

He nods, like this isn't a serious caveat. "OK. You understand that I can only meet in secure locations? I can probably never come to your apartment, for instance."

The idea of the vice president in my tiny studio apartment feels about as real as this conversation does right now. "I can come to your place."

One of his hands slides around so that his thumb can trace circles on the naked small of my back. My entire body lights up from the sensation and my internal muscles clench involuntarily. *Fuck.* I want to drop my dress on the floor here and now.

"You like that?" he murmurs, stepping into me a little more. His chin grazes my forehead.

"I'm very sensitive there," I whisper.

"Good to know," he replies softly. "Where else?"

I smile a little, afraid to move at all or lose the feeling he's creating. My core is empty, my internal muscles aching to be stretched. "I like," I pause to swallow. "This is something else I wanted to bring up. I like..." And then I can't keep talking. I'm bold; I'm called a crusader. But I'm being bold on behalf of other people. "Never mind. It's nothing."

His hand stops moving. He steps back, his hands going back to my hips. "What?"

I meet his eyes, hoping to distract him. "STDs? Anything to worry about?"

"I am happy to have a fresh panel done, although it might take awhile to do in secret. Most of my doctor appointments are on record. But I haven't been sexually active in a couple of years, so it shouldn't be a concern." He answers me, but I can tell he's still waiting for my response.

"Same here," I say. "A couple years. I tested clean after."

He slides his hand up my side until his thumb is under one breast and my breath catches in anticipation. "What else?" he asks, gently.

I silently self-talk the same way I do before a big meeting. *Speak up. Trust your instincts. Say what you want.*

"When you pushed me against the mirror, I liked that. That's what I like," I say, holding his eyes. *Come on, Cindy, be specific.* But my throat is closing up. I've only had this conversation once with a sexual partner, and it didn't go well. I'm 45 years old, yet suddenly intensely afraid of the vulnerability of telling another human being what makes me feel good intimately. *It's too early!*

But if we're going to have sex, and I hope we are, I want it to bring us closer. And he can't know me if I'm not honest with him.

I see the understanding in his eyes. I'm simultaneously relieved he gets it and terrified that he does.

"You like to be pushed around," he suggests. "In the bedroom, obviously, not in real life, where you are more than competent at taking care of yourself."

He says it simply, without judgment.

I still want to step back, away from my fears. Away from the realization of how much I've revealed. Away from how much power I've given him. "Is that something you can do?" I ask, instead of running away. "That you are comfortable with?"

He presses his fingers into my hips so that I sway toward him, then back onto my heels, like a puppet he's moving with a light touch. *At his mercy.* But I like it. I want, desperately, to be naked with him. Right now.

"Do you trust me?" he asks.

Staring into his blue eyes, I consider it. There's a certain amount of mutual destruction involved in our relationship if anyone finds out we're together. My adversarial reputation. His spotless one. But I don't know him that well. I settle on: "I'm starting to. Do *you* trust *me?*"

He gazes down at me without smiling. "I trust you enough to tie you to my bed and fuck you."

My whole body comes to attention. My nipples ripple the tape holding my breasts up in this dress.

"Without worrying about you taking it directly to the press," he adds, his voice several degrees lighter than before. The corner of his mouth quirks up.

I smile. "Well, not *directly,*" I joke, a bad habit to deflect a significant moment. "I'm sorry, what I meant was I would never do that," I add, looking him in the eye. "You threw me with that tie-me-up comment."

"In a good way?"

I bite the inside of my lip. I make my voice sound like a dare, but it's difficult when I want to beg. "Show me, and we'll see."

He smirks and lets me go. "We've got to get back or this agreement will be moot before it's even started. You go back before me. But first..." He sweeps me off my feet with his hands around my hips and pushes me into the wall hard enough that the mirrors shake, pulling my head back by my hair so he can run his lips up my neck. His jacket falls off with the motion and the cold zips up my spine.

A gutteral noise comes straight from my abdomen. It's desperate. Needy.

His mouth reaches mine as I run one calf up his side, trying to get my core closer to him. His hand slides up the slit of my dress and I arch as he slides right past my underwear. My body has been waiting for this, maybe forever. One finger slides inside, then two. Sliding easily into my liquid channel. I thrust against him. I want so much more.

He releases me and steps back. I reach out and grab his tie, bringing him back to me. Then I hesitate. What I want is going to take so much longer than we have. His eyes drop to my mouth, then bounce back to meet my gaze.

We stare at each other, absorbing the moment. *Are we going to be responsible or...?* His jacket slides the rest of the way off my shoulders onto the floor.

"Sorry about your hair," he says. His voice is breathless.

I reach a hand up to the wisps falling around my neck. My fingers are numb. "You'd better go first," I say. I need a minute or 10 before I can stand properly.

He reaches down and picks up his jacket. "I suppose I'd better. An agent will stand outside the door until you leave. No rush." He wraps one arm around my shoulders and pulls me to his chest for a hug. "You're alright?"

I smile into his chest at the unexpected gesture. His hardness is digging into my hip and I have to swallow before I can talk. "I'm alright. But there's something you should know about me."

"Oh?"

I tilt my body back to meet his eyes. "I'm extremely impatient."

He laughs. "Why does that not surprise me." He leans down, pressing his forehead against mine, and traces the curve of my breast. "Soon."

He steps back, throwing the jacket over one shoulder with two fingers in the collar. "I promise."

I watch him leave, still shaky. I want to yell after him, make him come finish what he started, anything to stop this sense of desperation.

How is it possible I've made a sex date with the vice president? Impossible that he could deliver even after I told him what I want. Our surreal moment in this bathroom could be merely that: A moment I'll remember the rest of my life. Never to be repeated.

My mother always says I'm a doubter. But in this case, I'm willing to be proved very wrong.

fourteen

Alex

BECAUSE I'M the vice president, I have little control over my schedule. So while what I *want* to do is clear the way for a full weekend alone with Cindy, what I end up doing is planning a trip to Detroit for a tour of a new factory.

"Why don't you come with me," I tell Cindy on the phone Tuesday night. I'm standing in the park, as usual. Ted is close enough to overhear the conversation but I'm not worried about him sharing it. "We can debrief on the bill. We'll have a chance to talk privately. And I'll have you back on Sunday."

"Seems risky," she says.

"Nah," I insist. "It's Air Force *Two*. People barely notice who's flying around with me."

"You still have a press pool."

"And they'll check you out, but it'll remind people that the cannabis legislation is still happening. It's a good thing. Raise the profile."

Her voice sharpens. "You think people have already forgotten the bill?"

I wrestle the ball away from Thor so I can throw it again, buying myself time. I need to be diplomatic here. "I think Washington has a short memory."

She sighs, and when she agrees I'm not sure if it's for my sake or business. But that's OK. I'm a master of reframing. I have, more than once, turned an argument about censorship or school choice at a fundraiser into a donation. Finally, I'll be able to use my powers for good.

* * *

Cindy

"*He invited you on Air Force Two?*" Lizzie's voice achieves a pitch I've only ever heard for votes after midnight. "What does this mean?"

"He said it underlines the White House commitment to a legislative compromise," I recite, thankful I'm on a conference call and Lizzie is the only member of my staff physically in my office. My face can't be very convincing. "It's mostly time-efficient. I asked for more face time and he said this was how he could give it to me."

I roll the pen between my fingers, staring hard at it while using the phrase *give it to me* and hoping I'm not blushing.

"How much publicity do we want?" Max asks, over the speakerphone. "I'm not sure how impressed Coloradans will really be that you're on a fancy jet flying to another state, to be honest."

"Right, I agree," I say quickly. "I wanted you two to know but I don't think we want to spread it around that I'm going. It's a quick trip, no public appearances. I'm just going because the only time the vice president has available is while he's traveling. The White House will release my name to the media, along with the topic we're discussing, but I don't expect any major announcements out of the trip. And I don't want to be one of those lawmakers who posts a picture with the presidential seal every time they're near one. Does that sound good?"

"Sounds reasonable to me. But send *me* a selfie with the seal," Max suggests. "Are you taking staff with you? I am so jealous right now."

"You are not," I retort. "You get 300 days of sunshine a year."

"Hey, April is D.C.'s one good month," Lizzie pipes up. "Max is missing out on cherry blossoms."

"I am not going to take anyone with me," I say, answering the question and my own guilty conscience. "It's a taxpayer-funded trip, technically, and I can't justify staff."

I'm walking a narrow line here, between constituent and personal priorities. In my defense, it's a line I walk daily as a human being who is also a symbol of the public interest. Taking time to eat, sleep, or use the bathroom could be considered stealing time from the reason I'm in this office. In this case, I promise myself I'll earn enough benefit for Colorado taxpayers from the trip to make anything *else* that takes place a bonus.

We hang up with Max, and Lizzie perches on the edge of my desk. "Can I help with anything else?" she asks.

Is Lizzie suspicious? I'd considered telling my staff this trip was sort of...kind of...a date. I could safely tell Max and Lizzie, my two closest and most trustworthy staffers. But it could also turn into a one-night stand, in which case I don't want the information I had sex with the vice president to spread.

"I don't think so?" I tell Lizzie.

Her brow wrinkles. "You don't want...a proposal drafted or the spreadsheet on votes to take with you?"

"Oh!" I manage to smile. "Sorry. I guess maybe I'm a little frazzled over this trip, even though I don't want it to be a big deal. Yes, please, let's tidy up our notes and print them for me to take with me. I don't know what the Wi-Fi situation is like on Air Force Two."

"Great!" Lizzie pops to her feet, smiling. "I'll work on that."

I put my head in my hands after Lizzie exits. This is the problem with mixing business and pleasure. I need to be counting votes, but all I want to worry about is what lingerie to wear.

The buzzer over my office door goes off, calling me to a vote on the Floor. I grab my blazer and purse and head down the hall, my heels harmonizing with all the others exiting nearby offices and heading for the tunnel to the Capitol.

The floor of the hallway outside my office is marble, but the rest of the decor is dull. Door after matching door is marked with a brown and gold plaque next to it spelling out the member's name, some with a flag or two on the opposite side. I nod and smile at several people joining me for the walk to the lower chamber.

Steven, one of the Freshman Six, falls into step with me.

"Getting some face time with the vice president this weekend," I tell him proactively. "I'm hopeful we'll make some progress. Did you talk to anyone about potentially dropping one provision or the other?"

He makes a face. "No one wants to talk about it. They think the time is right to go for everything."

I sigh. We pass the entrance to the cafeteria on our way to the tunnels. "I don't think we get to roll up in Congress one year and win everything we want the next."

He glances at me. "That's not what you used to say."

Low blow. "Well, I'm learning," I say, mildly. Steven doesn't have anything else to say after that. He takes the subway and I keep walking down the tunnel to the Capitol.

Keeping an eye out to ensure I don't run into anyone else, I'm thumbing through social media on my personal phone as I walk.

I pause to read a story about the vice president and Zack Ryder. "VP to Cameo in the Sequel to *Attack on the White House*?" reads the headline.

The members of Congress on their way to a vote have priority after the buzzer goes off, so the tunnel is clear coming from the other direction and I can be swept along in the tide.

Using my thumbs, I zoom in on the picture on my phone. Alex Drake looks as delicious as I remember him in that dark suit with the pink tie. His hand is on Zack's shoulder and they're smiling at each other, belying how annoyed I remember the vice president seemed with the actor at the time.

The pink panties. The ones that match my bra. With the straps that come up over my hips. *Just in case he sees them.* I study the picture two seconds longer before I turn off my phone, decision made.

I don't remember what vote I'm going to. I switch to my BlackBerry, at the same time consciously switching my brain into work mode.

* * *

Alex

The cherry blossoms are beautiful, but my spring allergies are making themselves known as I walk up the long steps to Air Force Two. I focus on energetic posture and not tripping, the nightmare faced by everyone who is filmed on these long walks. Tim still says the president before him lost his second term because Americans judged him for tripping on the Air Force One stairs. Twice. Both times went viral.

It's a lot of pressure to walk up the red-carpeted steps safely.

After I check walking off the mental to-do list—again—I have time to worry about how pissed Cindy's going to be about the travel arrangements. I couldn't *not* invite the Michigan delegation to join me on a trip to their state. But now I'm going to have to share my public time with both her and her colleagues, or risk suspicion and rumors. The press would probably love to sniff out a story about me snubbing a committee chairman—and why.

Maggie, my traveling press secretary, walks with me to my office, carrying the print-outs of everyone on board she'll hand out to reporters. "Did you want to come back to talk to the press once we're in the air?" she asks, once she's asked me for updates on the topics she expects from reporters.

I catch myself before I run a hand through my hair. "No, I've got too much to do on this flight," I say.

"No problem," she says, noting something on her pad.

Is it selfish, as a full-time public servant, to want a bit of privacy to explore whatever I'm building with Cindy? In an ideal world, I'd have checked the "significant other" box before I became vice president. We would have agreed, together, that the job came first in this season of life, after already building a strong foundation between us. Perhaps I would have built my schedule, as much as possible, around my relationship, instead of the other way around. Now it's borderline impossible to fit one into my life.

It doesn't feel quite right, taking Cindy on a 500 mile joyride without giving her anything to take home from it. "This is the job," my father would say. "She better know what she's signing up for."

But she hasn't signed up yet. That's the whole point of spending time with each other.

I lean outside the door to my stateroom. "Maggie," I say, when she's almost down the hall. She turns back. "Would you suggest to the Michigan delegation that they might want to talk to the media on board? Could be a win-win."

She smiles. "Good idea, sir."

Win-win indeed, if it keeps the lawmakers from Michigan busy while I get, well, *busy* with Cindy. I didn't become vice president by being a complete idiot.

* * *

Cindy

I should have known. The House Judiciary Chair—Randy—is from Michigan. He's the first person I spot when I step off the Osprey at Andrews Air Force Base ahead of boarding Air Force Two. He must have been in the other helicopter. It would have been easy to miss him in the crowd at the White House, with all the staff shuffling us around and me trying to avoid questions from the reporters boarding with us.

It's loud by the twin Ospreys and I wave and hope he'll leave it at that, but Randy walks over and yells to me, "If it isn't the Freshman One!" He chuckles at his own joke and then explains it, "Used to be the Freshman Six!"

I pretend I can't hear him over the rotor blades.

We are herded away from the landing pad, White House staff diligently explaining the process even though I can't hear anything. It's moving lips and a lot of pointing.

"You here to talk to the VP about marijuana?" Randy asks, once we're far enough from the rotors to speak normally.

"Yes," I say. "We need to discuss a new date to release the cannabis legislation." I knew we were going to blow past the deadline weeks ago, sometime in March when the House adjourned and I realized I couldn't schedule any meetings with members who were back in their districts. Not without the leadership of my party jumping behind the bill or Alex stealing the baton in a way I *don't* want. It still burns to acknowledge to Randy that we missed it.

He's scoffing. "You're never going to get the votes if you stick with your bill. Washington works slow for a reason and your crusade will be short-lived here."

I nod, like his point is thoughtful, watching the concrete landing pad as we're crossing it. "I think there's room to find common ground and make progress."

He shakes his head, like he's disappointed in me. "There hasn't been common ground in Congress for the last five years. I'd think you'd have picked up a few more things in your time here."

We're interrupted by one of his aides—Randy apparently does *not* travel alone—so I don't have to defend my experience.

I walk a little faster to move ahead of him and glance up at Air Force Two standing on the airfield in front of us. The blue and white Boeing startles me with how massive it appears, bigger than in pictures. I've never been on it or even near it.

The White House staffer keeps leading us forward, and the surreality of the trip sinks into my mind. The man who kissed me in the bathroom is on that plane, or somewhere nearby. I don't know if the vice president boards first or his guests do, but the moveable steps with a red carpet are set up at the front door of the plane. I can't stop obsessing over his hands, those long fingers and how he touched me with them. The way he smelled like a hint of smoked wood and tasted like chocolate. The *vice president*. I can't believe I'm allowed to touch him at all. Who the hell am I—just some girl from Colorado who, according to Randy, doesn't understand how politics work.

We board through the middle door of the plane, along with the media. The journalists are escorted toward the back, while I'm taken, along with the other lawmakers, to the equivalent of first class. I sit down in a cushioned chair and take out my phone to hide how I want to gawk at my surroundings. I start reading a celebrity gossip site. A little light reading doesn't disqualify me for my job.

Zack Ryder is in the news again for allegedly romancing the co-star of his new movie. There are pictures of him shirtless on some tropical beach. But I'm distracted, irritated at yet another man casually challenging my abilities. It wouldn't matter what I tried to do in Washington, there would always be a Randy to scoff and doubt and feel justified doing it. Yet I do worry that Alex and I are trying to reach a compromise starting from different places. I worry about that for more than the bill.

But it's not like the compromise has to hold forever, right? Only long enough to get this one thing done. I sigh softly, because now I'm making accidental double entendres about myself. Sex *and* legislation—is that asking too much?

I try to keep focusing on the celebrity vacation pictures I'm scrolling through on my phone, but I'm wondering—no, *knowing* —what Randy's reaction would be if he found out my presence here was in response to a booty call from the vice president.

He's already harrying the staff, his rounded belly taking up his entire seat. There's no way Randy flies economy in a regular airplane, even when flying on the taxpayer's dime. I try not to judge on appearances, having been judged many times that way myself, but from what I know about Randy, it's hard not to view him as an entitled, comfortable snob.

I won't back down because someone smug tries to shame me out of my plans. It's hardly the first attempt. Holding my phone though I'm no longer using it, I tap my fingers against the little table by my chair until I notice I'm doing it and stop.

Maggie, the primary press aide for the vice president's office, walks back into our section and smiles at me. "Good afternoon, congresswoman." She turns to the others. "The vice president wondered if the Michigan delegation would like to speak to the press today? Give some background on the factory and the state economy, that kind of thing."

From under my eyelashes, I observe as Randy and his fellow representatives react enthusiastically. If the vice president planned this, he's clever. The Michigan lawmakers will clear out of this section long enough for me to see him without anyone the wiser. If they come back before I do, they might not even realize why I'm gone. My need to touch the vice president again—something we can only do when alone—pulses under my skin.

I hide my smile, but inwardly, I'm pumping my fists in victory.

fifteen

Alex

I'M in multitasking mode by the time my staff lets Cindy into my stateroom on board Air Force Two. I signed off on a *Wall Street Journal* op-ed while on the phone with the CEO of a tech giant who wants me to become a user of their new social platform. Earlier, I spoke to the Majority Leader about drop-dead requirements for supporting the cannabis bill. When she walks in, I consciously tell myself to slow down.

She's wearing a soft gray skirt and matching jacket with a pink blouse that makes her appear more demure than she is. Her hair is in a sleek ponytail and I want to tug it, as if I've reverted to a school boy.

I walk up and put my hand on her shoulder before I ask, "Are we at this stage yet? The casual kiss hello stage?"

She smiles and bites her lip a little. I love when she does that. "You tell me."

So I do, by wrapping one hand around her shoulders and pressing the other into the small of her back so I can pull her to me and kiss her on the mouth. She tastes like the custom-made candy they offer guests on board.

Her eyes open slowly once I let her go. "Not that I don't appreciate that, but...is anyone going to walk in on us?" she asks, eyeing the closed door she came in.

"I asked them to give us 20 minutes." My staff is too professional to show surprise.

"Yikes. Time pressure." She turns away from me. "As if this wasn't already a lot."

I note her ramrod posture, shoulders thrown back and neck stiff. She's in a new environment—heavily sanitized and with weird lighting and a lot of people around—and not exactly a sexy one. "Are you nervous?"

She turns around and smiles, but it's as sanitized as Air Force Two. "Not to talk about this bill."

"Listen," I say, and walk toward her so she backs up against my desk. "Why don't you sit here." I push her gently and she sits down on the edge. "I will sit here." I pull up a chair in front of her. "And you can tell me where you're at on the bill while I do this."

Reaching down, I pick up her foot and ease off her high heel. The pointy toe cannot be comfortable, but my sisters would inform me that's not the point. In fairness, her discomfort was appreciated when I checked out her legs.

I take her foot into my lap and start digging my thumbs into the ball of it.

She closes her eyes and holds onto the desk. "OK, if you insist, Mr. Vice President."

I laugh. "You can call me Alex, you know."

She leans back, her eyes still closed, stretching out her leg. "How many people call you Alex?"

"Tim—the president. Anita. My mom. My sisters. Thor probably does, too, but not out loud." I move my thumbs gradually down the center of her foot. She moans quietly, making me smile. "So tell me where you're at."

She keeps her eyes closed, her face tilted toward the ceiling, as she says, "I have more support for keeping the banking, so let's go for that. We can attach expunging records to another bill in the future."

"Well, I've got bad news for you." I press more firmly with my fingers, flexing and pointing her foot. Her fingers cling to the edge of the desk as I tug on her limb. "The Majority Leader says the provision she will consider is deleting past records."

"Oh my god, of course she did."

It's bad news and I can do nothing about it but distract her. "You know, this is much more effective with more access," I murmur, sliding my hand up her leg.

She goes still. "Is it?"

"Let me show you how much more," I say, sliding my hand around to her inner thigh. I pick up on the moment when she thinks about closing her legs, but then she lets them fall open. She's balanced on a few inches of desk with one foot in my lap and the other on the toe of one shoe, an awkward position that gives me all the access I want. "Tell me more about the bill," I suggest, my hand tracing the taut muscles leading in the direction of her core.

She takes a little sip of air, her head still thrown back. "Someone's going to revolt to prove a point. I can't guarantee all six of our votes."

"That's alright. If the whole party votes with us, we only need five. Do we have five?"

"I...think so," she says. She's frowning. Can't have that. I stand up, placing her foot back on the chair, and she pulls her head forward and opens her eyes.

"One second," I say. I put my hands on her hips and start lifting her tight skirt up, slowly folding it over in my hands, revealing an inch of her legs at a time. I glance up at her before the final fold that bares her pink panties to my eyes, checking to make sure she's still with me. She's curious, maybe more curious than turned on. But she doesn't stop me.

I lift her a little so I can get the skirt under her, and put her back down on the desk with her skirt hiked up the way I want. I pull her shirt up around her waist a little. Then I step back and gaze at her, perched on my desk looking disheveled, her legs spread and her panties showing.

"Ah yeah, this is it. Whole reason to become the vice president."

She smiles a little, a knowing smile, nodding with her chin at the way I've posed her. "Is this all?"

"Not quite."

She meets my eyes. "Are you watching the time?"

I glance at the clock over my desk and nod. "We're OK."

"Then show me what else you want." Her voice is a dare. She doesn't move, like she's enjoying playing doll for me.

Stepping back between her legs, I help her take off her jacket. Putting my hand around her ponytail, I pull her head back with her hair using small, testing tugs. I want to test the limits of how aggressive she likes it. She gasps, her chin pointing up at the ceiling. "You like that, hm?" I say, and run my lips along her exposed neck. I use my other hand to check through the thin fabric of her panties. "Oh, you like that a lot."

The pulse in her neck beats hard against my mouth.

"Tell me," I urge.

"Yes, I like it a lot," she agrees. Her eyes, raised toward the ceiling of the plane, slide closed. I put pressure on her head until she lays back on my desk, and I push her shirt up over her breasts so I can see her bra. Pink as well.

"I think you hoped I'd see this," I murmur, running one finger over the curve of her breast where bare skin meets lace.

"It crossed my mind," she whispers, opening her eyes and looking at me.

I step back so I can get a good mental picture of Cindy Wight stretched across my desk. Vulnerable and wanting. She raises her other leg, dropping her shoe onto the floor, and putting the heel of her bare foot on the edge of the wood.

"What are you doing?" she asks.

"Enjoying the view," I reply. I glance at the clock again. We might not have enough time, but I'm going to give it a shot.

Pulling her leg back off the desk, I reach under her skirt to take her underwear off. She watches me as I do it, but neither of us say a word. I put the panties in my suit pocket, step back between her legs and slide both hands down her thighs. She arches her back, a delicious sight with her shirt pulled up, and closes her eyes again. She has a landing strip of hair between her legs, and I suspect it's freshly trimmed.

"Thanks for this," I murmur, sliding one finger down her slit. She cuts off a moan by biting her lip. "Not necessary, but appreciated."

Resting both hands on either side of her pussy, holding her pelvis spread open so I can see the folds of her labia and the opening below it, I blow gently. She shivers and her legs quiver.

I glance at the clock again. Definitely not enough time.

Lowering my face between her legs, I plunge my tongue into her opening.

"Mmph." She slaps a palm over her own mouth.

"That's good," I say. "Keep your hand over your mouth."

Checking long enough to make sure she follows directions, I then lick up and around her clit and draw it into my mouth to give it a strong suck. She murmurs against her hand and lifts her butt off the desk toward my mouth. Her actions say: *more*. That's good, since it's been a while since I did this.

I raise my head and check the clock as I shove two fingers

inside Cindy without warning her. She's swollen and wet; I knew they would slide right in and I'm right. I twist them back and forth as she arches up and into me, eyes closed, hand over her mouth, so debauched already.

She pulls her hand away. "That's good," she whispers.

I put my face back into her pussy and lift her up into my mouth with my wet hand, bracing my other hand on the desk so she stays arched away from the desk. I make fast circles around her clit, then slow, alternating pressure.

"Jesus, Mr. Vice President," she whispers. "Alex." She puts her hand back over her mouth to silence herself.

My own cock is hard from the sound of her, from the visual of her spread out in my workplace, from the signs she'd let me do anything I want right now. I decide to test this, again.

With my two wet fingers, I find the second opening below her pussy and circle it, lubricating, before I press inward with one.

She breathes in hard. Her free hand flies to the top edge of the desk by her head and clutches it. She's pressing hard enough against her mouth with the other hand that her fingers turn white.

I push my finger inside of her and turn my mouth into a suction at the same time. Then I catch sight of the clock again and pull back. "Fuck," I whisper.

She drops her hand and opens her eyes. "Fuck?" She follows my eyes and hers widen. "Fuck."

I release her back onto the desk and help her sit up, drawing her shirt down.

"I'm so sorry. Someone could come back at any moment." I pull her off the desk and she smoothes her skirt down.

"No, yes, I mean, I completely lost track of time." She's breathing hard. Her face is flushed. She yanks her ponytail down and starts trying to redo her hair.

I'm so hard I involuntarily lean into her, letting the head of my cock brush against her side through my pants. I clench my teeth in response to the sensation. It's not enough. She pauses and I rest my forehead against hers for a moment, sharing this excruciating sensation. I smooth my fingers over the shirt now covering her breast.

"Use the bathroom," I suggest after a few moments of breathing together, pulling away and pointing to the door in the corner. She leans down to grab her shoes and hurries toward it.

The door has just closed behind her when Deena knocks on the outer door and steps in. I duck behind my desk to hide my hard-on. "Sir, if you're about finished..." She pauses and scans the room for the missing Cindy.

I gesture at the bathroom. "About finished," I agree, wishing to put my head down on my desk. I straighten some of the papers on it. "When are we landing?" I ask.

"In 30 minutes," Deena says.

Cindy steps out of the bathroom like nothing happened, clothes straight and hair smooth. She locks eyes with Deena. "My time up?" she asks, a little too cheerfully. She doesn't look at me.

"I'm afraid so, ma'am."

Before she can leave, I clear my throat. "We can perhaps find some time this evening to continue this conversation. You have my number."

"I do." Cindy nods at me crisply. "Thank you." She picks up her jacket and Deena ushers her out the door. I smile, tidying my desk quickly before Deena comes back, because Cindy looks like the most professional woman on the plane but only I know that she left behind her panties.

* * *

Cindy

Legs still shaky, I take my seat with the members of the Michigan delegation. Leanne, a woman 20 years my senior, leans over and says, "Was that the most amazing experience?"

My eyes dart to the other woman's. I fold my legs carefully to one side, to avoid flashing anyone with my bare lady parts.

"Flying on Air Force One *or* Two never gets old," the woman continues with a smile. "If it ever does, that's when it's time to give up this whole business."

I nod and smile. I'm thankful I didn't have to walk through the reporters on the plane to get back to my seat. I looked normal, if a little flushed, in Alex's bathroom mirror, but who knows what a gaggle of reporters might sniff out—possibly literally. Between my legs, it's still wet.

My stomach is clenched, like I reached the top of a roller coaster and am teetering on the drop. I'd been close when he stopped. Shockingly close. I haven't come that fast since my early 30s.

Once we land, my group, as well as the press pool, disembark before the vice president does. I don't join the photo op of the Michigan delegation and Detroit mayor greeting Alex. I have two conference calls scheduled, so I head back to my hotel room.

The first thing I do is put on fresh underwear. I wonder if Alex left mine in his pocket while taking photos. The idea leaves me half embarrassed, half smug. I'm proud that I can still surprise myself with stolen moments of intimacy. But also embarrassed because of how the public would perceive it if anyone ever found out. I'm the one who would be branded a slut in this scenario, no matter that Alex had all the power.

After all these years working in one of the least sexy industries in the country, what we did on Air Force Two is weighed down with a layer of prohibition beyond the fact that it's a government plane. If someone ever found out, there might be an ethics investigation.

Stop feeling guilty, Cindy! Historical records show presidents have had sex on Air Force One in the past—I'd looked it up. Is a government official wasting taxpayer money every time she goes to the bathroom or sleeps at night? Voters are not electing robots.

But I already have enough challenges on my plate, enough criticism just for daring to exist and use my voice in this world.

My first call is on video, and as I'm setting up my hotel desk, I silently promise I'll let myself have this—these stolen, sexy moments—so long as they remain secret.

sixteen

Alex

I'M KNOWN for my level head and calm amid a crisis. That's one of the reasons Tim said he chose me as his VP—that and the many electoral votes represented by my home state.

But I'm pissed, *pissed*, that a certain segment of the media is coming after my dog.

I march down the hallway to my hotel room, surrounded by staff and security, ranting about the video going viral online. "My dog makes people think I'm gay, huh? If I was gay, I would just be gay, this isn't the fucking *Handmaid's Tale*. I don't need to tell the world by owning a tiny mammal, like some kind of captive sending up flares from my little gay prison in the White House."

The viral video completely overwhelmed my visit to the new factory opening. So much for the White House's planned emphasis on manufacturing this week.

"Can we issue a statement *from* Thor? Completely laugh them off?" I wait for an agent to open the hotel room for me.

"It will breathe more air into the controversy, give it another day of conversation," says Maggie.

"It's pretty likely to come back up anyway," says Dan. "Better to shut it down now."

"I don't mean to be a dick about it," Maggie counters. "But do we even have anyone who can write a statement like that? We're not funny people."

She and Dan go silent, exchanging looks. Some of the best things about my staff are their comfort with staying behind the scenes, writing in my voice, and fear of making waves. Until now.

I roll my eyes. "Thank you for being honest," I say. "You have many other fine skills. Now go find me someone funny." I pause, rewinding what they'd said in my head. "But why is it likely to come up again?"

They both blink back at me like deer in the headlights. Of course. It's because a single man can't remain single without people coming up with conspiracy theories.

"Never mind. Go, get out of here." I pull off my tie and throw it onto the desk before I move into the bedroom of the suite.

People are going to mock me for my little dog and my suspect masculinity for as long as I'm a bachelor. America is more comfortable with married leaders—preferably heterosexual ones. Managing my singleness is a catch-22. The other extreme, dating a lot of women, might earn me high-fives from the people snarking it up on certain streaming channels, but it would earn me criticism—and outright distrust—from the Bible Belt. There's no way to win.

Besides, dating requires intense energy, and my job is greedy.

I flop onto my bed face-first for about five seconds before I remember the next thing on my to-do list and roll over to find my phone. I don't see it, so I pop my head outside the room and ask Ted.

Ted hands it over. "Apparently your mother called."

"Has she seen the video?"

Ted raises his eyebrows, like I'm an idiot. "I didn't talk to her. But who hasn't?"

I sigh and take the phone back into the room. Before I close the door, I add: "Oh, I might have a guest later. If I can convince her."

Ted nods. "The congresswoman?"

"No, my other secret girlfriend." I make a face.

Ted is impassive, all business. He says, "Don't tell her your room number. We can send someone for her."

I nod and close the door so I can call my mother back.

"I just feel terrible," she says after greeting me. "Your father was right all along, that dog makes you look like a *you-know-what.*"

"Mother." I rub the spot on my forehead between my eyebrows, pacing by the sofa in my hotel room. There are too many assumptions to parse behind my mother's lowered voice. "If you mean it makes me gay, there's nothing wrong with that. And Dad shouldn't think there's something wrong with that either."

"But you don't want to *look* like something you're not, do you?" She pauses. "*Do* you?"

"I don't want to look like I'm ashamed of being something that I don't happen to be. But Mom, you know there's no inherent way of *being gay*, don't you? It's not like everyone who happens to be gay immediately buys a tiny dog or, I don't know, assless chaps."

"Alex!"

"Mother. You're from California, you should know better." I was a grown adult before I discovered teasing works on ingrained prejudice, at least from my mother and a number of donors. My father, though, is still immune to being called out.

"We're from *northern* California," she corrects me, but her voice turns contrite. "I suppose you're right."

"I'm definitely right, *and* I'm right that you shouldn't blame yourself for this dumb criticism. Thor is tough and so am I. We'll handle it." Funny how having to calm someone else down helps me soothe myself. I can't *believe* anyone would use my innocent dog against me.

She moves on to asking where in the world I am and what I ate for dinner. Then we reach the subject my mother really relishes: My other little sister's upcoming wedding.

"I went ahead and gave you a plus one because it balances out the table, but don't worry. If you don't have a date, I'll get you one."

Refusing to take the bait, I smile, kicking off my shoes and taking off my belt. "I wasn't worried."

Her voice does the mom equivalent of going in for the kill. "Does that mean you *do* have a date?"

"Not currently." My mind is full of Cindy Wight, and the way she got vulnerable with me the last two times we saw each other. I'm almost afraid that I'll blurt out her name. "But maybe by August I will."

My mom says nothing, but I get a mental image of her clutching the phone to her side and screaming silently as she bounces up and down. "I'm so excited!" she finally says, her voice completely even.

I laugh. "Well, let's take it slow for now. It might fall apart in four more months."

"Don't predict bad things," she warns sternly. "Speak only good things and good things will happen. And it's about time, too. I hate to think of you all alone in that city."

"Believe me, Mom, I'm *never* alone."

"You know what I mean."

And, to be honest, I really do.

* * *

Cindy

The vice president offers wine when the hotel room door closes behind me. I take it, but walk to the table in the front room of his suite and sit down without drinking it.

"We should talk about the bill," I declare. I'd decided on the way over here we needed to have this conversation. It might be 11 p.m., but this is *not* a booty call. I came for work. I even left my work clothes on from earlier, heels and all. Discomfort is good for determination.

He nods and pours himself a glass before he follows me. "I don't want to guess how you're feeling, so would you mind cluing me in?"

My gaze darts up to him as I'm taking the folders out of my file-sized purse. "What?"

He pulls out the chair across from me so that it's facing me more than the table and sits down, crossing his legs. He's wearing the same clothes, but he's taken off his tie and jacket and his shirt is unbuttoned at the top. "You seem tense. I don't want to make any assumptions, but it's making me think you aren't happy about earlier."

"Oh." I put the folders down and stare at him, trying to gather my thoughts. His face is open, like he's willing to wait on me. Like he's interested. "I've never been asked anything quite like that before."

He pauses as he's bringing his glass to his lips. "You've never been asked about your feelings?"

"Not as straightforward as that, no." I run my finger over the edge of the folder. I try to be a straightforward person in general, but sometimes, in relationships—or whatever this is—it's easy to retreat behind a shield. It's hard to put words around my thoughts. "I'm not unhappy about earlier at all. I feel kind of vulnerable and a little embarrassed."

His eyes on me are so intent I can't quite keep his gaze. "I'm the one who didn't make you come—isn't the embarrassment mine?"

I smile, because my instinct is to reassure him, and doesn't that illustrate the whole problem in our dynamic? *Speak up, Cindy.* I press forward. "It's more a reaction to, um, feeling like we got distracted. Like I'm doing this other thing with you when I should be focused on negotiating this legislation. For my constituents."

"Ah." He nods. He puts the wine glass down on the table and uncrosses his legs so he can sit forward, clasping his hands between his knees. His eyes are locked on my face. "Do you think I'm doing it deliberately? Distracting you from what you want?"

Who knew I could be this turned on by someone having an open and direct conversation with me? I'm distracted from the actual conversation by how thrilling it is to have someone's entire attention. "Are we having a DTR right now?"

He cocks his head. "What's a DTR?"

Feeling like a teenager again, I laugh. "A defining-the-relationship talk."

"Oh, right." He smiles. "I went to an all-boys school; I missed out on a few things." He pauses. "I don't want to have a DTR if what you want to be doing is working on this." He points at the folders on the table.

I stare at him hard, because what I want and need to do right now are very far apart. "I want to make some tangible progress on this," I agree. "But maybe after that, we can...make some progress on us?"

"Incentive. I like it." He sits back again. "OK, let's do this."

So we discuss the language I refuse to remove from the bill, the votes I can guarantee with one provision, and each of the votes I think I can secure if we're careful about language and messaging around both of them. Naturally, I argue for going bigger; Alex argues we have to be cautious to make any progress at all. I'm starting to understand, despite myself, why he can't get carried away by one cause. He has so many to balance.

He tells me he can convince the Senate Majority Leader to support a slightly more ambitious version of the bill *if* it passes the House with overwhelming support. I acknowledge that support depends entirely on whether the issue remains popular between now and when our legislation finally comes up for a vote.

It's 1 a.m. when we're done, and he stands and stretches and tells me, "There's never going to be an ideal moment for us, but if you want to take a raincheck, I certainly understand that."

I think about it as I stand. I'm pretty tired. But I also don't know when this moment will happen again. The way he's stretching, with his shirt untucked, I can see a sliver of his bare stomach. I step toward him and slide my hand under his shirt. It's like crossing a forbidden line. From *wanting this* to *doing this*.

"Alright," he agrees, and smiles. He puts his hands on my shoulders and slides them down my arms, brushing my breasts with both thumbs on the way.

He raises both hands up to my hair and gently takes it out of the ponytail. I close my eyes and enjoy his fingers massaging my scalp.

"Take off your clothes," he orders me softly. I open my eyes. "All of them," he says simply. It's not a negotiation. Then he steps away and stands there, watching me.

Taking a deep breath, I obey. I don't know how I can hate being ordered around everywhere else but in the bedroom, in a space of mutual consent, it turns me on faster than anything else. In my fantasies, when I'm alone, I imagine being tied up and surprised by what a man—who, historically, looks a little like Brad Pitt—does to my body. Helpless to his touch. Lately, the outline of that imaginary man is morphing into the shape of Alex, though still with shaggier hair and a mild Missouri drawl.

I peel off my clothes, one item at a time, leaving my panties and heels for last.

In general, I like my body; it has stayed strong and curvy as it's aged and that's more important to me than some cellulite and sagging. Still, I'm not used to someone watching me take my clothes off with all the overhead lights on.

He steps forward, once, after I take my bra off, and caresses my naked breasts, running his thumbs over the nipples in a way that sends sparks through my body. His eyes are intent.

I pause with my panties and heels still on and I'm not sure what to do with my hands. Fortunately, he gives me more direction.

"To the bedroom," Alex says. He touches the curve of my butt as I pass him and walks behind me down the short hall.

"One knee on the bed," he says, and I climb onto the edge, kneeling with both hands and one knee on the mattress and my other heel on the floor. I take a peek over my shoulder at him, arching my back. I know the vision I'm presenting. I hope he likes it.

He puts one hand on my bottom, caressing it. He gives it a very light pat. "Do you like this?" he asks.

"Sometimes," I say. "Not too intense."

He nods, and slaps my butt again, harder this time. Then he slides his palm in between my legs. "You like it more than you'll admit," he says. He runs one finger back and forth, over my panties, down my slit.

"It's you...telling me what to do," I admit. It's intensely vulnerable to tell him how he affects me, even though he can feel the evidence. My fingers are shaking against the bed. I can't remember the last time I got this turned on by nothing more than the low, steady murmur of a man's voice and the confident, attentive way he assesses me.

He nods. He slaps my ass one more time, causing another blurt of desire.

"Then turn over, spread your legs, and put your hands above your head," he says.

I swallow hard and lick my lips, enjoying the rush of heat at my core, before I do what he says. Part of the turn-on is wanting to please him. Allowing myself to reach the point where I'd do anything he told me to do. It's so sexy, my body feels like a live wire. I'm already ready for him to fuck me. I can tell how swollen my clit is from the way it throbs against my underwear.

Lying spread-eagled on the bed, I brace my hands against the headboard, tucking my fingers around the top of the mattress. "What are you going to do with me?" I murmur.

He takes my heels off, one by one, and drops them on the floor. "I'm going to fuck you," he says, unbuttoning his shirt. "I'm going to fuck you until you come, and then I'm going to make you come again to make up for earlier on the plane. Don't move," he adds, as I wiggle a little in anticipation.

"Alex," I say, rolling the syllables around my mouth as I adjust to calling him by his first name out loud.

"Yes?" he murmurs, pausing before he pushes his shirt off his shoulders.

"I want you to fuck me hard," I say. I want him to fill me up, get so close to me that our skin blends.

He drops the shirt on the floor. "I intend to, Cindy," he says. It's the same voice he's used in interviews where he talked about national security. Calm, reassuring, certain. He unbuttons his pants and my eyes are glued to his crotch as he pushes them down. The bulge in his boxer briefs is promising. I dig my fingers into the mattress.

"Do you have condoms?" I ask, suddenly worried. I didn't

come prepared. Now I'm imagining the vice president trying to buy condoms at a convenience store, perhaps trying to hide his purchases behind a soda and a lottery ticket.

He picks up his pants and I notice he's wearing blue socks with dogs on them. He pulls a wrapper out of his pants pocket before he drops them again. "Thank a Secret Service agent," he says with a grin.

I wince.

"Stop," he commands. He's looming over me, knees on both sides of my hips. "I didn't make anyone run an errand for me. It's a personal loan."

My attention is torn between him and everything outside these walls. "I hope they don't want it back."

He smiles before he grows serious again. "Close your eyes, Cindy."

Without asking questions, I do. The darkness instantly transports me back into my own body, to the sensation of being beneath him with every nerve ending attuned to the next time he will touch me. His mouth closes around one nipple, then the other. He bites it, a sharp bite that makes me gasp and open my eyes again.

"Yes?" he asks, looking up at me.

"Yes," I agree, appreciating how he keeps checking in with me. "I like it."

He slides back off the end of the bed and pushes off his underwear. His dick, thick rather than long, is standing at attention like the soldier he once was.

I hear myself whine a little, because I want it. But I follow his directions not to move. He smiles and rolls the condom on as he's standing there, too far away. I clench my toes in the bedding because I've never seen anything more attractive than this right now, the vice president of the United States naked and nearly between my legs.

Finally, he puts both knees on the end of the bed and pulls my underwear down. I lift my hips so he can take them off and then spread my legs again for him once they're free.

"Good girl," he says. He positions himself over me and nudges the tip of his penis against my opening. "I'm not going to be gentle," he warns me.

"Good," I whisper.

He slides in a little. My eyes are rolling back in my head. He pulls out again and I make that keening sound I've never heard from my own mouth before.

Then he shoves into me, all the way, so far he brushes against my organs somewhere deep inside.

All day since the flight, I've been conscious of the emptiness between my legs. I've longed for this. I forget myself and reach up with one hand to grasp his shoulders, but he grabs me by the wrist and puts my hand back above my head. Fuck, that's exactly what I wanted. He holds my hand there as he fucks me, thrusting deep and pulling out with every stroke. One thumb keeps brushing over my palm, soothing even as he plows into me.

On purpose, I move my other hand, so he'll grab it and stop me. "Fuck, yes," I say, the words forced out by a spike of pleasure. He is so big above me, like he could genuinely hold me in place if he wanted to, beyond the illusion of being held down. He clasps my wrists in one big hand and uses his other to pull one of my thighs up to his side, giving himself better access as he fucks me.

But I need more. I need pressure against my clit. I squirm, trying to build some friction against his moving body.

He pauses, half-way inside me. "What do you need?" he asks. "Speak up."

I squeeze my eyes shut, feeling another rush of desire from the evidence we're on the same page. "I need you to touch my clit," I whisper.

He lets go of my leg to reach between us. I moan as he starts circling the raised nub of nerves there. He slides in and out shallowly, creating delicious friction against my opening. I squeeze my internal muscles as hard as I can against him and my mind goes blank from how hard I come. His lips slide against my arched neck and I coast over another hump of pleasure.

I'm still gasping when he starts fucking me again, hard, deep strokes until he comes inside me. He collapses on top of me, the hand holding my wrists above our heads sliding up my wrists until our fingers are loosely clasped together.

He slides his other hand down my sweaty side to press my clit again. I jump. I'm not sure I can handle stimulation again so soon, but he strokes gently, leaving my center alone, until the need lazily starts to build again.

"Show me," he says. "Show me what you like." He releases my hands and guides one down my own body. I show him, watching him watch me give myself what I need. The intimacy between us gets me closer than what I'm doing alone.

"I think we've found another campaign slogan for you," I say, once I'm satiated again and smiling aimlessly up at the ceiling.

"Oh yeah?" he murmurs, unmoving at my side.

"Alexander Hamilton Drake: Orgasms."

He raises his head. "Is that it? Just orgasms?"

I close my eyes drowsily. "Yep."

His soft laugh is the last thing I hear.

seventeen

Alex

I'M USED to waking at the slightest touch, both due to my past as a Marine as well as my current job, so my eyes open to Ted before he says anything.

Holding up a hand, I check over my bare shoulder to find Cindy still asleep behind me, her hand on the bed between us. I throw a sheet over her naked chest and slide out of bed.

Dan is waiting in the outer room when I follow Ted out into the rest of the suite. I don't want Dan to get the right idea about what's going on in the bedroom, but I don't want to wake Cindy either, so I speak in a lowered voice but don't whisper. "Emergency?"

"No, sir, I'm sorry for waking you. The secretary of State is seven hours ahead of us in Jordan and wants a meeting."

I nod. "Sure." I pause and scan the room. "Let me change and meet you in one of the conference rooms."

"Yes, sir."

I glance at Ted as Dan leaves and nod, thanking him for

cleaning up the clothes strewn all over the room last night before letting Dan in.

Ted quirks his mouth and nods back. I go back into the bedroom to grab my clothes and watch Cindy's outline for a moment, in the dim light from the other room. I wish it were not the case, but suppose *immediately* is as good a time as any to find out if she can handle my schedule.

* * *

Cindy

"Ma'am."

Slowly, I surface from a dream about saving kittens from a flood.

"Please wake up, ma'am."

My eyes open. A strange man is standing at the end of my bed and my hand goes to the covers, because I'm naked beneath them.

The next second, I recognize him as one of the vice president's Secret Service agents. I gaze around in confusion. The drapes are closed but it's obviously still dark outside. One lamp is on, on the table on Alex's empty side of the bed. We're alone in the hotel bedroom.

"I'm sorry to wake you like this, congresswoman," the agent says. "But we need to get you back to your room now if you don't want to risk someone noticing you're here in the morning."

"Right. Thank you," I say automatically, while I try to force my brain back online. "Where is…"

Then it hits me. Alex sent the Secret Service to deal with me. *Is this what he does?* Am I the latest addition to the vice president's list of secret sleepovers? How is this belatedly crossing my mind as a possibility?

I sit up, holding the blankets to my chest.

"The vice president had to step out," he says, not comforting me at all.

"OK," I say, pushing the word out forcefully. Trying to keep all emotion out of my voice. "Give me a minute."

"I'll be right outside," he says, and leaves. I wait for the outdoor door to close before I scramble up, looking for my clothes until I remember leaving them in the other room. How humiliating.

I tiptoe naked out to the other room, but my clothes aren't there, either. I scan for them frantically.

OK, don't panic yet. I start systematically searching while internally chanting: *Calm, calm, I am calm.* I find my clothes in a rumpled pile on a chair in the bedroom, like they were gathered up and thrown there quickly. Like a metaphor for how I'm being treated right now.

I pull them on angrily, but the person I'm most angry at right now is myself. I should have left last night. I got my legislative update, I got the first good—great—sex I've had in years; I should have checked those off my day and put myself to bed in my own room instead of greedily trying for...what? Someone to cuddle with? A *boyfriend*?

A vice president is not a boyfriend.

That is very obvious this morning.

I'm an idiot. I'm dressed by the time I hear the hotel room door open again, and I stomp out into the other room holding my shoes, irritated that I'm being hurried on top of everything else.

It's Alex. He's wearing a button-down shirt over sweatpants, which I quickly identify as a last-minute video conference outfit. He smiles at me. I pause. It's the second time in the last 10 minutes that the certainty has fallen out of my world.

"I'm so sorry you had to wake up like that," he says. "I had to talk about the Strait of Hormuz with the secretary of State and approve a statement because people are still saying my dog represents the size of my dick, or something like that. Are you OK?"

No, I'm not OK. I'm cold on the outside and a fiery inferno on the inside. "I'm told I need to leave now, before someone realizes I'm here," I say. My voice seems to sound normal, but from inside my buzzing head it's hard to tell.

"Well, that's only if you care who finds out," he says, walking toward me and putting his hands on my arms. I'm paralyzed, caught between shaking him off and leaning in. "I assumed you didn't want the press to find out like this. With a so-called walk of shame."

He's standing right in front of me, but he might as well be a million miles away. "I don't want the press to find out at all," I say. That was my plan. I've got to stick to my plan. Otherwise, I'll keep waking up stumbling over pointless dreams.

His eyes flicker, like he's cataloging that statement in a new file. "Right," he says. "I understand."

I eye the door. I should go. But I don't want to go while I'm this confused. "I thought you were trying to get rid of me," I say, having to force the words out past my fear of admitting the fear itself. Straightforward worked for us last night and I have to find out if it still works in the morning.

Standing over me, his expression is serious but not exactly surprised. "I'm sorry I made you feel that way," he says. It's not reassuring. The anger rises again.

"So you *were* trying to get rid of me. Got it," I say, steering around him toward the door.

"Wait," he says, grabbing my arms again. "Look..." he pauses, gazing into the distance behind me for a moment before turning his eyes back to mine. "We don't know each other that well, so I understand why you don't trust me. You woke up alone and that sucks. But it's part of the package."

"What *package?*" I demand, my head starting to clear. He might be the vice president, but this level of assholery is common. "The one-night-stand package?"

He appears surprised. "No, the...*me* package. This is what my life is like. Getting woken up and pulled into meetings in the middle of the night. Not always being available. You need to understand that."

My confusion is wound around me like a ball of string at this point and I don't know how to reconcile the facts with my feelings, so I plow ahead with the anger: "Oh really, why's that."

He tilts his head, studying me. "If we're going to do this."

"Do *what?*" I shake him off and balance on one foot as I put my shoes on. He stands back, hand slightly extended as if I'd accept his help.

"Keep dating?"

With my shoes on, I'm a little more in control. I can look him in the eyes instead of craning my neck. It helps the anger clear enough to hear him. "We're dating?" I say.

"I thought so," he says. He might be re-evaluating that as he says it. A small, traitorous bubble of excitement catches in my throat at the idea he wants that.

A vice president is not a boyfriend.

"Alex," I say, and pause after hearing myself call him by his first name. I don't know what I want to say next.

"Did you think..." He frowns and turns his gaze away from me, then back. I see him swallow. "Did you just want sex?"

That sounds like an accusation. "I thought that's what *you* wanted!" I protest.

He's still frowning. He steeples his hands and puts them to his lips. "It's OK if that's what you wanted, I just wish we'd had that conversation before now."

I stare at him. My stomach is running away from me and I'm starting to develop a headache. "What did you want?" I hear myself speak in past tense and it's like losing something important.

He stares at me, like it should be obvious.

"You wanted to date," I say. I can't decide if I'm cold or hot. Two seconds ago, I wanted nothing more than to flee this room and now I'm frozen, like I couldn't leave unless I was carried out.

"I wanted to date," he confirms. "Privately. Without the press knowing about us."

The vice president wants to *date* me. Wanted.

"What made you think I didn't?" he asks.

Waking up alone. But it wasn't really fair to blame him for that. He's helping run a country. Maybe I overreacted. "You could have left a note," I say weakly. "Or woke me up."

He nods. His eyes are understanding. "Yes. I could have. I'm sorry."

"No, I'm sorry. I jumped to a conclusion and blamed you for feeling..." I trail off, but he waits for me to finish the sentence. "Used," I finish. Now that my temper is cooling, I realize how differently I could have handled this. It didn't have to become a fight. Now my impulsive defensiveness has up and ruined the happy glow of our evening together.

"It's not a good feeling," he says, validating my emotions in a way that, clear-eyed now, I can appreciate. "I enjoyed last night very much. I'm sorry this morning turned out so different."

I walk over to my purse and pick it up. I should probably leave before this gets worse. I turn to him, resigned. "Did I screw us up?"

He runs his hand through his hair. His nervous tell. "There's an 'us'?" he asks. "If there's an 'us,' nothing's screwed up."

Biting my lip, faced with someone who may be one of the best guys I've met in years, I hesitate. He's the vice president, yes, but right now he's also a *man* that I want in my life. A man I disagree with frequently on matters of policy, but so far never on personal topics. This is not going to be easy, but right now he seems worth it.

"There's an 'us,'" I confirm.

He smiles, a smile I've only ever seen up close and in person, never on TV or in front of a crowd. *My* smile. "Good."

This is going to be excessively complicated. But right now, I've never agreed more fervently with a member of the establishment.

eighteen

Alex

I'VE NEVER PARTICULARLY LIKED golfing, but years ago decided it was a necessary evil—first to spend time with my dad, then for a political career.

Tim and I don't golf together often because the optics of both executive branch leaders taking time out of the day for relaxation doesn't go over well with the public. But we take advantage of the days when our teams allow that the visual of the executive branch leaders getting along may outweigh other concerns.

"Nice socks," Tim comments first thing upon greeting me. We drove separately and we'll have separate golf carts with separate security, too. We're waiting by the carts for the final all-clear from the Secret Service.

Lifting one foot, I show off my *Got balls?* socks. Unlike almost every other pair of gaudy novelty socks I own—which is a lot—this pair is from Tim.

"You don't think they're inappropriate for a date with the president?" I joke.

"I don't know, it's been years. What's dating like these days?"

"Doesn't seem to have gotten any easier." I shrug helplessly.

"Ah, so Anita was right."

Internally debating protesting that the status is brand-new, I abandon my pride and shrug. "Anita's always right."

Tim cuts right to the chase. "How long you planning on keeping it a secret?"

"As long as she wants to, I guess." I've been thinking about this—a lot—and it doesn't seem like it should be my decision. "Being the vice president's girlfriend, publicly, seems like a big job. And she's already got a big job."

"You're right, it's a shitty job and one that doesn't come with a salary. Just ask Anita. In fact, you should have *her* talk to Anita, whenever she's ready." Responding to the Secret Service signal, we start walking toward the tee, continuing our private conversation despite being in the middle of a group of agents, staff and caddies. You learn how to pretend you're alone in this job. "You think you'll get that far?"

I shrug again. "How do I know?" It's not a rhetorical question.

"You're looking for a partner, not just a date," Tim says, rapidly summarizing the salient points the way he would in a national crisis. "You want someone with a strategic vision for your life together that goes beyond politics. But you also need someone who can help you through your next campaign. I'd advise you to set aside your feelings and consider your needs."

"It seems so transactional," I sigh, examining my nine iron.

"If she's smart, she's doing the same calculus," Tim says, raising his eyebrows at me over his sunglasses. "If you want long-term, you need to, too. If you're thinking short-term...well, make a calendar and stick to it, Alex."

I nod, stepping back for Tim's shot. Tim's probably right, but first I need to sort out the difference between what I want and need, because when it comes to Cindy, they're all mixed up together.

* * *

Cindy

"Have you told anyone?" Alex asks me when I come over that night. It's a "working meeting," in that we discussed the latest vote I locked down while naked and touching each other in bed. It satisfied me both professionally and personally—a rarity.

He'd made me talk about whipping votes while circling my clit with his tongue.

"No," I answer him. I'm wearing one of his shirts and digging in his fridge for omelet ingredients. He's rumpled and delicious, bare-chested with his soft pants hanging off his hips. "I want to tell one person on my comms team, to have some kind of just-in-case strategy prepared, but the comms person I most trust is out in Colorado and I don't want to tell her on the phone. What about you?"

"Tim knows. And my agents, obviously. And, well, some of the comms staff."

I dump my options on the counter. "This is already becoming one of those open Washington secrets."

Alex grimaces. He's sitting on one of the stools pushed up against the bar counter. His kitchen appears spotless, the appliances gleaming and nothing on the counters. "I swear it's not. All of those people are legally sworn to secrecy."

He's cute, but not convincing.

"Only a matter of time before some 'anonymous source' talks to the *Times* or the *Post*," I say. I'm predicting it calmly, mainly because my body is still filled with endorphins, but it's a terrifying prospect. Yet living in denial is foolish; we know how this works. "Then they'll be on red alert to confirm it, and we won't be able to sneak nights like this anymore."

He waves the scenario away. "We're not there yet."

"How long shall we say?" I ask. I pause what I'm doing in the kitchen and pull my phone out of my purse, which we'd dropped on the floor on our way to the bedroom earlier.

"Are you setting a calendar alert?" he asks. "You and Tim must share a brain."

I glance up from my phone. "I think like the president of the United States? Thank you, I'll take it." I ignore my many notifications—after scanning to make sure nothing urgent has happened—and open my calendar app. "I wasn't setting a reminder, but that's honestly a great idea. We can table this discussion for now, but we should have it later. In, like...a month? I mean, assuming we're still together then." I say it because I should, because I'm realistic, but bleakness settles over me at the idea of a future without Alex. Already, it's like he—and our time together—has filled a hole in my life I didn't know was there.

He doesn't respond directly to my suggestion, so I set a reminder in my phone for a month away. I've got to be smart about this, not afraid to examine it. I have so many goals outside this relationship. I can't lose track of them.

"Can I help?" Alex is standing in front of me now, taking my phone from me and putting it on the kitchen counter as he runs his hands up and down my arms as he eyes the ingredients on the counter. He's clearly trying to change the subject from our impending doom, but I'll let him. When I'm with him, thinking about anything else is a struggle.

"Do you know what you're doing?" I ask.

He scoffs. "I nearly became a professional chef. Long time ago, during my 'rebellious' phase."

"Are you serious?" I try to remember any profile I've read

about Alex that had this detail in it. "Your secret bad boy phase involved cooking?"

"Believe it or not, the long, long road toward a career in higher office did not always appeal to me." He nudges me aside, pulls out a shallow glass bowl and starts cracking eggs. "After the Marines, I considered going to culinary school."

"Why didn't you?"

He gives me side-eye. "I didn't get in."

"Are you serious?" I repeat myself. I laugh, delighted by this tidbit I never would have guessed about his past.

"My one big failure in life," he says with a grin.

"Oh, your *one*," I smirk. I take in the room with new eyes. "But your kitchen looks like you never use it."

"I never have time," he replies. "Or I never make time, I guess. Cooking for one was never my favorite. I used to cook for my entire squad." His eyes settle on me. "All my ingredients go bad faster when I'm only cooking for myself."

It makes me happy that I'm giving him an excuse to do something that he loves. "You don't make a batch of cookies for your staff every Friday?" I tease.

"I wish." He pauses, as though considering that further. "I should do that sometime."

Thor, up from a nap, comes running down the hall and winds between my legs, so I pick him up. Every time I see Thor's adorable face and chocolate eyes, I want to squeal like a little girl. I kind of want to steal him from Alex, but I'll settle for sneaking time with him whenever I get a chance.

Not that different from my strategy toward Thor's dad—or my reaction to him, for that matter.

"Did you cook for your family?" I ask, making faces at Thor. He keeps trying to lick me and I keep ducking out of his way.

"No..." Alex trails off and I tear my gaze away from the adorable dog. He's sliding a pan around on the heated stove with a practiced air that gives more credibility to his aspiring chef claims. It's starting to smell amazing, like garlic and rosemary. "My mom did all the cooking for my family. No men allowed."

I flick my eyes back at Thor to avoid reacting. "Too bad," I say, making faces at the dog again. "Seems very limiting."

He laughs. "You hate how gender-conforming my family is." He's caught me.

"I don't know your family," I protest. He's right, though: I've made a few judgments based on clues. "But are they?"

"My parents are, absolutely. Fortunately, they sent me and my sisters to progressive schools. And they think of their values as more of a generational issue than a moral one, so they're not judgy." He pauses to send a grimace my way. "About most things."

"I get it. My parents have some strong opinions as well. They think I'm too..." I trail off. "*Too*."

He keeps adding things to the pan and it keeps smelling better. "Too bold? Too progressive?"

"All of the above," I admit. "Even as an adult, I guess I still care a little bit what they think."

"Hey, I understand. I've spent my whole life being pushed into one mold or another." Alex comes around the counter with two plates, setting one in front of me.

"Wow, garnish and everything?" I put Thor down and examine my plate. "What is even happening here."

"Leftover salmon, goat cheese, capers on the side because I didn't want to assume you liked them." He brings two glasses and wine to the counter and sits while I wash my hands.

I glance at the clock on the microwave as I sit down. If I'm going to sleep tonight, I need to leave after I eat. I never stay over, of course. It would make our chances of being caught at least twice as likely. We've only slept together—actually slept— that one night. I shouldn't miss something I've only done *once*, when I'm much more used to going to bed every night alone, but I do anyway.

As if he senses I'm contemplating time restraints, Alex says, "I have vacation coming up."

"Ha." I raise my eyebrows at him. "The vice president takes vacation?"

He smiles. "OK, a 'no public events' long weekend back home in California."

"Oh, nice. Memorial Day weekend?" I take a bite of the omelet and have to pause to close my eyes. The texture is perfect. "Mmm." I open them again and he nods, intent on his subject.

"You should come with me." He promptly revises his words, "I *want* you to come with me."

I smile briefly, because I love how careful he is with word choice. But then I frown, uncertain how to handle his request. "Someone once told me you shouldn't plan anything farther out than you've been with someone."

"What does that mean?"

"It means that weekend is three weeks out and we've only been...doing this—a couple weeks." But I can imagine spending full days together, and nights. It sounds perfect and I haven't had a vacation myself this year.

"Dating," he corrects me, but absently. He takes a bite. "So you can't commit until closer, is what you're saying."

I'm creating obstacles out of thin air, but I hold my ground, staring at my plate so he doesn't see I'd cave to coaxing. I don't want to start looking forward to something I end up having to cancel because it falls apart.

That applies to the relationship as well as the trip.

"OK," he says easily. Not frustrated at all. "But in the hypo-thetical case you decide to go, I'm going to give you a list of the preparation we'd need to do. You shouldn't fly with me in that scenario, for example. But you can look at that and decide whenever you're ready."

One bite of eggs on my fork hovering mid-air, I stare at him. "Really?"

"Of course." He picks up another bite and raises his eyebrows at me. "What, did you think I was going to hold you ransom?"

"And you're so sure you won't change your mind?"

This level of stability in a relationship isn't something I'm used to. My relationships have often been volatile, insecure and prone to bouts of on-and-off-again passion from both me and the other person. The last person I'd dated for any length of time was several years ago and ended in a flurry of angry text messages that weren't even about our relationship—we were arguing about gun control.

Alex is so even-tempered and direct, I don't quite trust it. There are so many things we disagree about, and yet it's never been a problem. He listens to me; I listen to him. There have never been raised voices between us.

"Why would I change my mind?" he replies, a ridiculous answer. Why *wouldn't* he change his mind about me? I make his life more difficult.

"Vacationing alone is not exactly my favorite thing to do," he adds. He puts his fork down and turns toward me. I put my fork down, too, recognizing we're having a conversation that deserves full attention. He lays his hand on my knee. "I don't mean to make light of it. But I'm not doing this with you lightly. It's a lot of fun, but I want to take it seriously."

A whooshing sound follows his words in my ears. I'm not sure what to say. I'm not even sure what I feel. My feelings fill me up so tightly there's no space to examine them. So I jump to my feet. "Thank you for saying that, but I'm going to need some time to get back to you." The words come out without thought, something I'd say in a business meeting. Formality: my fall-back defense.

I catch myself and pause to look at Alex. "I'm sorry," I force out, hoping he understands for what. "You surprised me. I'm surprised."

He's still sitting there, like nothing insane has happened. "There's nothing to apologize for."

I'm not sure that's true, but I'm also not sure how to apologize for being who I am, so I say nothing. Doubt creeps in. Maybe my first instinct—to flee from this conversation—is the right one. "I really should go," I say, glancing at the clock on the microwave. "It's getting late."

He nods, never prone to read into things or question my decisions. "OK. I'll ask Ted to have them bring around a car to drop you off."

Watching him as he knocks on the inside of his front door and then talks to an agent, I start to relax because Alex didn't put any pressure on me over the trip. A weekend in California. With him. No suits, no meetings, no press. It doesn't have to mean anything more than we want it to mean.

My justification to myself is that I shouldn't make any real decisions about our relationship before seeing him like that— outside the context of D.C. and our jobs. I walk up to Alex, so I'm standing nearby when he turns around.

"It'll just be a minute," he says, and reaches to pull me closer to him.

I step into his arms. "Send me that prep info, will you? But I'm definitely interested in the trip."

"Yeah?" he runs his hand down my back.

Tracing fingers over his shoulders, I nod. "I can never say no to a beach trip."

He grins. "Northern California, so don't pack your bikini. I mean, unless you want to wear it around the house."

"I changed my mind then, I don't want to go." I grin and pull away without any real desire to stop touching him.

He pulls me to him with the hand on my ass and slides his other under my shirt. "I promise to make it worth your while. I can probably borrow some handcuffs from the Secret Service."

Surprised and turned on, I laugh. *Yes, please, Mr. Vice President.* "OK, I'll let you know next week."

He smirks. "Yes, ma'am."

I make a face as I slide away from him to go grab my pants and bag. "Don't call me 'ma'am.'"

"I'll call you whatever I want," he says, filling in the teasing notes of his voice with a promise he'll keep the next time I willingly put myself in his hands. I want to drop my purse and go back to bed with him. Only discipline keeps me moving.

Every time I walk away from him now, I look back to make sure I'm not imagining him. It's all too good to be real.

nineteen

Alex

I'VE BEEN TRYING to improve the coffee situation in my workspace since I took office. Ensuring quality for such a large staff is nearly impossible while also keeping to a budget. I'd settled for buying a single-cup machine with my own money that theoretically provides for the tea and hot chocolate drinkers, too. As far as I'm concerned, the coffee is still inferior to the French press I have at home.

Fortunately, I'm in a great mood the morning after a night with Cindy and I don't care how weak my first cup tastes. That is, until my chief of staff asks if I want to run a private poll asking how voters feel about the vice president conducting a hypothetical relationship.

"No, I absolutely do not want polling done." I say, carefully setting my shitty coffee back down on the counter in the kitchenette.

The staff that ambushed me first thing—Toby and Deena— now exchange glances. I have cultivated a workspace where people are encouraged to push back. I'd wanted that because there are limits to my own insight. Right now, I'm regretting it.

Toby, my chief of staff, must draw the short straw in their nonverbal battle. He speaks up: "Sir, it's a big decision. More information can help you make it. That's the reason we're suggesting this."

It's a good argument, damnit. I like having as much information as possible before I make a move, and right now I'm uncharacteristically myopic. "OK, I understand. But let's have this conversation later. No need to jump the gun when we're only a few weeks into this thing."

The two of them exchange another look, but apparently decide it's not worth arguing again and nod. They would have had an easy time if they'd tried; I've never made it this long in a relationship as vice president. My staff recognizes a few weeks is significant, especially when they've been some of the best weeks of my life.

I pick up my coffee mug and lean against the counter, even though everything in me wants to walk away. "You really think I need to get ahead of this?"

Toby's face tells me he does. "This kind of thing doesn't stay secret."

My brain shies away from the possibility of my relationship going public in a way that's out of my control. "What if we limit our in-person meetings," I suggest, hating the idea. Hiding a relationship by never seeing the other person seems like a good way to end the relationship. "We can talk on the phone."

Toby, one of the best strategists in Washington, is merciless. "Putting off the inevitable."

"Well, buying time is the goal," I counter. "I want this thing to be rock-solid before we go public. It's a *relationship*, not a contract."

On a bald, Black man who normally displays only tension

and determination, Toby's sour expression behind his glasses is jarring. I add, "OK, think of it as pre-contract negotiations, Toby. It's very delicate."

"Not as delicate as your evangelical endorsements. Which you will lose if this thing comes out looking sordid." Toby doesn't pull his punches, which is another reason I'd wanted him as my chief of staff.

"Don't call it a *thing*." I ignore the other comment, because no one has ever given me a satisfactory answer when I've asked whether my weak "family values" are the result of being single. I straighten. Deena, sensing an end to my patience, goes back to her desk but Toby falls into step with me on the way back to the VP's office. "Let's come up with solutions, not hypothetical problems."

"Yes, sir."

"Also, she's coming with me to California." Best to break all the bad news at once. I believe in optimism. Cindy is coming with me. It's just *right*.

"Sir..."

"Everything is negotiable except the fact she's coming. I already talked to her about traveling separately. We'll stay at the secure complex the whole time. It's private."

Toby sighs. We pause at my door.

"Why don't you come up with a list," I say. "Of risk mitigation ideas. Containment, not elimination." The other man looks reluctant, so I add, "There's more to life than politics, Toby."

"Is there?" Toby grumbles as he turns away.

I sit down at my desk and turn away from the door, because I don't want anyone to see my staff's doubts got to me. Perhaps I'm being greedy. I want a relationship that's passionate and healthy. *And* I want the office I've been working toward for 20 years.

But maybe even a president cannot have it all.

* * *

Cindy

Of course, the very first question is about family values.

I would already receive a higher-than-average number of questions coded as "family values" because I'm a woman, but add on the fact I'm single and politically progressive and the number is exponential. It doesn't matter whether I'm hosting a town hall in Denver or the suburbs within my district, I always get several.

This constituent is asking about "putting family first" in Washington. "My kids don't need more marjuana around, that's already all I smell every time I leave the house," he says. "I have to tell them it's a skunk in the city."

To validate him, I nod thoughtfully. I ask what school district his kids are in, and remind him how much money the district gets from sales of legal cannabis.

"Your concern for your kids is such an important part of being a parent," I add. "That's one reason I have opposed any measures to increase access or remove protections from legal cannabis. As far as I'm concerned, and I hope you agree, recreational drugs and alcohol shouldn't even be a choice for kids while they're still developing."

Thankfully, he's nodding, so I move on to the next question, walking across the front of the school gym we're borrowing for tonight's event. It still smells a little like sweat in here. I've done the armpit check twice already on bathroom breaks, paranoid it's me and not all the teenagers who usually use this venue.

As an organizer, I loved holding town halls and leading groups. Then I became an elected official and I became the bad guy to a lot more people. The straw man, rather than the rally point. I've been screamed at and spit at, and called a bitch, a

185

tyrant and Cersei from "Game of Thrones." It's hard to enjoy the abuse, as much as I believe in being accessible to voters.

Days like today, it's tough to tell if the job has changed or I have. Maybe I'm not the crusader I once was, not as willing to crash through all barriers to achieve what I want. Perhaps I'm softer in my older age, and choosier about my battles.

A few questions later, I get the "are you dating anyone?" question. It comes from a gaggle of high schoolers I'm positive were assigned to come to tonight's event, and probably invented a dare to make the time pass.

Smiling at them, I pivot. "You've done your research. I hope your teacher gives you credit for that because I don't have an answer for you. Unlike Zack Ryder, I don't make my dating life public."

I regret the sentence the minute I say it. I'd meant to joke about Hollywood, play it for laughs, but I shouldn't have named names. Zack Ryder's was the first to pop into my head.

Max, in the back of the room, makes a rolling motion with her hand. Keep going. So I do, through another grueling hour.

"I'm sorry for that dumb Ryder name-drop," I tell Max after.

Max is driving us back to the district office. I'm looking out the car window from the passenger seat. It's dark outside and I love the Denver skyline, the statues lit up in the park and the manageable cluster of tall buildings downtown. Denver, for all its options, is still a small town masquerading as a big city. It has that in common with Washington, a surprisingly claustrophobic town.

"It was fine. I'm glad you didn't make a bigger thing of it; the last thing we need is people thinking you are dating a movie star." Max is driving us in her car, which smells a little like a dog.

"He's nice, but not *that* nice."

She snorts. "It was nothing compared to that statement the

White House put out from the vice president's dog. Talk about keeping the conversation going."

I pause, aware of how strongly Alex had felt about defending his dog. "Oh?"

"You saw it, right?" Max takes a right after the Capitol building. "So many late-night jokes about the vice president's penis size."

"Yes." Alex told me about some of the jokes. And I also took one of the pictures of Thor his Instagram account shared in the wake of the controversy. I clear my throat. I almost change my mind, then push ahead: "Speaking of the vice president's penis, and I'm sorry for the segway."

Max laughs. "Yessss?"

"I'm..." I hesitate, but I need to do this. Someone needs to know and I trust Max, who has always been honest with me, even when it's messy. "Well, I'm dating him."

"I'm sorry?"

I wait for Max's brain to catch up.

"You're dating the vice president," Max says, teetering on the edge of belief.

"You're the only person on staff I've told," I tell her. "I thought someone should be prepared."

"Excuse my language, but are you fucking kidding me, congresswoman?"

I shake my head, struggling to gather words to affirm verbally. Max pulls the car over blocks from the office, under a street light shining into the car and illuminating her intent expression. "How long?" she asks, turning her full body to me.

"A few weeks. Well..." I hesitate. "I guess it depends on when you count from. We met in February. We've been talking off and on since then. But it became a *thing* at the White House Correspondents' Dinner. And then more official when we went to Detroit."

"OK," Max says. She grimaces. "I need to know what you mean when you say things like that. You had a DTR? You slept together? I'm sorry. It's important."

It's like I'm the teenager in the car and Max is the mom. I take my seatbelt off because it's constricting and plunge ahead, "We kissed at the dinner and slept together in Detroit."

Max nods. "When it comes out, you've been dating since February. We don't share details, we let people think it was love at first sight." This is why I chose Max: Her practical mind is strategic. And, maybe, I wanted to tell Max partly because I needed to share with somebody.

"Do you want to announce it?" Max asks.

"No!" I meet Max's eyes. They're not judgmental. "It's a secret," I repeat.

"For...how long?"

I shake my head. "Forever?"

Max laughs, an edge of scoffing to it. "I can't get you that number. Listen...is there someone on his staff I can talk to? We should coordinate on this."

"I don't know."

"You don't?" Max seems surprised. "Oh," she says suddenly, sitting back in her seat. Her expression melts from intent to warm. "I'm sorry, Cindy. I didn't realize you were telling me as a friend."

Abruptly, I want to cry. I blink up at the sky, above the apartment buildings lining the road. "I didn't either. I want you to be prepared. But I also hadn't told anyone yet. I didn't realize how it would feel."

"Are you...happy?" Max's voice is tentative, unlike her earlier tone.

I pause. I'm scared. Confused. Surprised. But. "Yes," I say.

"Well, he's adorable, and smart, and has a cute dog. So I hope so."

That prompts a small laugh. My hands are clasped in my lap, trying not to fidget from nerves over this conversation. "He's also a pretty good communicator. He's careful. And direct."

Max's eyebrows go up. "He sounds like a keeper, if you don't mind me saying so."

I smile and purse my lips. "You're not the only person to think so, considering he was People's Sexiest Man of the Year last year."

Max wriggles her eyebrows a little. "Not something I can say about my man." We are both quiet for a moment. "He also comes with some high-level challenges," she adds, her voice hesitant.

"I know." I swallow down the wobble in my voice, because, *wow, this is terrifying.* "To be honest, I've been ignoring those."

Max nods, like it's settled. She turns back to the front and puts the car into drive again. "Well, make that my job then. To stop ignoring those things. Then you can just enjoy yourself."

Blinking again at the surprise swell of emotion, I gaze out the window. I didn't realize the depth of my worry, hiding behind the excitement of a new and *working* relationship. My connection with Alex seems so fragile, like a miracle I'm afraid to hold too tight. Yet this whole time, looming beneath our little cloud of happiness is a deep pit of consequences that might swallow us up if we make a wrong step.

I'm thankful to have someone like Max on my team. I can finally take a deep breath again.

Alex

MY STAFF STOCKED my California home with groceries before I arrived, including specialty items I've had my eye on for recipes like homemade sushi and quiche. I decide to put together the latter while I'm waiting for Cindy to arrive on Friday night, so we can have it for breakfast in the morning.

I convince Ted to sit inside with me as I'm cooking, because I listened to podcasts almost the whole flight and the drive here, and I'm not used to this few interruptions.

Might as well pick his brain while he's here, too. "When you and your wife first got together, was it gradual or did you know right away where your relationship was going?"

"Oh boy." Ted sits back up from where he'd leaned down to pet Thor. "I didn't realize this was that kind of 'hang out.'" I can hear the quotation marks around the phrase when Ted says it.

Unrepentant, I grin back. "A number of people have made it clear to me that as the vice president, I never get to 'hang out,' which is the point of the question."

I keep cutting room temperature butter into cubes as Ted

thinks. "It's a little backward. Normally, you meet someone and decide where it's going as you're on the way. *You're* trying to decide where you're going before you even start."

"Tell me about it." I say. I put the butter and flour in my food processor. Most of the appliances in this kitchen are unused, so I have to examine this one closely before I figure out the controls.

"It seems like the most important thing is to make sure the two of you are on the same page. It doesn't matter what the page is, as long as you agree on it."

"Very wise." I pulse the dry ingredients, concentrating on my next step rather than the fact I'm having this discussion with my Secret Service agent. Ted technically works for the country, not me, so that makes it alright to force him into a personal conversation, right? Justified or not, I'm desperate for advice. "But what if we don't know what pages we're on?"

Ted rubs his hand over the stubble on his chin. "When I dated, I had a security clearance and a lot of guns in the house. I didn't want to mess around with women who didn't understand or respect that. So I made a list of requirements up front. Nothing wrong with a vision for what you're looking for. But then you got to know when you've found it, too."

I think about it as I put ice into the water in my measuring cup and start adding it a tablespoon at a time to the dough. It's not like I have a written-down list, but I do keep one in the back of my mind. *Understands politics. Can handle crowds. Gets along with Thor.* Plus things I didn't think I'd ever find in the same woman: *Adventurous in bed. Inspires me to cook again.*

Cindy's face appears when I close my eyes for a moment. *I've found it.*

"Fair enough, Ted," I murmur.

"If you don't mind me saying so, sir, it seems to me you're more concerned she's not looking for what *you've* got to offer." Ted's voice is level, the same way it is when he informs me that

I'm not allowed to step out from under the protective tent and shake hands and if I try it, he'll manhandle me into the nearest vehicle without a second thought.

I frown while I'm dumping the food processor out onto the parchment paper on the counter. My hands are in the dough I'm forming into a ball when I respond. "It's not what most women would consider the ideal relationship, is it?"

Ted raises his eyebrows. "I know better than to speak for most women. Or any women, for that matter. What part of it do you think bothers her?"

Thor is standing on his back legs in the kitchen, begging me to pick him up. Hands full, I try to nudge him out of his way so I don't step on him. Ted laughs and comes over to grab the little dog. Always ready for protective duty.

"Growing up, my mom had dinner on the table every night at 6 and my dad was always home in the evenings. My mom told me they made sacrifices to arrange their lives like that, because that's what you do to have a family." I shrug. "I will never be able to guarantee anyone I can make dinner every night. Not as long as I'm working in the White House."

"Hm." Ted sits back down, holding Thor. They make quite the picture together. Ted's biceps are bigger than Thor's entire body. "And that's a problem for her? For the congresswoman?"

It's a pointed question; Ted is telling me not to make up Cindy's mind for her. I push the ball of dough back in the mixing bowl and cover it. "She's not like my mom but...I guess I don't really know what she's like, yet."

Ted's even tone keeps me from expecting a gut punch. "So, have you decided no family for you at all, then? Because it won't look like your parents?"

Pausing over the cutting board I'm grabbing, I think about it. It's a jarring question, because I don't *want* what they had. I start working on dicing the ham. "I just don't see how other people make it work."

"It's not one big decision, it's a lot of small ones. Like what you do every day, Mr. Vice President." Ted puts the squirming Thor back on the floor.

I smile down at my dog, who still wants his dad to pick him up. "You're pretty wise for a guy who never talks," I tell Ted. I'm deflecting, but the conversation is getting *too* personal. I don't want to force my security agent to be my therapist.

Ted smirks and I shred cheese, and we both act like it's settled. But it's not. I know what I want. But I don't know if I'll lose everything if I go for it.

* * *

Cindy

"Well, I see what you mean about not wearing a bikini," I say, standing on a rocky beach with no one else in sight but me, Alex and several Secret Service agents. One agent is standing on a rugged black rock rising far out of the water, where he has a view of everything on the beach.

I've never been to northern California before. It's more like Seattle than the sunny southern half of the state that I've seen. The beaches are beautiful but stark. Tendrils of fog are wrapping around the enormous rocks on the beach, as if caught there earlier in the day and now hiding from the rising sun.

The beaches are also less busy than down south. We drove in an entourage to the edge of the land and picked an access spot. Perhaps the people in this town are used to the vice president hiding out nearby; no one lined the streets. It was that simple to find somewhere we could be alone.

Well, alone as we ever get.

Alex is wearing faded jeans and a soft, long-sleeved t-shirt. I'd rubbed my face on it when he put it on this morning, the first morning we've ever woken up together. I left the house without makeup and wearing a sweatshirt, comfortable with him. Now here we are, holding hands on an empty beach like a side-step out of real life.

We take a long walk down nearly endless sand, talking about everything but politics. We take our shoes off and walk barefoot near the edge of the water, where the sand is packed. We pick up seashells and put them back. We uncover sand crabs. We joke about having good luck if we find an unbroken sand dollar and then find two in a row. Even though I don't believe in luck, I hope it's a good sign.

It becomes our ritual every afternoon. We take a long walk, dressed in sweatshirts, the noise of the waves loud enough we might be unaccompanied. We take our shoes off and I leave my long hair down to tangle in the wind.

We talk about our parents and the similar ways they screwed us up. "I felt like I couldn't have children because my mother would criticize me for not staying home with them," I say.

And he tells me about his parents setting him up with every local woman ready to be a stay-at-home wife from the age of 16, even during his time at the U.S. Naval Academy. "I hated the idea of having someone constantly waiting at home for me while I lived my life," he says.

We talk about the fact I might be too old to have children, and whether we'd *hypothetically* be open to alternatives. I ask him when his hair started going gray and admit I have more than a little gray hair under my dark touch-ups. I ask if Thor would get along with a cat, because I've always wanted one and worried I travel too much. We talk about what we want our political legacies to be, and then turn the same question on life.

"This is going to sound soft," he says. "But I want it to be 'he created something people loved.' I don't know what that thing is. But I want people to really love it."

I smile at him, because I love that dream and it's not what I expected. "I want mine to be 'she spoke up.'"

"Do you have plans to run for higher office?" he asks.

Making a show of looking for the camera, I put on my best "politician" charade, avoiding the question. He makes a face at me that has me dropping the deflection. "I want to make a difference in the world," I say. "Politics has never been my end game. But right now it's the right tool. What about you?"

"You know my ambition."

"Yes." Yet I'm not sure *why* he wants what he wants. "Well," I say, choosing my words carefully. "What do you get out of becoming president? What does it mean to you?"

"Ah." He takes a step forward, so for a moment he's ahead of me and I can't see his face. "I guess when I first launched my political career, it was all about duty. Duty to my family, to my country, to myself, because I knew I could achieve big things. Don't look at me like that; yes, it sounds arrogant."

"You *are* one of the most successful politicians in the world."

He shakes his head. "That's just it. Tim is the successful politician. I still feel like, in some ways, I haven't been tested."

"Is that what you want? To be tested?" I pause before I take a guess. "To find out if you can pass the test?"

He shrugs, looking out at the water. It doesn't seem like a very good reason to me. He supports the president, he makes jokes, he toes the center line, but who is he when he isn't playing the nice, neutral guy? I hesitate to continue down this conversational path.

I want to be free—to be able to pivot if I need to, to take whatever next steps I want—as much as he wants to be president, and those two things are not compatible for long-term partners. I'm trying to focus on the moment, but the future keeps getting in the way.

We hold hands as we walk, like teenagers, and build things out of driftwood. We take photos—on my phone—of the sun rising or setting. I don't share them anywhere online; they're personal mementos. We never take any pictures together and we don't talk about why not.

And then we go back to the house and eat whatever delicious meal Alex prepared. Eggs Benedict one day, pasta carbonara another.

The weekend goes quickly.

The sex is somewhat tame—the Secret Service could be listening to everything—but the quiet makes it more intimate. One night, we lay facing each other side by side in the moonlight, touching each other until we come. In the shower, I drop to my knees and we let the pounding water drown out the sounds he makes.

We laugh a lot. He laughs at me for bringing high-heeled shoes—which, fair. I tease him for having medicated shampoo. We share simple joy over Thor's antics.

He lets his facial hair grow and practically becomes a different person, exchanging the clean-cut politician's face for a stubbled, ruddy-cheeked and wind-swept one.

Eventually, we talk about the legislation, finalizing the language and telling each other, yes, it's ready. Time to move forward. I admit I don't quite know what my next project is after this. "I've been working toward this legislation so long," I say.

Alex jokes that I'll still have it on my plate for another few years at this rate, and I throw a baby carrot at him over dinner.

When I ask him about other serious relationships, he tells me about Wendy, the woman he almost married. Daughter of his father's partner. He grew up with her. Everyone considered it the right choice and he almost made it. But Wendy didn't want him to go into politics. Alex considered giving up the idea—he wasn't fully committed at the time—but ultimately he wanted marriage to be about creating options, not shutting them down.

"At least that was my dream concept for marriage," he adds. "But after Wendy, I assumed I'd been wrong, or that marriage wouldn't be about new things for me, and set it aside for later, after I'd accomplished everything I wanted."

I understand. "I've been in a lot of controlling relationships," I say. "Nothing ever got that serious because I would always rebel. Sometimes it got messy," I admit. "Because instead of breaking up with them, I would pick fights. Try to change the relationship in spite of fundamental incompatibility."

Then we talk about fundamentals. We talk about what our ideal relationship looks like and decide it's a lot like what we have this weekend: Shared time, the space to let conversation come easily, working together on projects like dinner or sand castles or legislative bills, having enough energy leftover for inventive sex.

That night, I let him tie me to the bed with the belts from our robes and gag me so I can't scream when he goes down on me. I've never done this before—been tied up—but it's been a fantasy for years. Alex makes me comfortable, protected even while naked. Then he uses his hands to penetrate me both ways and it's the best orgasm I have all weekend.

"What about when it's not like this?" Alex murmurs into my hair after, once he's untied me and wrapped me in his arms and the blankets, and we're cuddling. "When we go back to the real world and can't hide away from everyone?"

I don't answer right away, because I'm not sure. I run my fingers over the soft hair on his forearm that is wrapped around my chest. He's so certain and we're so close when we're in bed like this, but in D.C., there is still so much between us. I'm not sure I can throw myself further into this mess for someone who seems a little lost himself, even if he is so privileged and powerful.

When I speak, it's in a whisper because I'm not sure: "I guess we figure it out as we go."

* * *

Alex

Monday afternoon, the last day we're here, my sister shows up on the front porch.

"Sasha," I say, opening the door further and taking in the grim faces of the Secret Service agents making a wall between me and the view beyond her. "What the hell are you doing in California?"

"Visiting Mom and Dad." Then she holds up a plastic baggie and smiles. My protective detail carefully does not look at what's in her hand.

I gesture her in and close the door behind her. "Cindy," I say, as she joins us from the other room. "This is my sister, Sasha. She brought us weed."

Cindy's expression is similar to mine: *Oh, shit.*

"Well, I knew you couldn't buy it yourselves and you definitely weren't going to send the Secret Service out to get some, but what's a vacation without a chance to turn off your brain?" Sasha puts the baggie on the end table and looks around. "Where's Thor?"

"At home. Sasha...it's not a great idea for the vice president to get high." I look at Cindy for affirmation.

"What would happen?" she wonders aloud. "If there was a situation."

"Oh please," Sasha shuts us both down. "You're on vacation. The president is healthy and in charge. And you drink wine! It's the same thing. Just moderate your consumption." She extends her hand to Cindy. "So you're the girlfriend."

Cindy and I lock eyes, startled.

"What?" says Sasha, looking between us.

Cindy takes her hand. "No one's called me that yet. It's nice to meet you, Sasha."

Sasha shakes her head. "Man, your relationship is weird." She walks into the kitchen.

We smile at each other a little in her wake, because she's not wrong.

I follow Sasha to the kitchen, wondering how long she plans to stay. We only have a few hours left, and I planned on Cindy being naked for part of the time.

Sasha's head is in the fridge. She comes back out with the dish of our leftover carbonara. "Wow, really pulling out all the stops, huh, big brother?"

"He didn't think being vice president was suitably impressive," Cindy says, sitting at the counter that looks into the kitchen. Alex realizes she's brought the baggie with her and is examining the blunt inside.

"Are you considering it?" I ask her.

"You know, I am," she says, and sounds surprised herself. "I haven't gotten high since I took office. But your sister makes a good point. I do drink. And my whole thing is that cannabis should be treated similarly to alcohol."

"I knew I was going to like her." Sasha is eating cold pasta out of the container now. "This is delicious, by the way. And I'm not even high yet."

"You're planning to stay?" I recognize my tone is whiny but it's too late.

"Come on, Alex, I just drove like five hours to save you from your boring weekend of, whatever, like walks on the beach and eating pasta? Is that all you've been doing?"

Cindy smiles at me. "We watched almost a whole movie yesterday."

Zack Ryder starred in it. I made it my personal mission to distract Cindy from watching.

Sasha is eying us like she has a box of popcorn in her hands instead of pasta. "Go ahead," she says to Cindy. "Alex won't judge you, will you, Alex?"

"Of course not," I say immediately. "I'm just not certain I want to become the first vice president to smoke pot while in office."

"That you *know* of," Sasha and Cindy say at the same time. I grimace, watching them share a grin. Now I'm outnumbered by beautiful women with an agenda.

"Do you think it helps our cause or hurts it? I can't decide," Cindy muses, even as she takes a joint out of the bag and reaches for the lighter Sasha managed to unerringly pull out of the first drawer she opened. "After all, we're white people. Our privilege is that our only real concern is optics, not arrest."

I shake my head, watching her and the delicate way she brings the joint to her mouth with two fingers.

"I haven't done this in a while, so don't judge," Cindy says. But she only coughs once after she inhales and holds the smoke in her lungs for a few seconds before she releases it. The kitchen fills with the pungent smell of skunk and I go to open a window, remember I need to discuss adding a potential entrance with the Secret Service, and then abandon the idea.

Cindy hands Sasha the blunt and my sister takes her own puff. She doesn't cough at all. I roll my eyes. "Finishing school really trained you well, huh?"

Sasha makes a face at me. "Sure, like I bet you never smoked in high school. Actually, never mind, I wouldn't take that bet." She looks at Cindy. "He always had to be the perfect candidate, right from the beginning."

"Had to be?" Cindy asks. She looks at me, as if asking whether this line of questioning is OK.

I take a deep breath, trying to get as high second-hand as possible. Sasha offers me the joint, but I shake my head.

"Poor Alex," Sasha says. "Always worried about something. In junior high, he ran for class president and everyone wanted better lunch options. But our dad got in his head about how everything he asked for could be used against him, so his campaign ended up being options, full stop. Not lunch. Not classes. Just more options for everyone. Did you win that campaign?"

"I did." It was my first lesson in pleasing the masses. If you're a blank slate, people can impose anything they want on your values. I sit down on the other stool beside Cindy. She nudges her knee against mine as she takes the blunt back from Sasha and inhales once more.

"That's enough for me," she says. "I don't want to get too high and I feel like I'm being a bad influence."

Sasha laughs. "Alex could use some influence, good or bad. It's a miracle you ever got him to be alone with you, you know. He's always so careful. Where's the bathroom in this place?" She wanders down the hall.

Cindy gets up and finds a plate to rest the joint on. "So the being careful...that comes from your parents?" Her voice is casual, but I can feel how close her attention is.

"That and not taking a stand on any controversial issue." My voice sounds bitter to my own ears, and the words are sharper than I intended. Maybe I *am* high? I shrug. "My dad always told me I need to be like Obama and appeal to everyone."

Cindy sits back down with me, her movements looser than normal. "I don't know if I should tell you this, but..." She whispers in my ear, "People hated Obama."

I grin. "But he was still president."

"You'd hate being hated. At least, for the wrong reason. For something that a million other people didn't love."

Stunned into silence, I'm grateful for Sasha's return. My sister, catching at least part of what Cindy said, shouts, "You know him so well! Also, I love that you brought like 30 face serums with you. No way that's stocked by the Secret Service."

The two women discuss skin care routines as I stare at the joint sitting on the counter. It's not a surprise that I've somehow gotten this far in life without ever taking a stand on a divisive issue. I was trained to always see both sides and negotiate the middle. Not getting emotional about right or wrong has been a strength in many ways. But to realize that not taking a stand means never aligning with a cause I—or anyone—really *loved* hits hard.

"I want to create something people loved," I'd told Cindy about my future legacy.

I may never have that if I continue like this.

twenty-one

Cindy

I HAVE a lot awaiting me at home, so it shouldn't be so hard to leave this bubble we've created outside the real world. But late on Monday afternoon after Sasha leaves and I'm packing, I have to sit down on the bed—our bed—for a moment and stare at the wall.

This was never going to last, but we'd established a routine over the last few days that felt natural. I've never had that with someone I dated. "If it's meant to be, it'll feel easy," my mom told me my whole life. But nothing I wanted has ever been *easy*. I'm used to fighting hard for everything. This is different. I can't *achieve* a relationship with the vice president. I shouldn't even want to.

What am I doing here, moping about change? I am the champion of change. Usually. I push myself up and finish packing.

When I leave the bedroom, carrying my weekend bag and with my monster purse slung over my shoulder, Alex is still sitting at the table where I left him working on a speech about roads, bridges and broadband networks that he has to give the day before the release of an important jobs report. "The sword of Damocles is hanging over Infrastructure Week yet again," he'd said.

But his tablet is closed and he's staring at it, dark on the table.

"Still feel a little high?" I tease him, pausing. I see some of the same softness in him I did earlier, the lazy movements so unlike Alex. He'd let me shotgun some smoke into his lungs—"plausible deniability," he'd joked—and then admitted, after Sasha left, that he always felt held to a higher standard, his motives for everything from serving in the military to staying single scrutinized.

He stands. "All set?" he asks. His voice is casual, but his eyes are shadowed. I nod, and walk toward the door to drop my bag there.

"Cindy..." He's coming after me. I drop my bag and turn around and he stops.

The Secret Service is taking me to town, where I'll order a rideshare car. We're trying to avoid using government resources for personal errands like taking the vice president's girlfriend to the airport. Not girlfriend. Mistress? The available labels don't fit me in this situation.

I should concentrate on the ones that do. Congresswoman. Activist. Thorn-in-the-White-House's-side.

"I shouldn't make them wait," I say.

Alex fidgets his hands in front of him, looking down at his fingers as he stretches them backward one by one. "I'm glad you came."

"Me too," I reply. "It's been really nice." Nice? "It's been an escape," I try again.

He looks up. "It's been more than that."

He's right. Even though I don't have a label for it. And

although I'm scared to kiss him goodbye—it's too final—I drop my purse by my bag and step toward him.

He enfolds me in his arms and the way his body fits mine, the heat of it and the smell of the soap we used in our shared shower this morning, triggers sharp nostalgia. I'm already missing something I only had for a few days.

This goodbye is going to get soggy if it drags on. I kiss him hard, holding his chin in one hand, the other clutching his bicep. The next time I see him will probably be in public. I won't be able to touch him.

Stepping away is one of the harder things I've done in my life, among laying back at my Lasik appointment or that first mammogram. But I nod and keep my voice brisk, like I did on both of those occasions.

"See you back in reality," I say.

* * *

Alex

I'm trying to focus on work, but Cindy is on my mind on the way back to Washington. I wish she'd flown home on Air Force Two with me. I can't shake the sense I'm failing her by forcing her to travel alone.

I call Toby and Deena in. "Can we make sure Cindy is on the guest list for the state dinner in June? She's on the House Foreign Affairs committee, it'll be fine," I add, before Toby can object.

"Of course," Deena agrees, taking the easy road and leaving me alone to face my chief of staff.

Trying to jump ahead of Toby's wrath, I tell him, "I want to make a plan to go public." I come around my desk to perch on the side nearest the other man. I'm momentarily distracted remembering using this desk with Cindy, but Toby is glowering.

"Can we do some testing first?"

I didn't become vice president by rushing into things, but I also didn't become vice president by tiptoeing around. And anyway, haven't I always been careful? Haven't I done everything the "right" way? I snap: "This is not a political strategy, Toby, this is my real life."

The other man shifts, but he's standing his ground. "I'm not saying you dump her if the polling is bad, I'm saying let's be prepared. We'll go public, but let's find the best way to do that that sets us up for success."

"Can we do it for the state dinner?" I ask eagerly. I imagine Cindy on my arm as we enter the East Room in the White House.

"We'd step on the message of the dinner," Toby warns. His face is impassive, like a man who knows he's right but also realizes no one believes him.

"Right." I cross my arms and frown, reminded of my place. Am I getting too carried away? Toby is right, I need to think about optics. I have commitments to Tim and to the American public.

"Alright," I say. I'm caving—it's ruining my excitement about what Cindy and I built together on this trip—but listening to my staff rarely steers me wrong. "We'll do it your way. Figure out the best way to announce it and let me know. We don't have to be in a hurry."

Toby sighs. His shoulders loosen, a sign of more concern than he let on. "Thank you, sir."

I unfold and go back to my chair, but Toby doesn't leave. "One other thing..."

"Yes?" I sit down and pull the print-out of my Tuesday schedule toward me, putting on reading glasses.

Tomorrow's going to be a long day. Cindy is releasing the cannabis legislation and submitting it to the Clerk's desk and I have to approve a statement. I'm also swearing in a new senator who won a run-off election. And attending the president's Daily Brief and remarks in the afternoon on small businesses.

"You understand that the legislation you're working on with Congresswoman Wight may be compromised."

"What? Why?" I look up.

"Because of the relationship becoming public. It would be better to pass it before announcing, but that's unlikely to happen. Congress will be in recess all August and there's no way we can accomplish it before then. Plus, I don't think we can wait until fall to go public."

"Do you think our relationship will hurt the chances of the legislation passing?"

Toby hesitates. "Let me do some polling on that, as well." He rocks on his feet a little, which is what Toby always does when he's trying not to listen to his conscience.

"Say it, Toby," I say, taking my glasses off. "Whatever you don't want to say."

"The negotiations over the bill are already tenuous and I'd imagine some party members would pull their support as a statement." Toby, still standing in front of the desk, widens his stance like he's already planning for a fight.

I frown, bracing myself. "What kind of statement?"

"I think you can imagine, sir."

I can. We're not married; we represent different political stances; she's a junior member and I'm the party leader. There's plenty to criticize about this relationship, and what people won't say out loud, they will cloak with political reasons. "In the House or Senate?"

Toby shakes his head. "Both? Either. Worst case scenario, we fracture the party and lose any votes from the other side of the aisle. It's not the sort of news that brings people together and it's been years since Congress wanted to look like a big, happy family. Probably not since that State of the Union when the parties mixed seating."

I grimace. "That's so long ago, I forgot it ever happened." I slap my hand on the desk. "Damn it! You just can't win in this town."

"I could be wrong." My chief of staff never says stuff like that because he almost never *is* wrong.

I'm out of denials for the day. I should have thought about all this before, but I'd been so caught up in the delicate magic of finding the right woman at the right time. I breathe out slowly, as anxiety winds its way around my relaxed, post-vacation muscles. "Thanks, Toby."

"We'll find a way around it, sir. But I wanted you to be prepared for the possibility we have to sacrifice the legislation."

My mind rebels against the words. I can't lose this legislative win. I need it going into campaign season. It's part of my big-picture strategy to prove I can unite the party. But I can't lose Cindy, either. "You're saying it's either/or?"

"I could be wrong," Toby repeats, softly. His face wears an expression I've never seen on it before. It looks like...sympathy.

I shove the papers in front of me out of frustration. "Well, aren't you a blast of post-coital bliss."

"I'm sorry, sir." Toby starts to back away. "I'll start that research."

"You do that." I turn my chair toward the airplane windows. It's blue sky for miles out there. But inside, a storm is building.

The truth is, given a choice, I'm not sure which one Cindy would choose: Me or the bill. She ran for office specifically to push this legislation through, after all. I don't want her to ever be faced with such a decision.

So much for the afterglow.

twenty-two

Cindy

IT'S amazing how fast I can adjust to sleeping with someone when it's the right person. When I wake up alone on Tuesday morning, I miss Alex.

I palm my hand across my face and stare up at the ceiling, which leaks during D.C.'s most humid summer months.

One weekend is not real life.

Our lives are complicated and I have priorities—long-standing priorities—that I'm not sure align with being with someone like Alex. He's going to be president and that's the kind of job that completely subsumes everything and everyone else. He might have the best intentions now to support me and what I want, but once he takes that office, for four to eight years, everything else will take a back seat.

And yet I'm still smiling into my hand, lost in memories of the soft light slanting across the beach and how Alex brought a fork of chocolate cake to my lips and then kissed it off.

My phone buzzes. It buzzes again, angrily, from the nightstand.

I have a text from Lizzie. "We have a problem," it reads, with an attachment. It's a photo of the gossip column "D.C. Tea" in one of the daily commuter papers.

"SPOTTED: What congresswoman was seen far from her snowy state over the weekend at the closest major airport to a certain vice president who went home for a long weekend?"

Sitting straight up in bed, I forward the picture to Max.

She calls me back. "If they printed this, there's more to come," she says.

"They didn't use my name though. And there's no photo. Most people won't know who they're talking about, right?" Most of my own staff didn't realize I was in California this weekend, and Lizzie thought I went south for the beach.

Max's voice is filled with tension. "People who matter know. I'd better fly back for a while."

I fall back onto my pillow. I have whiplash after my long, lazy weekend. Things can't be spiraling this quickly. No, this must be an overreaction.

"No, no, it's not that urgent. I need you handling things if it comes up at home." I crawl out of bed. I need coffee.

"OK, but you need to put me in touch with the VP's people right away."

"Right. He gave me a number for you." I find the paper in my purse by the door and read it off. "It's fine, though, right? I mean, they only have enough for a blind item."

"They'll be on the hunt for confirmation, so don't give it to them," Max warns me.

"Right." I nod, although I'm on the phone and Max can't see me. "We'll lie low."

"Let me talk to his people and I'll call you back once there's a plan, OK?"

I let Max go and finish making coffee. Staring at my phone

while I take my first few sips, I debate internally. I want to call Alex, but I also don't want to make too big a deal out of this. It's gossip and innuendo of the type we deal with every day. Last week, I saw an item on the cover of a tabloid at the store that suggested Alex was having an affair with the gay son of the French prime minister. No one actually believes these headlines.

Still, this is much more mainstream. This is much more trouble if other outlets start digging.

Using the number I have for Alex, I pick up the phone and dial. Someone answers right away. "Hi, congresswoman. Everything OK?"

"Yes, hi. Deena?" I take a wild guess, because it's a woman's voice. A woman answering my quasi-boyfriend's phone is jarring, but I'm starting to adjust to Alex's lifestyle.

"Yes, ma'am."

Ugh, always with the ma'ams. "Good morning. And yes, I'm fine. Is he there?"

"One moment."

After the sound of movement on the other end of the line and a long pause, Alex's welcome voice says, "Good morning."

"Hi." Despite everything, it's soothing to hear his voice. It's almost like we're still on the other side of the country and I woke up to his face, creased from the pillow, his hair standing up straight with all the gray more obvious because I'm so close to him. "Um, there was something in the paper."

His voice changes. "It must not have had names, or someone would have showed me by now." That last part is obviously for the benefit of whoever is with him.

"No, no names...it's a blind item. But someone could follow the clues."

"OK," he says. His voice is calm, as I'd hoped it would be, but for some reason I'm not reassured. "We can handle it."

Max had taken it so seriously. Maybe Alex and I are in denial. "Someone from my office is going to call the number you gave me."

"Great. Try not to worry about it. I'm sure it'll be fine." He sounds distracted, and I try not to take it personally. He must have so much to catch up on, back from vacation. We both do.

"We should probably avoid being together for awhile, just in case," I say slowly, hoping he will protest but knowing it's the right thing to do for both of us.

"Right," he says. "That's true. For a while."

Flinching, I start twisting my coffee mug back and forth on the counter by the handle. "Right," I repeat. "For a while."

"Can I call you back later?" he asks.

"I'll be at the Capitol most of the day," I say, reminding myself I'm not some moony teenage girl. I have things to do and a busy day ahead. "Tonight?"

"OK, that sounds good. I'll call you tonight. Love you," he says and hangs up.

Yanking my phone away from my face, I stare at it.

Love?

A mistake, said offhand by accident. But how many people did Alex say that to, and why did it trip off his tongue?

I put the phone down carefully on the counter, because my fingers might be shaking a little, and lift my mug with both hands to my mouth.

It's much too soon to be using the L-word. I've been in other relationships that used that word and almost every time, I've been able to review later and realize it wasn't love. There were some intense emotions involved, but every time things went wrong, as soon as the endorphins disappeared, so did the loving feelings. Love is something that lasts. It doesn't flame out with the relationship.

The phone rings. It's him calling back.

Cautiously, I answer: "Hello?"

"Hi, it's me," he says. "I didn't mean to say that."

We should talk about this, but I think about how busy he seemed before, how distracted. "Where are you right now?" I ask.

"I'm about to walk into the Oval Office."

I put my free hand to my forehead. This requires a longer conversation, but not at the expense of a meeting with the Executive Office. "Right," I say. "It's OK. Don't worry about it."

"It's a little early," he says, and I'm not sure if he means in the morning or in the relationship.

"I agree," I say, rather than pressing him. It's true either way.

"OK," he says. "I gotta go."

"Have a good day," I say, sounding like some kind of robot.

He ends the call and I say, outloud to my empty kitchen, "Love you."

It's scary to say but sounds right when it comes out.

* * *

Alex

I'm in the middle of a gaggle of Secret Service and reporters as I cross in front of the Ohio Clock in the hallway outside the Senate Chamber when I hear the question: "Mr. Vice President, are you in a romantic relationship with a member of Congress?"

My first mistake is glancing up at the questioner. The fact I'm only being asked about it by a British tabloid is an encouraging sign. It means the story isn't being taken seriously by the papers of record yet—and won't be, as long as I don't feed it.

"No comment," I say, and hustle into the Senate lunch, a weekly open invitation for members of the party conference.

A senator from North Carolina catered today's lunch and the

room smells of barbeque and deep-fried pickles. The gilded arches of the room's interior are echoing with friendly banter, and likely a fair amount of barbed negotiation.

I haven't surprised anyone by "dropping in" on one single event since I got the Secret Service detail, so although I decided to stop by at the last minute, no one is stunned to see me.

"Slumming it, huh?" jokes a senator I used to chat with often, what feels like centuries ago, when I worked in the Senate too.

"I heard there was free food," I joke in return.

Sometimes I miss the camaraderie of the Senate. In this community, my job was similar to that of 99 others and always offered someone else's example to provide direction—often of what *not* to do. Plus, on my off days, I could disappear into the crowd and no one would bother me. Every day is an "on" day, now.

The Senate Majority Leader approaches me. She's a nearly 80-year-old woman who could recite the Senate rules and gained power the hard way: Through years of maneuvering around them, shaking hands and kissing up to people she probably doesn't like very much.

That's the kind of thing I remember every time I start to miss the Senate. Capitol Hill is like a big game of king-of-the-hill. Members get so preoccupied with playing the game it's easy to forget real lives are impacted by policy.

We greet each other by our titles and brush cheeks in a half-hug. "I'm glad you're here. I have a few reluctants for you to chat with and an idea for winning them over," she says.

I'm surprised she's diving right into the legislation we've been talking about, off and on, for months. I've gotten the impression it was firmly on the back burner of her priorities and then she begrudgingly spent time on it because the White House cares.

It's more than a few "reluctants." I have to give an impromptu speech to the whole room, pitching the cannabis bill, while senators are licking their fingers clean from barbeque sauce.

Then she springs it on me: "A number of us are interested in a clean bill."

Weeks ago, I thought I'd successfully pushed the Senate Majority Leader toward the bigger bill. I'd confidently told Cindy that I could get the Senate to vote for at least one provision. The Majority Leader would fall in line with the White House; if I wanted it, she did.

Maybe not.

"This is a surprise," I say, trying not to blink.

"There's some new concern about caving to special interests."

New concern? The question I got outside the room crosses my mind. "Oh? I think the push is coming from within our own party, from voters."

"We're on the right side of history on decriminalization. If we overextend ourselves, we might lose the whole vote," she says.

It's a disingenuous answer and we both know it. Very few people in Congress care about "right" when the kind of results you can put in a campaign ad are the product of expediency and power. I was once part of this body, and I too sometimes bowed under the pressure. My best days were the ones where I found a path that won me success but also suited my conscience.

Like many others, I tell myself, "I can do more good if I stay in power." And it's possible I have. *Unlike* many others, I worry I haven't.

But wasn't this the plan all along? To take the win and force Cindy Wight to line up with the rest of the party? Then I let it get personal.

I can't ignore the Senate Majority Leader of my own party, so I ask her to send me the revised text and give me a few days to look it over.

I'll figure out a way to discourage it later. My own party won't want to go against the White House on this unless they have some reason to make a statement like that. And our unity as a party has never been better in the Senate. It's the House that I expected would be the problem, and that's why I relied on Cindy to secure the progressive votes.

After I leave the Capitol, my motorcade proceeding noisily across the front drive through security across from the Supreme Court, Deena shows me the online homepage of the British tabloid: "'No comment' from VP over secret affair."

"Terrific," I sigh. I'd slipped up by saying anything at all. "Send it to Cindy, would you? And tell her I'm sorry."

I wonder if I should pick up the phone myself, but decide I'll call her later. My schedule today is packed and I already made a fool of myself with that verbal slip while distracted earlier.

All of the research my team is doing now presupposes the two of us stay together long-term. But it's not fair to dump that commitment in her lap this soon because of external pressure. I won't fit Cindy into a mold created by circumstances.

But I'd struggle not to admit how much pressure I'm under if I talked to her again now.

* * *

Cindy

I flop down on the sofa in my office. "I understand you're excited about the semester being over, but you didn't have to come all the way here to talk about my silly writer's block."

"I like coming to visit your office, it makes me feel important," Sara says, browsing the books on my shelves. They're mostly biographies I haven't read that were written and given to me by other members of Congress. Soon I may be represented the same way on shelves throughout this building.

"Did you avoid getting lost this time?"

Sara laughs. "I only get lost in the House office building with the courtyard. Which one is that, Rayburn? I somehow end up in there every time, confused and desperate to find the street again. I managed to find my way today without too much trouble."

"Thanks for coming. I'm waiting on a vote so..."

"You get buzzed, you gotta run. I'm in no hurry. It's a nice night," Sara adds, standing at the open window. "I'm surprised this isn't sealed shut."

"Some of them are, but I insisted on one I could open. I'm a Colorado girl at heart and we need our fresh air. If we're lucky, we might hear some music from the concert on the Capitol steps."

"I watched them setting that up." Sara sits in my leather chair and runs her hands up and down the armrests. "This office doesn't suit you at all. I'm slightly intimidated."

Sara is right. Sometimes, I read my gossip sites to ground myself and remember I have interests outside this building. To remember I am not my surroundings. "I have to follow a lot of old-fashioned rules here," I say simply.

Sara, always full of nervous energy, stands to switch and join me on the couch. There are notepads and a computer spread out on the low table beside it. "That's what I feel like you're doing in your book. Following rules. The Cindy I know, knows when to break them."

I make a face and spring back to my feet to retrieve my flavored water off the desk. "I have no idea how to fix it. I am totally blocked."

"Hmmm," Sara says. She taps her fingers on the table. "Why?"

"There's a lot going on in my life right now. Some upheaval." I shrug. I'm great at handling multiple tasks at once, but not when they involve emotions I need time to process.

"I have been known to read the gossip sites," Sara says. She stops tapping and raises her eyebrows meaningfully at me.

Dread fills me as I lower my seltzer can from my mouth. "Is it that easy to figure out they're talking about me?" I wonder if my staff knows. Lizzie hadn't asked if the blind item was true. I wonder if I need to tell her, and perhaps more than her, and mentally add that to my long list of decisions to make.

"No. But you mentioned going to California last weekend to me. And I saw you on TV with him back in February and I thought, 'don't they look nice together.' And because at heart I'm a mom, I had hopes." Sara grins. "Also, *hello*, this is so juicy. Are you really having an affair with the vice president?"

"Not an affair. We're *dating*. Secretly." I feel my cheeks heating like a teenager's, but I'm not sure if it's embarrassment or pride. I like being able to talk about Alex to someone else. I have to stop myself from gushing that *he's great, he listens to me and doesn't think my hopes and dreams are stupid,* and also, *he's hot under those suits he wears.*

"Well, I think we've identified the block!" Sara says.

Frowning, I sit back down on the couch, causing it to emit a muffled fart sound. "My love life? But the book has nothing to do with that."

Sara raises her eyebrows again.

"I don't want to have anything about that in the book," I insist.

"But why? A married woman in a position of power would talk about how her relationship supports her work. Take Sheryl

Sandberg. Or Michelle Obama! People are interested in whole people, not slices of a person."

I sigh, putting my can down. The only person who understands how precarious my situation is, is Alex, and I'm not sure about him sometimes. "I guess because there's nothing there. My romantic life *hasn't* supported my work. Dating has always been a distraction."

"Until now?"

"Even now. Why do you think it's a secret? He's in leadership. I'm trying to make my mark on Washington."

"It's such a good story!"

I groan. "I don't want the arc of my book to be 'single woman goes to Washington and gets a husband.' Not that we're getting married," I add quickly.

I'm tempted to scan the office, as though Alex could have heard me plotting to marry him after dating for a month. First that moment in the kitchen this morning, now this. This relationship is going to my head. I can't be Alex's first lady; it would ruin my career. I'd have to give up all my own plans to sit in the White House and look supportive at events.

"That's fair. But I think you might have to tackle exactly that perception. In tackling it, you make the book more interesting." Sara leans forward. "Also, *are* you getting married?!"

"No! I mean, we barely know each other yet. And he has all these political aspirations."

"He's going to be the next president," Sara notes, like it's a fact. Alex will benefit if the Meyer administration stays popular.

"Right," I say, rather than argue against what I suspect will be true. "And I don't want to be somebody's first lady. I want to have my own life."

Sara rears back, offended. "First Ladies have done some amazing things. Launched policy initiatives, furthered their own careers. They should collect a salary for all the work they do."

It's true, but I wave her off. "Maybe some first ladies can make that thoughtful and deliberate."

"Don't limit yourself, Cindy," Sara says, shaking her head like she's disappointed. "You don't want to turn down an opportunity because you think you can predict how it will turn out."

I want to brush Sara off, but I've learned that when the older woman's advice is uncomfortable, that's when I most need to consider it. I finally nod. "OK, I'll think about it. But until whatever happens, happens with Alex—I mean, the vice president—I can't put any of that in my book."

Sara slaps her hands against her thighs and stands. "So, tell your agent you need to put it on pause. Tell her it's going to be a much better book a few months from now."

Cringing, I shake my head. I'd never use my relationship with Alex as some kind of hook for readers. Our relationship could end without anyone the wiser. In that case, I'm certainly not going to reveal in my book that I once went on a few quiet dates—and had some great sex—with the vice president, as if it's somehow representative of my success.

"Remember what I said," Sara says, collecting her purse from the coat stand by the door. "Don't pass judgment while things are in process."

After Sara leaves, I close myself in my office to sit on the inside of my wide window ledge, listening to the faint sounds of the National Symphony Orchestra on the West Front lawn.

I hold my phone, but hesitate to call Alex because of what happened earlier. I don't want to interrupt his important work. But he'd said he would try to call me back and it's around the time he usually goes to the park with Thor.

My phone vibrates. It's a blocked number and I pick it up with hope it's him.

"Hi Cindy, it's Deena," she says. "The vice president wanted me to pass on the message he's tied up and won't be able to call this evening."

"Oh," I say. Disappointed, but reminding myself "vice president" is more than a title. It's an all-consuming lifestyle. "Thanks for letting me know."

We hang up without more fanfare—what am I going to do, ask "has he talked about me?"—and I sit quietly, listening to the music and wishing that, for once, I didn't have to share my boyfriend with the rest of the country.

twenty-three

Alex

ANITA STANDS up from her knees in the dirt when she sees me coming. The White House garden looks like it's about to produce everything at once, the growth nearly overwhelming the edges of the raised beds.

"Are you dating Cindy Wight or not?" Anita stands with her fists on her hips, gardening gloves leaving streaks of dirt on her khaki pants.

"Is this on the record?" Startled, I try to make it a joke.

She frowns at me. "I need to know about the state dinner. Is she your date?"

Now I frown. "Uhhh."

"Alex. I'm project-managing this shindig and it is *not* a simple matter to leave one seat empty at the president's table."

"She was supposed to be!" I blurt, in my own defense. When I got the request to stop by, I'd expected Anita wanted to talk about the state dinner, since her office manages the production of it. But I didn't have time to come up with answers for her before I walked over. "And then my staff said it would distract from the prime minister, and I never talked to Tim about it. Plus, I haven't seen her since we got back after that item in the paper about us."

Anita starts taking her gloves off, like this conversation is going to take awhile. "Have you talked to her? Is she ready for people to know?"

"I don't think she's ready," I say. I've gotten that impression from my phone conversations with Cindy so far this week. She hasn't pushed to get together, given the risk that we're being watched for that kind of movement. She still wants to hide.

Anita sighs loudly. "Then I need you to bring someone else."

"*What?*" I'm shocked. Anita always supports me when it comes to my single status on guest lists. She either manages to find another appropriate person going stag or arranges the tables to hide my aloneness.

"Alex." I can tell she's glaring at me through her sunglasses. "The state dinner is a week away. Do you have any idea how many details I have to put in order before then? You think running a country is hard, try event planning." She turns and starts walking up the wide lawn to the White House.

"Can't Cindy still sit at our table but not by me? So it's subtle."

"A 'subtle' date?" Her voice drips with sarcasm. I've really made her life harder, judging by how irritated she is. "This brings new meaning to the idea of casual dating, Alex. You want to invite her to a dinner and then sit her across the table from you so people don't get the *right* idea?"

"I'm sorry. I don't know what to do." I have the impulse to prostrate myself across the lawn. I'm exhausted, like I've been spinning in circles. I've barely slept since California. "Help me," I add, shoulders slumping.

"Wow, that was pathetic. I hope no one else saw that." Anita stops halfway up the hill and glances at the Secret Service agents standing at a respectful distance. She sighs again. "You realize if I do this, it means no one at the table can sit next to their significant other. Even the prime minister and the president. Otherwise it's not 'subtle' at all."

Cringing away from her waving finger, I hang my head. This situation is becoming a mess for more than Cindy and me. "It's not doable?"

"It's *unusual*. We haven't separated couples at dinners since the last administration. And state dinners, if nothing else, are supposed to be *usual*." But she shrugs, and the irritation drains out of her voice. "This will go down in the history books as 'that one time' Anita Meyer changed the seating arrangement. And I can't guarantee people won't figure it out!" she adds, waving her finger again. "It's still an honor to be seated at the president's table and people will wonder about her being there."

"She's on the Foreign Affairs committee. And she's been working with the White House on legislation."

Anita turns to keep walking up the hill. "A good enough reason if there wasn't *already* a more persuasive theory floating around."

I walk alongside her for a moment, silent, enjoying the warm sun against my back after working inside all day.

But Anita is one of the most emotionally intelligent people I know, so I have to ask: "What do *you* think I should do?"

She doesn't answer right away, watching her feet as we climb. She pauses at the top, where the grass levels out to the sidewalk near the Oval Office. "You need to figure out what future you want and work backward."

We step into the shade from the White House and I can look at her again without squinting.

"It sounds counterintuitive from all the usual advice to live in the moment and whatever," she says. "That's fine advice when it comes to worrying about things. But this is a decision to start something that will last a long time. You need to have a picture in mind before you can build it."

I recognize wise advice, but worry I'm lacking some of the tools I need for it. "How long did it take you and Tim to...agree on a blueprint?"

Anita smiles and takes off her sunglasses to assess me. I see the sympathy in her eyes that I crave, at last. "We still work on it all the time, Alex. That first 'blueprint' we came up with wasn't perfect. It's been amended many times. At one point, when Tim wanted to go for the White House, we threw it out and started over. You can't expect perfection right away from a new partnership."

"Or ever?" I suggest, thinking of my yearslong partnership with Tim. We get it right a lot now, but not always.

"Or ever," she agrees, too quickly for comfort. "But you've got to start somewhere. The important part is being in agreement on the plan." She raises her eyebrows at me. "Can't do that without talking."

"Right." I've talked to Cindy on the phone since California, of course, but mostly about Thor and the weather already edging into swampy summer territory. We've avoided the topic of "us" and what to do about it. She hasn't brought up my slip of the tongue, the cringe-worthy "I love you" that slipped out from nowhere.

Last night, I'd called her after midnight, crossing my fingers she wasn't asleep. She'd been in bed and asked sleepily if this was a booty call.

"Only presidents get to make booty calls," I joked. "And then only to their wives, in the bedroom across the hall when the daily agenda is finally clear."

"Reasons I never want to get married," she'd grumbled, and I *thought* it was a joke but rather than let it go, I'd responded: "I'm not sure how America would react to an unmarried couple in the White House."

After a pause on the line, she said, her voice less sleepy, "Are we talking about this?"

I've conversed with despots and tyrants, and once even with the pope, but in that moment, I felt real fear. I'm not ready for us to end. "I don't know, are we?" I asked, and she backed down.

"It's probably too early," she said. "Or too late."

We'd ended the conversation after that.

Now, I tell Anita thanks and walk back to my office, where I ask Toby for an update on the polling. I sit down at my desk and see the adult coloring book I sent to Cindy weeks ago. The note on it reads: "This was returned marked failed delivery." I flip it open to a page that says, in flowery outlined letters: *Fuck this shit.*

Toby walks into my office looking annoyed, but I try not to take it as a bad sign because that's Toby's usual expression.

"People hate the idea of you dating," Toby announces.

I collapse in my chair. This is the worst-case scenario I feared.

"It's the in-between part they hate," he adds. "You coupled-up in a committed relationship, people like that. You single, people are used to. The 'maybe' part, they hate."

"Me and them both," I sigh.

Toby slaps a file on my desk. "I gave you toplines as well as the details. But that's the main takeaway. The good news is people got excited about the idea of you getting married. Across the board, no matter who you marry. Huge bump for your like-ability and, weirdly, your hypothetical job approval score goes up, too, because this country makes no sense."

Agreeing, I pick up the folder and open to the first page of results. It's true, the country is out of its mind. A person's relation-ship status shouldn't have anything to do with the perception of how well they do their job. But of course it does. Just as the color of their skin does. This is why politicians are so obsessed with optics. It's impossible to accomplish anything if people hate you.

"And the *bad* news?" I ask.

"The bad news is you take a huge hit on both stats for dating a member of Congress who is perceived as influencing your policy. For example, by being further left than you. You take a hit for dating, period, but that's the worst result of all the hypotheticals we surveyed."

"Great," I say, dropping the folder onto my desk. "My life is a worst-case scenario." I consider asking one of the staff aides to find me some colored pencils so I can work on the open page in this coloring book.

Toby pauses, which is how I know he's about to make a suggestion I won't like. Toby doesn't hesitate if his ideas are going to get pushback, but he does when they'll make someone cry. I'm dangerously close already, and I never cry.

"Can we bring her in here?" Toby suggests, charging on. "Talk about a way forward that helps everyone? I've talked to Max, from her office, and she appears to know what she's doing. But that's containment strategy stuff. We need to talk mitigation."

I can't tell my chief of staff I'm nervous to have a conversation about the future with my girlfriend. It's the truth, but it's not good optics.

"Sure," I say. "We'll do it after the state dinner."

That will buy me some time to figure out what the hell I'm doing.

* * *

Cindy

My calendar reminder goes off with a *ping* as I'm walking back up the National Mall from a pre-work run. This early in the morning, the Mall is filled with other locals on morning jogs, like me, and entirely empty of the tourists that will pack it later in the day.

The reminder reads: *Talk to Alex.*

I remember adding this to my phone. My smile tastes bitter in my mouth. I'd been so optimistic that we would know what we were doing and what we wanted within a month.

And I'd thought that if we still weren't sure by now, I'd be able to walk away. Impossible. The idea of never having another weekend like the one we spent in California creates an ache in my heart.

Deciding it was time, I'd told Lizzie the night before. My chief of staff had been more horrified than Sara but less shocked than Max. "Are you trying to keep it secret until the legislation passes?" she'd asked.

I hadn't framed the timeline quite like that, but it makes sense. We both need this legislation to pass, and our relationship could be a distraction. If I'm going to blow my career up, it might as well be after one of my biggest achievements rather than before.

My phone rings and I answer, picking my way at a walk around people on the gravel path leading back toward the Capitol looming up ahead of me.

"Please hold for the first lady," a woman's voice says over the phone after confirming my identity. I pause, taking stock of my running capris and yanking on my sweaty shirt, as if the White House can see me. I step off the path to a bench nearby.

"Cindy?" Anita Meyer comes on the line.

"First Lady Meyer. Good morning."

"Good morning!" Her voice is cheerful. "Anita, please. Alex

told me you were an early riser, as am I, so I thought I'd try you now. I hope I didn't catch you at a bad time?"

"No," I say. "I'm cooling down from a run. Any excuse to walk, really. My knees can't take long runs anymore."

"Are you out on the Mall? I used to love to run on the Mall. Now I'm only allowed to exercise outside at Camp David." Anita is chatting so casually it's almost hard to remember she's the first lady and we're not friends. Almost. I watch people pass, the Washington Monument in the corner of my eye, and somehow the setting won't let me forget this conversation is loaded.

"I won't take too much of your time," Anita says, her voice taking on an extra layer. Still friendly, but more to the point. "You're coming to the state dinner, yes?"

It doesn't sound like a question. "Yes?" I'm not sure it's a smart idea, but I'm also not going to turn down an invitation to an official White House event. I'm a junior member of Congress and it's a room full of decision-makers.

"Wonderful. I'm looking forward to seeing you. Here's the problem: The vice president has a few official functions to perform at a state dinner that require a partner. I would love to be going through the explanation of how to perform them all with you right now, but I understand from Alex that you're not quite at that point yet. So I wanted to confirm with you that you realize for the purposes of this dinner, there are no formal or informal obligations between you and Alex?"

I'm trying to catch up to Anita's words, but I understand the gist of the first lady's tone and it's, *Don't make a scene.* "I understand he does not belong to me," I say. I'm being paranoid, but I avoid saying his name aloud in such a public space.

"Unfortunately, that would be the case even if you were married, but we can talk about that some other time," Anita says. Her voice is like steel wrapped in velvet. I'm holding my phone so tightly, trying to catch everything she says, I can feel my ear getting hot. "When we spoke, Alex indicated there's no under-standing between you two yet, no rules to be broken, and I wanted to confirm that's also your take on the relationship."

I frown, watching the people passing me: Joggers and walk-ers, earbuds in, holding phones or water bottles. "I'm not sure I know what you mean by that."

"Would you say that you are dating?" Anita asks the question without inflection.

"Yes," I say.

"Do you have an end goal in mind?"

"Um…" I flounder. I take a sip of my water, because my mouth goes dry.

"That's what I mean, then," Anita says briskly. "In our line of work, we don't talk about a deal until it's signed. I'll have my social secretary send you a few notes on what to wear and I look forward to seeing you at the dinner." She hangs up without saying "goodbye."

My hand grips the phone, now sweaty from being next to my face. I wipe off the screen with a corner of my shirt. I understood the meaning behind Anita's sheathed, Southern-sweet words: We're all running out of time.

* * *

Alex

I still haven't told Cindy about the Majority Leader's reversal. I've been on the phone all week with the leader and the whip, trying to convince them they can go a little further with the bill.

The Majority Leader keeps saying, "Why give up the win, sir?"

The problem is, it's a good argument. The midterm elections are coming up. A popular middle-ground vote will lure more people to sign on than a risky vote that gives ammunition to the other party.

Our party, led by Tim, has sky-high political capital right now. Between that and the popularity of the topic, we might peel off a few votes from the other side of the aisle. We could pass the bill without Cindy and her progressive, do-more coalition and it would still be progress.

And, yes, it would do a lot for the country.

But it's her bill. It would be a betrayal to pass it without her participation.

I should call Cindy and talk it out with her. Maybe find a solution I'm not thinking of. Or maybe, with her quick temper, she'd accuse me of using our relationship to double cross her and refuse to listen to a word I said.

Head hurting, I call out to anyone in the other room in my office suite to bring me ibuprofen. Deena hurries in, pills in one hand and phone in the other. "It's your sister, sir."

"Sasha or...?" If it's one of the others, it's an emergency. Sasha knows my schedule is too tight for a personal call during the middle of the day, but she doesn't care.

"Sasha," Deena replies.

"Sure, OK." I'll talk to her while I wait for the medicine to kick in. I can call Cindy later.

"Big brother," Sasha greets me, barreling forward without waiting for a response. "Since you told her you might be bringing a date to the wedding, Mom is already talking about how she'll have to relocate to D.C. to help plan *your* wedding."

I'm appalled. My mother visited Washington, D.C., for both inaugurations. And both times, she complained about the weather, the traffic and how "cottage-like" the White House is in person.

"We're definitely not there yet," I say. Years of diplomatic experience keeping my voice calm when I want to freak out are coming in handy. "It's not even public."

"Obviously, or all of the tabloids I'm looking at in this store would be full of your face."

"You're calling me from a store? Sasha." I sit up and scan the room, like my Secret Service detail will come flying in the windows to stop me from this security mistake.

"Blah, blah, ears everywhere," she says, her voice mocking. "You can't keep it a secret forever if you're bringing her home to meet the family."

"I'm hanging up now." And I do. I'm not about to make another dumb media mistake over the most important relationship in my life. Well, one of the top two relationships in my life, alongside the president.

I could call and ask Cindy whether August is too soon to go public with our relationship. But I remember her resistance to the idea of going public at all. I don't want to rush her, and yet the problems with secrecy are starting to pile up. It's not fair to her; the bias toward stability and pressure on me to settle down with a wife shouldn't force Cindy into choosing before she's ready to decide whether she wants to share my complicated life or not. I need to give her more time.

So I'll keep putting off the conversation, not wanting her to realize the pressure is increasing. Besides, I have a briefing to attend in the Oval Office in 15 minutes, so clarity will have to wait.

twenty-four

Cindy

I'VE NEVER BEEN to a state dinner and never expected to go to one. Presidents only hold a handful in their time in office and about 40 guests are invited to each, so it's one of the most coveted invitations in Washington.

The reason I made the list makes me more than a little uncomfortable. But I haven't seen Alex in two weeks, and I'm not going to turn the opportunity down.

I'd worried about how it would appear, and he'd reassured me that we wouldn't be sitting next to each other or walking in together. "It's not being packaged as a date," he'd said. I knew that from Anita, as well.

And I'm disappointed, even though I agree a public date is not a wise idea. Of course it's not. I wanted to be consulted about it, though. So far I've been "handled" by the White House staff, up to and including ideas on what to wear. Under no circumstances am I to wear the same shade of green as the vice president's tie.

The blue I'm wearing brings out my eyes and I'm carrying a

bag that's big enough for my phone. So long as I'm seated by someone interesting, it's going to be a fun night.

I'm seated by Zack Ryder. Again.

"You're becoming quite a regular in Washington," I tell him.

He gives a lazy full-body shrug. "I'm lobbying for something or other. It's a good look right now."

I laugh. "You don't know what you're lobbying for?"

He raises one eyebrow. His very flexible face manages to emote a lack of concern with the appropriate lack of effort. "I don't know what I'm doing from one day to the next. I don't know how I got here. I have no idea what my next line is."

"Is this a call for help?" I whisper. "Do I need to alert one of these people in uniform? I think they're social secretaries, but they seem official enough to save you from your fate."

He grins. "You mock my pain."

"Good line. I don't mean to mock it." I lean back and try not to "mom" him too much. "But you should consider asking your people more questions."

"Eh." His brow remains unwrinkled as he dismisses my advice. Then he gives me a full-blown movie star smile. It's distracting. "It's something to do with supporting the military, so it's not controversial. I'd rather focus on my next role."

I indulge him by asking about his next role for a few minutes, while casting sneaky glances at Alex across the table. He's deep in conversation with the prime minister of Canada and barely eating anything. He's handsome, as always, but there's a hint of dark circle beneath his eyes. He's had a busy couple of weeks—judging by how short our phone calls have been—and I wonder if it's been worse than he's admitting. There must be a lot he can't tell me.

The thought makes me sad, so I turn my attention back to Zack.

"How did you end up at the vice president's table?" I whisper to him.

His response is a doe-eyed stare. "They just put me here."

I laugh. He's young and oblivious, yet he must be in his late 20s and old enough to know better. Perhaps he's lived in a bubble his whole life and doesn't realize his own privilege. Still, I'm somewhat charmed that he isn't constantly scanning for someone better to talk to, like the majority of Washington would do when seated at a table of more important people than me.

I'm not excited about doing the usual schmoozing this evening, either, so I exchange a few obligatory words with my other seatmate, the secretary of Transportation, and then turn my attention to another round of teasing Zack and learning about his plans for a sequel to the movie where he played the vice president. We also talk about filming rights, and he becomes more passionate discussing something he is clearly more personally invested in.

When the president leads the first lady onto the small dance floor after dinner, I have a mental flash of doing this same thing—starting the dancing at a state dinner—with Alex someday. My brain shies away from the very thought of that kind of pressure. Not the dancing in public while significant people are watching, but what it symbolizes. Representing the entire country. It's one thing to be chosen for that responsibility, like a president is, like the way my constituents chose me to represent them in Congress. It's another to marry into it and face the same pressure without knowing whether the majority of people you're representing have your back.

"May I have this dance?" Alex is standing at my side, shifting from foot to foot as though ready to get out of his three-piece suit. If only.

"Are you sure?" I ask. I glance at Zack, on my other side,

whose eyes are starting to glaze over. This party is probably too tame for his movie star tastes.

"That I want to dance with you? Absolutely," Alex says, ignoring my real concern about doing so in front of this crowd. He takes my hand and leads me out among the other people joining the first couple.

"Seems risky," I murmur, making a strong frame of my arms to keep plenty of space between us.

"Riskier would be letting you keep flirting all night with that movie star," he replies, directing his eyes over my shoulder.

Giving him side-eye, I keep my gaze fixed properly on the other side of the room. "You're not seriously jealous."

He keeps his face directed away from me, reducing the intimacy of our positions. "Define *seriously*."

I huff. "You're the vice president. He's an actor."

"Which is the most interesting job description? Not to mention more glamorous and less likely to make one an old man before one's time."

Is he truly insecure? It's ludicrous; when I'm with him, it's as though there's never been another man in my life. I laugh, but gently, for his ears alone. "Have you seen him do stunts? He's going to wake up with the aches and pains of a 60-year-old any day now." I tap his shoulder with the hand on it. "Besides, unfortunately my type is vice presidents."

He smiles, nudging me across the floor. He's an excellent lead, subtly signaling his moves before he makes them. Taking care of me so I don't stumble over my own feet. "All vice presidents?"

"Yes, I also have a real thing for Dick Cheney." I keep my voice expressionless and my gaze beyond his face.

He snorts and tries to cover it by clearing his throat, turning his head away from me.

"Al Gore also gets me hot," I continue, deadpan. I can't help noticing, with my nose nearly in his neck, that he smells delicious, with that spicy scent I've come to love.

"And what happens if I'm not always vice president?" he asks quietly, cutting through the silly joke. It's easier to tease him than talk about serious things, while all these eyes are on us.

"I don't know what happens," I admit, not quite looking at him. I'm sure he's not talking about quitting. He means what I was thinking about earlier: Being in a position to lead the dance. There are questions I haven't quite dared to ask. *Speak up, Cindy.* "Is that what you want? We haven't really discussed it directly."

"That's what I want," he confirms, gaze still focused past me. "But I can't do it alone."

A man in need of a wife, then. Not a wife—a first lady. The woman who walks silently beside him and waves. I start to stumble at the confirmation, but he keeps me upright.

Did his team diagram the appropriate marital partner for his presidential aspirations and conduct a search? I have a hard time believing I'm an ideal match, with my background. I have some messy personal history and a past of advocating for unpopular causes. Once I even called Tim Meyer "the cardboard president" in an interview with *BuzzFeed*.

"I feel like I'm being recruited to join your campaign," I say. "What would I bring to your ticket? The mountain west? Progressives?"

He breathes in and out once, slowly. "Those are both helpful," he agrees, exactly what I didn't want to hear. "We've done some polling..."

I stiffen until my back could snap. "What does it say?" I demand.

The dance ends and Alex lets me go. He takes my hand between both of his. "In general, it's not good," he says, looking me in the eyes finally. "But they predict a big bump if we make it last."

We can't continue this conversation here. I have to walk away. But it's like someone opened the curtains while I'm standing in my living room naked. He's brought the whole world into a moment of intimacy.

"Cindy." The president is suddenly at my elbow, extending a hand to me. Alex nods and moves off, called away by someone standing nearby.

"Thank you, sir," I say, and take the president's hand.

"Thank *you*," he replies, putting his arm around me and taking my other hand. "It's a privilege to dance with someone who doesn't want to talk about appropriations or tariffs. You *don't* want to talk about appropriations or tariffs, do you?"

"Well, I did, but now I guess I'll keep it to myself," I say, taking the distraction and running with it. He's successfully managed to hook my mind away from the troubling conversation with Alex.

"What's on your mind, congresswoman?" he asks, keeping us to the edges of the dance floor where we're less likely to be overheard.

I hesitate. Something about Tim Meyer—perhaps the knowledge that he's the father of two daughters or the way he keeps his grasp meticulously appropriate—makes this space between us seem safe. But he *is* still the president. A man I've insulted behind his back in the past.

"Oh, just...foreign relations with Canada, I guess," I say weakly. It's such a cop out, but I don't want to start a fight in the middle of this state dinner.

He smiles. "Sometimes it's the countries that share our language where we have the most tricky relationships." He pauses. "Have you ever noticed that about relationships?"

Impressed by his persistence, I make a noncommittal noise. This must be why he's known as a master of negotiation. "That they're tricky? Yes, that's definitely true."

"What strikes you as the most tricky part?" he asks.

His conversational skills outmatch mine. I can't avoid answering him without being rude. So I settle for a partial answer hidden in a question: "Did you do any polling about Anita—the first lady—before you married her?"

"Ah." He considers this for a moment. "No, but we were in a different phase of our careers. She was a teacher and I was a member of the state legislature. It was a simpler time and fewer people were involved than are with you and Alex. I wouldn't worry too much about polling a hypothetical. People are more easily won over than they predict." He ducks his chin to give me a quick glance. "Everybody loves a happy ending."

"What about a happy beginning and who knows where it goes from there?"

"Well, that's life. Packaging and messaging are all about making messy processes more tidy."

I wonder about how casual he acts about the whole affair. "Does this messy process affect you, sir?"

"Me?" He shakes his head. "I'm on the downhill slope of my career. Thank God. What does concern me, however, is my party keeping control of the White House. Alex is our best chance for that."

A whole other concern I haven't paid proper attention. I might criticize the administration, but ultimately I would rather my party stay in power. I don't know what kind of president Alex would be, but he deserves a chance. I'd no more want to stand in his way than I would want him to get in mine. I want to see him succeed—for both personal and professional reasons.

Tim continues, without visibly bracing himself. A man who can have a confrontation without giving away discomfort. "What puzzles me about you is—you're a leader in the party. You've made quite a stir during your time in Washington. People are looking to you to shape the future and take down the establishment. To some, you're dating the enemy. Some might wonder how much of that is about power."

Am I imagining it or is there a little more tension in the way he's holding me, the push-pull of our hands?

"I've always been more concerned with organization than power," I say carefully. "It's a cliche around here, but I believe in checks and balances and I like that my underdog coalition checks the power in the hands of the old white men who have been in office for 20 years or more. I believe in the party but, unlike most, I'm also willing to admit when my party is wrong or needs to do more. That's the only reason I 'create a stir' around here."

He nods, like it's settled. "As an old white man who's been in office more than 20 years, I don't disagree." The dance ends and he lets me go. We clap lightly for the band. "You might think of a potential partnership in the same way. Maybe Alex needs you to check and balance him. Maybe that would benefit our country, as well."

I stand near the dance floor alone until Zack walks up. "These parties are way more interesting as a montage scene, it turns out," he says.

Trying to focus on him, I smile. My first two dances weighed me down and now my brain and my heart are both heavy. "Was it worth getting dressed up?" I ask.

Zack considers this. "I guess for the experience. Now I'll know for the movie. You? Worth it?"

Focusing across the room at Alex, who is dancing with the wife of the Canadian prime minister, I admit, "I'm not sure yet."

* * *

Alex

240

I should've called Cindy myself, but I had a staff member warn her about the requests from *US Weekly* and *The Daily Mail* so that I could fall into bed after the state dinner.

I'd had them tell her the same thing I'd told myself: We're fine until it's the *Times* or the *Post*.

When I wake up the next morning, *The New York Times* has called.

"Why the hell is a respectable media organization writing about my love life," I rage to Deena and Toby, walking toward a conference room in EEOB for a meeting with Kaylee.

"They're taking the 'is it a distraction' angle," Deena explains. "'Do these rumors make him less effective,' that kind of thing. It allows them to cover the rumors as if they're incidental to the point, but they're still spreading them."

"How did we get here already?"

"There's a picture."

I stop in my tracks, the worst possibilities filling my mind— telescopic cameras and open window shades in California. Or something on the beach. "What kind of picture?"

"From the state dinner." Toby pulls out his phone and displays a picture of me standing with Cindy near the dance floor. I study it. We're not even looking at each other. "You know the cliche: A picture's worth a thousand words, sir."

"This picture says we were both guests at an event." I roll my eyes and keep walking. This is *nothing* compared to the private moments we've shared.

"Not in combination with the other stuff."

Again, I halt. "What other stuff?"

"The *Times* quoted an anonymous quote confirming you went to California with the congresswoman," Deena says.

"Who the hell told them that?" I demand, glaring at the two of them, like it's their fault. I know better, but I'd thought they had a *plan*. "Does anybody know?"

"It could have been almost anybody, Mr. Vice President. A lot of people knew," Toby says. The subtext is: *I warned you this would get out.*

"Are we in touch with her people?" I ask, because there's no defense. Toby had warned me. *Repeatedly.* Now we need to come up with solutions.

"Yes. It sounds like they're fielding questions from local media in Colorado as well."

"Why is everyone so interested in who's dating who," I grumble. "This isn't an episode of *The Bachelor*."

Deena shifts, gaze darting away.

"What?" I demand, too sharply. Taking a breath, I tell myself not to be so defensive. This was bound to happen. But I'd hoped we could put it off longer.

She takes a deep breath. "Well, it sort of is, sir. *The Bachelor*. It's all happening in real time and Americans get a vote. Plus, Americans are obsessed with royalty and you're as close as we've got in this country right now. It's like you're choosing the next first lady and they get to weigh in by social media. It's the perfect intersection for memes and media."

A deep, dark hole opens up in my stomach. I take another deep breath and smell the cleaner recently used in the hall. It makes me a little sick.

"Let's not be dramatic," Toby cautions, like he's talking me off a ledge. "Nobody's getting kicked off the island, or whatever it is."

"That's *Survivor*," Deena says.

Toby shrugs. "We need to present a united message. That's what this meeting is about."

"Shouldn't her people be a part of this?" I ask. I put a hand on the wall to hold myself up. Usually, I avoid being this reactive in front of my staff, but I need a moment. My entire career could be washing down the drain because I led with my feelings instead of my brain for a few weeks. A few weeks! How could I have let this go for *weeks?*

"Don't spiral," Toby snaps, as if he can tell what's going on in my head. My staff is *handling* me. "Step one, we unify on our end. Step two, we coordinate with her office. Deena told them to turn down media requests for now."

Deena nods. "I talked to people in both offices—here and Colorado. They sounded very organized." She sounds surprised. "For Congress."

"And have we heard from her? From Cindy?" I try to remember who has my phone. I pat my own pockets. "Did she call this morning?"

Toby and Deena shake their heads.

"OK," I say, deciding to deal with this crisis one step at a time. "Let's go do this meeting."

Thirty minutes later, I'm agreeing to the strategy of "ignore and wait" for now.

"If we're not ready to give the press a firm yes or no, we send the message it's beneath us to answer," Kaylee concludes. "Something else will come along to distract them. There's not much mileage here for any serious journalism outlet. No scandal, no ethics violation. And then if, down the road, we want to confirm you're together, we say it was a private matter and you weren't ready to share with the world yet."

"And that will work?" I want to believe the experts, but in my experience, trying to bury news makes everyone look in that direction.

"That will work for now," Kaylee says firmly. "But they are still watching. You cannot chum the waters any further, Mr. Vice President."

"So I don't see her in person for a while." I sigh, putting a hand over my eyes. *Everything is impossible.* How am I supposed to figure out if we are solid enough to go public if I can't even spend time with her?

"And I don't recommend inviting her to any more White House functions for now," Kaylee adds.

"We shouldn't punish her for being in a relationship with me," I say, lowering my hand. "No one's going to leave her off any lists she's supposed to be on, right?"

The room falls silent. Kaylee, Toby, Deena and Maggie won't meet my gaze.

"We can't guarantee that," Toby says, throwing himself on the bomb. "If it comes down to her or the White House..."

Holding up a hand, I stand. "Don't say it."

Cindy and I need to talk.

I can't fight for *us* until I know there's an us to fight for.

twenty-five

Cindy

"THE INTERNS HAVE BEEN CATEGORIZING letters and calls from constituents. Over the past two days, the majority are falling into the same buckets as our press inquiries."

My Washington communication director, Nathan, paces in front of my desk. Lizzie is sitting across the room on the couch and Max is on speaker phone from Denver.

"People want to know if you're sleeping with the vice president," he sums up.

Lizzie, Max and I all roll our eyes. I can sense Max doing it through the phone line. Nathan grimaces and presses on.

"They also want to know if you're sleeping with Zack Ryder," he continues.

I sit forward. "They what now?"

"Did you see that cover spread with the pictures of you two at dinner and at the party earlier this year? The 'Is she stepping out on the VP?' headline," Max says. "They haven't even established you're with the vice president and you're already cheating on him."

245

"Give me a break," Lizzie scoffs.

"And they want to know if you slept your way to your position," Nathan finishes.

We all fall silent. I meet Lizzie's eyes, and we're on the same wavelength. This one is the career-killer. The reputation that could haunt me the rest of my life in politics if we don't shut it down immediately.

"No one serious thinks that," Lizzie says, but it's a question.

"Martin says the votes are slipping for the marijuana legislation," Nathan warns.

"Who?" I demand.

"Somebody from Iowa. Apparently they can wrestle marijuana to fit their definition of family values but not a single woman sleeping with someone powerful. No offense, ma'am."

"If there's one, there are others," I say, leaning back in my chair. I'm frustrated that all the waiting around to drum up support is now worthless. All because of a picture of me with a man. "I need to talk to the Freshman Six as soon as possible. Am I losing progressive support along with the more moderate votes?"

"I'll get it on your calendar," Lizzie says. "I haven't heard from them."

Bad sign. "Let's do it now," I say. My chief of staff nods. "This is ridiculous," I vent as Lizzie starts typing on her phone.

"It is," Max agrees. "But it sounds like the White House won't help. They're not planning to comment."

Nathan nods. "That's what we're doing so far, as well: No comment-ing. But Max and I don't think we can ride this one out without saying something. So we might as well make a contingency plan."

"We don't necessarily have to address the rumors," Max adds. "We can address the criticism."

"OK, that sounds good," I say. *Focus on what you can control.*

"The only drawback," Nathan continues. "Is that people aren't as interested in measured responses as they are wild speculation."

"Well, a bully pulpit might help," Lizzie grouses, without raising her eyes from her device. "The White House really won't say anything? Did you ask them?"

"It was more of a..." Nathan hesitates. He's the new guy in this group, having taken the position in my D.C. office after Max moved to Colorado. He hasn't quite won my trust, yet; Max is still my first call for important communications strategy.

"Less a conversation than being told the plan," Max offers on the phone. Nathan nods.

"I'll talk to the vice president tonight," I say. "Find out what's going on."

Hopefully. I haven't talked to Alex since the state dinner.

But first, I have to shore up my wavering coalition. I make a series of calls that afternoon, starting with Steven Wilson and ending with the Reverse the War on Drugs PAC.

I have to fake an unflustered example to bolster the courage of my little underdog group of contrarians, channeling my inner Anita Meyer with a matter-of-fact, unflappable voice on the phone. "This is all a distraction," I say. "Ride it out. Focus on the goal."

It doesn't work. Steven is the only outright panicking one, saying "our cause is ruined, no one will take us seriously now," but the others are distant and noncommittal.

Without being told as much, I sense I've been categorized as *damaged goods*. Hard to be an ally in the war when you're starting scuffles on the sidelines.

I send my campaign manager a warning about outside money potentially drying up. I tell Steven, "This is a blip. I'll turn it around." The weight of that responsibility comes home with me that night. Not wanting to put it off, I drop my bag but don't change before I dial Alex.

He answers his phone for once. "I've been thinking about you," he says. After a long day, it's always irresistible to hear his voice. It makes me feel more secure than I have all day.

"I still rate when there's a crisis in the Middle East? I'm flattered," I say with a smile I hope he can hear over the phone line.

"There's always a crisis in the Middle East. There's never been a you," he replies, and we both pause at the sweetest *and* cheesiest thing he's ever said to me.

"Anyway," he continues, with a little laugh. "How bad is it on your end?"

Pacing barefoot in my kitchen, I hesitate. I don't want to be dramatic about this. My job itself is not threatened and I'm not getting more death threats than usual, as far as I know. "It could be better," I hedge.

"Yeah. Same. The worst part is they're saying we shouldn't see each other for a while. In person."

"They" are the strategists on his staff, I assume. "I figured. But, Alex, do they really think it will blow over?"

"Well, they think it will settle down long enough that we can make our own decision about whether and how to go public," he replies.

I don't like how far away that decision sounds when he talks about it in such a pragmatic tone. But I'm not sure I want to go public, so it wouldn't be fair to ask his position on it. Still, I can't resist probing a little. I didn't become a member of Congress without asking questions. "And when might that be?"

His laugh sounds a little stilted. "Whenever we want. *If* we want. Sometime after the legislation passes, I suppose." He makes it sound like it might never happen. Maybe he expects our entanglement will decrease along with the rumors. Suddenly, I feel much less secure. *I'm just a prop. Useful until I'm not.*

If only I could see his face, touch his hand. Go back to the lazy mornings we spent in bed together in California, and walking on the beach with the sun giving perfect light as it set—all golden, like a sepia photograph. I don't like having these conversations over the phone and yet that's all we have. At this rate, I don't know when I'll see him again.

Should I break up with him? Now that our relationship and reality have crashed together? It might be the right thing to do. But the things I miss about being with him are the reason I can't cut him off. I miss how carefully he plans what to make for dinner. The way he will casually touch me on his way past. How we can talk politics without it becoming an argument. That he's as interested in cuddling as he is inventive sex.

So I don't argue with the strategy. Distance, although it's the last thing I want. But I tell him I want his staff to check in with mine daily for the next few days. He agrees.

I dream about being with him that night—being close to him, skin on skin, not even having sex. When I wake up, I make the mistake of checking my social media replies. I want to take the temperature of my reputation. To gauge how long it might be before it's safe to meet Alex in person again.

My mentions are full of threats of rape and harm. According to social media, I'm a bitch for "seducing" men or a "traitor" to my progressive ideals, or much worse words for a woman who sleeps her way into power. It is all much, much worse than last time I checked my own social media feeds. I sometimes write my own content but I usually let my staff handle engagement.

They've clearly been protecting me this week.

Putting my phone face-down on the counter, I sit in my kitchen over a cup of coffee for a long time after I read the comments and search my own name.

I'm going to go to work and do my job. This is one very bad

week in what I hope will be a long career, a career I'm betting is interesting enough to write a whole book about.

The pep talk to myself continues through my shower and on the walk to the Capitol: I'm one of the most powerful female members of Congress in my party. I have important goals. I'm healthy and strong. In fact, I have small crow's feet for my age.

Walking between the concrete security barriers, showing my badge and putting my bag through the X-ray machine as I go through security, I try to spin the insults: People think I'm betraying my ideals, so at least I've done a good job communicating my principles.

Time to be proactive. At my desk, I call the House Rules Committee chairman's office myself and ask for a meeting. With Randy as my comparison point, anyone would be less dismissive, but Harold—whose support I need to clear the first legislative hurdle—is slow-walking it through his committee. Now I'm ready to go to war.

Martin and I are shown into Harold's office, where he's accumulated a lot more office furniture from the catalog than I have. The room is stuffed with cherry wood and leather.

Harold takes my hand between both of his and asks, "How are you holding up?" That starts the conversation on the wrong foot.

"What's holding my bill up, that's the more pertinent question," I say, smiling to keep from looking irritable. Women accomplish more with aggressive positivity.

He laughs, like I'm joking. "You've heard about the Senate bill, of course."

"Senate bill?" I glance at Martin, who shakes his head. He hasn't heard, either.

"Sure," Harold says, sitting back down at his desk. He gestures at the chairs across from him and I reluctantly sit. "Rumor says the

Senate Majority Leader told the White House the current bill goes too far and it can't pass the upper chamber. There's talk of a new bill in the Senate and the Majority Leader is urging the House to back something similar so we don't have a long reconciliation process."

"What's in the bill?"

"It's a clean bill, just decriminalization, without any of the additional provisions in yours," he says.

Martin sits forward. "But the progressives won't vote for that."

He turns to me. I can't return his gaze. I don't need help to realize what's going on. I'm being shut out.

"They think they have enough votes without progressives," Harold says. He shrugs. "That's what happens when the White House steps in. It's likely above your pay grade, now, Cindy."

A burning sensation builds behind my ears. "The White House is involved?" I ask quietly.

"That's what I'm told. It'd be a lot easier for your bill to pass the House if our members can limit their vote to the most popular parts, and still get cover from the Senate and the White House." His expression strikes me as patronizing. Like this concept might be a little too hard for me to understand without help. "I'll schedule hearings and a mark-up session for your bill, but I can all but guarantee that your extra language will be stripped before it makes it out of committee. Welcome to Washington."

He sits back in his chair, done with his lesson.

My entire body locks up in response to his tone.

"Their version isn't finalized yet," Martin says, sitting on the edge of his seat like he can chase down the new bill as it's coming across the street from the Senate office buildings.

Harold glances at him. His distracted gaze says he thinks it's a done deal and he's humoring our objections. "The White

House wants it stripped and the Senate party is so unified, I doubt there's any way to stop them from passing it."

"Right," I say numbly. I could ask him to bury the House version of the bill, effectively killing it. It's *my* bill and it's being stolen right out from under me to become Frankenstein's bill instead. I don't have to sit here and let it happen. Let the Senate pass their own bill with no teeth in it, and then I can point to my failed bill and make an example of them for their cowardice, their determination to stick with the status quo.

But the legislation could do a lot of good even if it doesn't go far enough. This moment, this tough compromise, is what I've got to learn to live with to be a lawmaker instead of an activist. Rather than indulging my petty and ruthless side, before I leave, I secure Harold's promise to schedule hearings soon.

I march back to the Cannon House Office building with Martin in tow—him barely hurrying to keep up, thanks to his long, skinny legs, damn him—furious at being talked down to despite my position. At how my support can be yanked right out from under me over a rumor. At how long and hard I worked to get to where I am only to be told I got here by laying on my back. At Alex, for never taking a stand.

Well, that's not me.

Back in my office, I sit down at my desk and start writing notes. Then I call Lizzie in and tell her: "I need to give a Floor speech."

* * *

Alex

Easy event, they told me. Nothing controversial, they said.

So I roll into the State Dining Room in the White House and get blindsided by Zack Ryder sitting side-by-side with uniformed officers in the chairs set up in front of the decorative fireplace below the portrait of Abraham Lincoln.

I turn to look at Deena. "Ryder," I hiss. She takes a step back, surprised. I've been volatile lately, prone to irritation, and yes I know it. Every time my staff reacts like this, I regret it, but I can't seem to stop.

"He's very popular with the troops," she replies, eyes wide. "He typically plays military roles. They say it raises awareness."

Right. I roll my eyes, keeping my back to the room. I've seen Ryder play a Marine and he got most of the details wrong. Awareness is what people promote when they aren't bold enough to take real action. "What's he lobbying for?" I ask Deena.

She checks her notes. "Health care waivers for veterans."

Of *course* Ryder would be on the side I agree with. It's wishful thinking that the movie star could be the bad guy for once. "So I have to be friendly."

"It's the best way to reset the media narrative," she says. "To be photographed as allies, not enemies." She nods, barely moving her head, to the pool of photographers set up near the chairs. We're being watched.

"Right." Those bullshit stories about a love triangle between me, Cindy and Ryder. Of course the rumors are now *my* problem. While Ryder made another notch in his dating tally.

"OK, but I'm grumpy about it," I say, before turning to the room to wave at the mix of media and military families.

"Noted," Deena says, following me to the front of the room.

The cameras start clicking as I extend a hand to each person in turn, including Ryder.

"Been seeing a lot of each other," I tell him.

Ryder grins. That'll be the shot the press runs with from the event: Zack Ryder flashing his movie star smile while shaking hands with the vice president.

"Too much?" he asks.

"Depends who you ask," I reply, managing to say nothing while appearing to carry on a friendly conversation. I let the cameras take their shot and then release the actor's hand and turn to the crowd to repeat what Deena fed me before we walked in.

"We're planning a screening of the new movie this week and I'm looking forward to watching it," I conclude. I can't remember what Ryder's new movie is called. "I think the first lady's the most excited of all, though. She's a big fan," I add, turning to the star. "She wouldn't mind me telling you that."

Ryder grins again. "I'll leave her an autographed picture."

"I'm sure the president will appreciate that," I reply dryly.

The crowd laughs. Poor Anita, suffering through "my wife said" jokes from both her husband and his bachelor running mate. I wonder if Cindy realizes committing to me means signing up for a lifetime of being used as a foil in public. A good reason why *not* to commit. One of many good reasons.

After a few more minutes of small talk for the cameras and a minimum of celebrisplaining on the complicated issue of veteran health care, I leave Ryder and the assistant undersecretary from Veteran's Affairs to do a Q&A while I go to my next scheduled event.

"Sir, Congresswoman Wight called while you were on camera," Deena tells me as I'm scanning the brief she put together for the meeting.

"What did she say? Everything alright?" I ask. The press has been demonizing her for allegedly both seducing and cheating on me. It's sexist bullshit, turning me into the victim of her wiles. I hope she didn't break up with me via my staff. I'd understand why, if she did.

"She said she's planning on giving a Floor speech tomorrow and wanted to give you a heads up." Deena is somehow typing away on her BlackBerry and iPhone at the same time, one in each hand, while balancing a wedge of files under one arm.

"OK. Any other details?"

"She said she plans to denounce sexism."

"I support denouncing sexism. Did you tell her to call back later?"

"Yes," Deena says, looking up. "But she said she'd be working late."

Of course. I have no idea how I'm supposed to deepen or strengthen a relationship without time to talk. If we lived together, it'd be different. We'd at least run into each other once in a while.

I laugh to myself, handing the brief back to Deena. Here I am contemplating moving in with the woman when we're desperately trying to take it slow. I shake my head, compartmentalizing the topic before I walk into the next room.

twenty-six

Cindy

I DECIDED to give my speech in the morning, before legislative business begins. When I'm ready, I walk to the front row of seats on my side of the House floor and sit. A few other members are waiting today, and the short queue is good because it means the speeches won't be cut off for too many people wanting to give one-minute remarks in the limited amount of time.

I'm wearing red. Red lipstick, red blazer, red skirt. The pin marking me as a member of this Congress is positioned on my lapel.

Standing at the right moment, I speak, clear and loud enough to be heard throughout the chamber. "Mr. Speaker, I ask unanimous consent to address the House for one minute." A minute is not much time, but it's enough to say what I want.

"Without objection, so ordered," the day's Speaker pro tempore answers. The chamber is silent. There are few people in the room and no one is paying much attention.

Walking up to the podium amid the silence, I wet my lips. I

didn't write out a full speech. I have a few note cards. I remind myself of the House rules that stipulate that, no matter how much I may be tempted, I'm not allowed to disparage anyone specific or direct my remarks at anyone but the Speaker.

Speak up. Own your voice. I'm not doing this for myself alone.

"Thank you, Mr. Speaker," I say. My voice is crisp in the microphone. "This week, I've been the target of the type of harassment that thousands or more women face every day in our country. The reasons are not important. I am not here to discuss what motivates some people to call a woman a c-word on social media, or to speculate about who she is sleeping with and whether that is why she achieved success in her career."

I take a beat to make sure my voice stays steady. Despite the fact the Speaker pro tempore is focused on something on his desk and the press gallery looks empty, I know the C-SPAN cameras are on me and people will watch this later if I do it right. My office sent out a press release announcing I'd be speaking today in response to all the other inquiries.

"This kind of public harassment is accepted not because it is acceptable but because it disproportionately impacts women." My voice grows louder, stronger, ringing through the chamber. I want to make it clear this is *unacceptable* for all women. "When a woman, particularly one who is a public figure, speaks out about this harassment, she is criticized. Being a public figure does not make me less human. As a public figure who is a woman, I have been accused of sleeping my way to a position of power. As a public figure who is a woman, I have been threatened with rape. As a public figure who is a woman, I also have more access to security than the average woman who is subject to these kinds of threats for actions as simple as sending a tweet or speaking her mind. Living daily under this kind of threat destroys lives. Our lives are treated as more disposable than a man's because we are women. This is not right."

My nerves are starting to tremble and it's hard to focus on my notes. I know I need to bring it back to my personal story. To why this matters to *me*. "The idea that this kind of harassment could be triggered by dating a certain man should offend all of us. It is triggered by an age-old belief that a woman can be owned. No man should assume a woman can be owned through dating her. No man should assume that an interest in dating means a woman is less of a whole person on her own."

I grew up hearing motherhood lauded as more important than working outside the home, and that led me to avoid serious relationships for fear of having to give up the career I wanted. I'd dated men who thought my career and my needs—in bed and out—should mean less than theirs.

"As a society, we should be eliminating reasons women fear speaking up or being on her own by teaching men to respect women as equals," I add.

The Speaker pro tempore raises a hand to warn me that I'm out of time and I finish my next sentence quickly, "And we should be publicly exposing men who don't. Thank you."

Walking back to my seat, my legs are sturdy. I sit to wait for others to speak. Several female members come up to me and congratulate me quietly, with a hand on my arm or a nod of recognition. I said most of what I wanted to say, even if there wasn't nearly enough time to address all the problems.

I hope it resonates.

* * *

Alex

I don't fully understand what "trending" means or how much it matters, so I usually ask my staff for more details when a hashtag appears on my morning comms briefing.

"Wait," I say. I can feel my forehead drawing in confusion, as I balance the cell phone between my shoulder and my face, holding Thor's ball and my briefing papers in either hand. "Cindy called me a pig? On the House Floor? And I'm just hearing about it now?"

"She didn't call you a pig, technically," Deena assures me on the phone. "But that's how people are taking it."

"And #VicePigoftheUnitedStates is trending?" I pull my phone away from my face, trying to figure out what apps are on it so I can pull this up for myself. I put the phone back to my face. "How...trending is it?"

"It's...pretty trending," she says, deliberately vague.

"Terrific. My one job is to be non-controversial and not distract from the president's message and here I am in the news again." I put a hand to my forehead, realize I'm still holding Thor's soggy ball and my dog is now up on two legs trying to reach it, and give it a toss. Thor runs for it, but the lackluster throw doesn't go far. "Can you send me something with the context of this? I don't understand where it's coming from."

"Yes, sir. I'll send you the video of her speech."

I'm the worst boyfriend ever. I didn't have a chance to call Cindy last night to ask how it went. Ted found me a clip—more of a gif—in which Cindy was as poised and articulate as I expected.

Thor brings the ball back to me and I bend to take it, dropping half of my papers in the process. "Deena, can you send that to me before I see the president, please. And is this big enough that Kaylee's going to take questions about it?"

"Um...yes?" Deena, I can tell, is cringing. White House daily briefings are usually full of policy questions; it's never a good thing when someone's personal life becomes a subject. "I'll have Kaylee call you."

"Great. Thanks." I hang up so I can rescue the papers from

my dog's tiny mouth. "You want to go to the White House today, buddy?" I ask. If people are pissed, Thor calms them down. "I have a feeling I'm going to be there awhile today."

I watch the video of Cindy's floor speech on a phone on the way to work, Thor curled up in my lap in the back of the black SUV.

She's fired up, direct and personal. I frown as she speaks about harassment, frustrated that she's been facing this kind of shit without sharing the burden with me. I'm sheltered from these kinds of threats in my position, due to my Secret Service detail. And the threats I receive are clearly different from those that would be directed at me if I were a woman.

"And we should be publicly exposing men who don't," she concludes on the video, and I suspect she got cut off before finishing the thought, but I understand now why the internet took it as a dig against the person she's reportedly dating. It took another small step to jump to the conclusion it was directed at me. *Too bad people aren't calling out Ryder.*

Kaylee meets me as I'm walking through the West Wing toward the Oval Office. "It's a problem," she says.

"Let's ride it out," I suggest, tightening my tie as I walk with her. Thor is on his leash at my side. "She's not going to confirm it was about me. We're not going to confirm it was about me. People will get tired of drawing their own conclusions."

"We can try that for now," she says. "But frankly, if she keeps talking, that strategy is going to work less and less."

I can feel the pressure piling up on my shoulders, but I'm not going to unfairly shift it to Cindy to escape the hot seat. "She's taking a lot of heat. I'm not going to tell her to shut up about it."

"Mr. Vice President, all due respect, but at some point we're not going to be able to shut up about it, either." Kaylee leaves me at the outer lobby to the Oval Office.

"Like sand through the hourglass..." Tim jokes when I walk

in, quoting the theme from a soap opera. He's sitting at the desk, his chief of staff standing in front of it. "Here's our daytime drama in the flesh."

"Ha, ha," I say, then adds, more seriously: "I apologize for the distraction, sir."

Tim waves me off. "Anita and I didn't need to watch our stories last night, we just opened up social media."

Tim is joking—the president doesn't have time to keep up with soap operas—but I suspect he's also annoyed. Tim was supposed to spend the week talking about infrastructure.

"How's my favorite nephew," Tim says, patting his lap for Thor to hop into it. Thor happily curls up into a ball of fluff on the president's lap. "Somebody needs a good grooming." He raises his eyebrows at me. "Letting a few things slip, Alex?"

I straighten my tie and run a hand through my hair to hide a flare of irritation. Tim is being unusually sharp for 7:30 in the morning. "Having a personal life and doing this job at the same time isn't easy," I say, in what I hope is a neutral tone.

"Especially not if you do it all alone," Tim agrees, turning his gaze down to Thor. "Is it, buddy?" He ruffles the dog's fur and Thor pants adoringly back up at him. Tim might not be great at kissing babies, but give him a room full of dogs and he'll win all *their* votes.

"If we need to take some things off your plate, let us know," says the White House chief of staff. I glare at him, because I can't glare at the president.

"No, thank you," I bite out. "Give me a minute to make some adjustments."

Tim stands, holding Thor up to his chest like he's burping a baby. He moves toward the couches and chairs positioned over the seal in the carpet. "It's not an insult, Alex, and it's not permanent. If you need some time right now to deal with things, we can help arrange that."

"I'm fine, thank you," I maintain, sitting once the president does. The outer door opens and intelligence officials enter to go over the daily briefing.

"If you say so," Tim says. His gaze loudly speaks doubt. Then he looks up at the men entering. "Gentlemen, I have conferred upon our guest the highest level of security clearance. You can speak freely in front of him," he says, holding up Thor in both hands. Thor gives them the full force of his big brown eyes and floppy ears and the two men pause to take it in.

"Certainly, Mr. President," they murmur before they sit.

"Traitor," I grumble, watching my dog trade up for the most powerful lap in the world while I sit abandoned and comfortless across from him. I open the daily brief and try to put everything else out of my mind.

* * *

Cindy

Alex finally calls the day after my speech. I've put off calling him, because every time I do, he's unavailable and I have to have an awkward conversation with his staff.

"Hello, this is the Vice Pig speaking," he says when I answer the phone.

"I'm so sorry," I say. "I hope you know I didn't mean it like that."

I might be angry with him, but I'm not mean.

"Your speech was amazing," he replies, ignoring that. "I'm sorry I didn't have a chance to tell you before."

"Thank you." I've been surprised by the delayed response to the speech. It went viral on social media hours later, amplified by fellow female members of Congress in both parties. Over the last day, I've had meetings with female members I hadn't thought to prod on voting for the cannabis legislation before. Suddenly, my bill is trendy.

"They want to present a united front under the social justice umbrella," Martin had mansplained to me earlier that day. "They're with you on sexism and they want to support you on minorities, too. It's inter-sectional."

I don't let Martin talk to any media for a reason. Still, whatever the cause, I've got momentum on my side and I plan to capitalize on it.

"Listen, we need to talk about this clean bill they're discussing in the Senate," I tell Alex, standing alone in my kitchen asking myself whether a glass of wine every night this week is too much. It's been a roller coaster and I've needed the chance to slow down in the evenings. "I still believe we can pass my version in the House."

"Ah, right," he says, sounding distracted. Increasingly common when I talk to him lately. "Sorry, I'm not up to date on that since the Senate Majority Leader mentioned it. Where are we at on that?"

"You spoke to the Majority Leader about it?" *What else has he failed to mention?*

"Yes, just a couple times. I didn't think it had progressed very far. I tried to shut it down."

"It's progressed far enough that I've got chairmen telling me my bill won't make it to the Floor without being stripped down. My little squad of five is now warning me they'll vote present if they don't get to vote on both provisions. They aren't interested in a bite instead of the whole apple."

"That's nearsighted."

I ignore that. "If we can only do one provision, I think I've managed to replace them, though. I'm popular all of the sudden around here." I would hate to pass the bill without the full

Freshman Six. But I'd rather have a bill become law than keep all my ideals pristine.

"Because of the speech?" he asks.

I try not to read into his tone, but it's as if he's surprised other people thought my speech significant. "Yes," I say. He doesn't say anything immediately, so I continue: "It's not a small issue. What I talked about. It resonated well beyond the House floor."

"I'm sure it did," he says. Like he's placating me. "I'm sorry I haven't been around to hear about what's going on. The press keeps asking me if you're going to be my first lady. I haven't even announced I'm running yet."

All at once, I'm impatient with this conversation, which we've danced around for months and now are finally going to have, damnit. "But you are. And you do need a first lady. Right?"

He's quiet for a moment. "Right," he says.

"That's what the polls say?"

"That's what the polls say."

"Is that why you haven't announced yet? Because you don't have a wife?" This just dawned on me. Of *course*. Has our whole relationship been a rehearsal to find out if I'm good enough to be a first lady of the United States? Just a prop. That's all he needs.

I can almost hear him running his hand through his hair. "Sort of. The polls say a bachelor can't be elected president and I just...haven't felt ready. I feel like something's missing."

"Why would you let a poll keep you from doing what you want? Or at least trying? Do you know what the press is asking *me*? They want to know when I'm quitting Congress to be your full-time girlfriend. They want to know if I ran for Congress in the first place to become your first lady."

He's frowning, I can tell. "I'm sorry they're asking you that. That's insulting and I wish I could do something about it. Your speech was great but I'm sorry you had to give it. And I'm also sorry some people are turning it into a referendum on me because it's causing some problems for the White House."

"It's more than insulting, Alex. It's becoming the narrative and it will be the narrative forever if..." I catch myself. He hasn't *asked* me to be his first lady. We've only been dating a few months. And his polling would reject me, according to what he said at the state dinner. I hate that it hurts a little that America doesn't think I'm "first lady material," although that's never been my goal.

"It's not just because of you, you know," I say. I can't stop poking at the issue. "That's not the only reason people are interested in me or the bill. There's more to my career than you. My career is about doing what's *right*, not just what will keep me in office."

I've gotten threats since before I became a policy-maker, since I dared stand up in front of people and imply "my thoughts are as valuable as a man's." Unlike Alex, I don't let what other people think run my life.

"No, of course. But I put a bigger target on your back," he says. "I'm sorry about that. And I'm sorry if you've felt alone in that."

I pace back and forth in my kitchen, not sure what about his words or his tone is bothering me. The way he's talking—it makes me think the end isn't just coming, it's *now*. Better to rip the bandage off. "Is that why you called?"

"No," he sounds frustrated. "I called because I haven't talked to you in awhile. I'm sorry about that, too. Look, do you need me to keep apologizing? Because I will, but you're going to have to tell me what I did that irritated you."

Gritting my teeth, I stop at the fridge and pull the bottle of red off the top of it. I don't understand what Alex expects—for me to stand by, nothing changing, waiting for his calls? Time is passing in the meantime and we aren't moving anywhere and I didn't realize how much that frustrated me. "Stop putting it on me, like I'm the one tasked with the emotional labor of sorting out our problems."

"We have problems now?" He sounds confused. *Good.*

"I'm not sure what you *want*, Alex." I pour a healthy glass of wine and take a drink.

He takes a deep breath. "OK. OK." Then it all comes rushing out. "I *want* to become president. I *want* a first lady. I don't want to be alone in the White House running the country and surrounded by people who call me *sir*. I want a partner."

"Which means someone who polls well."

"That's not fair," he protests.

"But the support you want would help get you into the White House. So that person has to be popular with your voters." He's not asking me because it's what he wants, damn the polls, or even because it's right. He wants a *prop*. Something I refuse to be. For anyone, ever.

He breathes out slowly over the phone. "I thought we were on the same page on this. We need to present a united front."

I huff. "A united front? To who? As far as anyone knows, we're not together. Meanwhile, you've been distracting me from my job and looking for a different way to pass the legislation this whole time!"

"I meant on the bill but I...I thought we agreed on the relationship, also? That we're keeping it under wraps." His voice is hesitant, but there's something else there. I'm not sure what it is. Maybe understanding. We're not in California anymore and he knows the pressure of being back in Washington is fracturing us.

"I'm not sure we even have a relationship, Alex. I haven't spoken to you in days." I slap my hand down on my countertop by the glass of wine. "You call me when it's convenient. You can't use your job as an excuse for everything. I'm a person, not a..." I cast around for the right metaphor. "A piece of legislation."

"OK," he says, dragging the word out like *I'm* being unreasonable. I hate that. "I don't think you're a piece of legislation. I didn't call to argue."

I didn't plan on arguing, either, but here we are and I'm not sure how to back out of this corner we're in. "Maybe we shouldn't talk at all, then," I say.

"Fine," he says. He doesn't hang up.

"Fine," I repeat, and end the call. Instantly, I regret it. If I try to call him back now, will his staff answer and make me explain the whole thing to them? I groan and say aloud, "What is *wrong* with you?" Every time I think I have my temper in check, I do something like this without thinking first. Slamming up a shield when I need to be vulnerable. I slump onto a stool at my counter.

My impulses sometimes flare quickly and die out, like this one, but there's usually a strong instinct behind them. I've relied on my instincts my whole life. Alex and I have been trying to coast on attraction alone, avoiding honest conversations about whether there's more between us. I know it's my fault as much as his. And I should have *said* that the lack of clarity bothered me, rather than picked a fight with him.

Taking another drink of my wine, I look at my phone, silent on the counter. He's always been certain in the past, constantly stable and reassuring. But tonight I'd pushed him into telling the truth about what he wanted. We want different things. He wants to be liked and I want to make a difference. The end was coming no matter what. I just confronted it. *Finally* and yet *too soon*.

A future of being condemned to see him regularly and never touch him again is devastating. I'll be close to him, yet so far, for the rest of my life.

I finish the wine, tapping my other hand on the counter in time with my fast-moving mind. Then I call Sara.

"What if I frame the book around this speech," I ask. "It would be about the harassment I've faced my whole life, and how dating someone high-profile made other people pay attention to it. And about how harassment, and fear of it, is the background noise of every woman's life and can shape our decisions whether we want it to or not."

There's no pause. "That would sell," Sara replies.

After hanging up, I sit down with a glass of water and write. I write about being prepared to face harassment as a young girl and never not being afraid of walking alone at night. I write about having a management strategy for harassment in my office, about creating a compartment for it in my mind and how that imaginary box can still get so heavy it feels like it's crushing me into a small, scared little girl.

I leave my cell phone on the counter in front of my computer, and then on my bedside table when I take the computer to bed. I almost send it flying across the room in my hurry to pick it up when Kari texts me that my speech even went viral where she is, in Nevada.

But it doesn't ring. Alex never calls me back.

twenty-seven

Alex

I'M MID-AIR, about halfway to Atlanta, when Deena tells me Kaylee is asking for a few minutes of my time.

"Is this about the vice pig thing again?" I ask her. I'm trying to make sense of Georgia's election law because the topic is bound to come up at the state Capitol.

"Yes, sir," Deena says, hovering by my desk. "A lot of think pieces are being written. One published in *The Guardian* today, so it's gone a bit international."

Tired of this topic, I rub my forehead. "They think I'm a sexist pig in the UK now?"

"Well...the theme is generally that calling out sexism doesn't change anything, even at the highest levels of power."

The nuances of legislation in Georgia are making my head hurt so I close the folder. "Has Cindy said anything to clarify the speech?"

Deena grimaces and I guess her answer before she says it because it's clear she doesn't want to disappoint me. "No, sir. Radio silence."

I hesitate before asking, "And we haven't received any calls from her today, right?"

"No, sir." Deena's eyes fall to the floor.

Of course. Someone would have told me before now if Cindy called me back. She doesn't want to talk to me; she made that clear by hanging up on me yesterday.

I'd thought it might have been an impulse decision, that she would take it back, but her silence now that she's had time to think about it proves it's how she really feels. She doesn't want me. She's tired of all the baggage I bring into a relationship.

We didn't have enough time to build trust before we were tested.

"OK. Put her on." I straighten in my chair. Time to focus on work, not another failed attempt at a personal life. "Hi, Kaylee," I say to the phone. Deena points to the door but I wave at her to stay.

Until recently, I'd rarely talked to the White House's press department. Deena and Maggie coordinate with them, but in general, the president's messaging strategy doesn't require the vice president's input. "I'm about ready for this thing to be shut down, can you do that?" I ask.

"I can, sir," she says. She sounds like she hoped for this question. "There are two ways to do it. One is a full-court press involving you and the congresswoman."

Cindy already made it clear that we are not on the same page. So much for a united front. "And the other?"

"The other is less polite," she says. "I suggest I make a statement the next time I'm asked about it and then we say nothing else. Similar to what you did when they came after your dog, sir."

The dog statement created a media circus that lasted a week —a century in media time. But my strategy isn't working, so might as well put it in the hands of the experts.

"Great. Let's do that."

Kaylee hesitates. "Are you sure, sir? We can take control of the narrative, but we do run the risk of looking aggressive on an issue we're not currently highlighting."

I'm done with how careful I've been the last few weeks, with letting things develop at their own speed and not pushing for what I wanted. It landed me in this mess and lost me Cindy. Now it's threatening my actual job performance—my ability to support Tim—and I need to take care of it. "Which way distracts less from the president's agenda, staying silent or addressing it?"

"At this point, addressing it is the best way to shut it down, sir," Kaylee answers.

"Great," I say, drawing a line in the air. I meet Deena's eyes. "I didn't become vice president without being aggressive. Do it."

Three hours later, I finish my speech about infrastructure to a round-table in Atlanta and am shaking hands when Deena sidles up and murmurs, "She did it, sir."

"How did it go?"

"There will be some follow-up questions, but I think the media will drop it now they have an answer. Assuming the congresswoman doesn't respond. Should we talk to her about it?"

Smiling and nodding at the man in front of me, I tell her, "Do whatever needs to be done, Deena. From now on, I'm focused on our agenda. No more distractions."

The press pool waiting for me outside the room in the state Capitol didn't get the message, though. The pooler for the day— the person who will write up notes from the day's events to distribute to the entire White House press corps by email—asks: "Was Congresswoman Wight only interested in publicity, sir?"

I nearly stumble and give her a reaction to the question, it's aimed with such precision at my thoughts. But I manage to wave her off without saying anything and climb into my vehicle heading back to the airport. I ask Deena to pull up the White

House press briefing from earlier that day and watch Kaylee respond to the correspondent asking, "Does the White House have any response to accusations that the vice president is sexist?"

"What are you basing that accusation on, Justin?" Kaylee asks from the podium.

The camera switches to Justin, a dark-bearded man who reads from his phone: "Congresswoman Cindy Wight's viral speech on the House Floor that led to the trending hashtag #VicePigoftheUnitedStates."

"The congresswoman is welcome to use her platform to drum up publicity for any cause that is important to her, but the White House is not working with her on that particular agenda," Kaylee responds calmly. "That's all I'm going to say on the matter, let's move on."

I hand the phone back to Deena. "Did she shut it down?"

"I think so, sir. I'm seeing a few pieces headlined 'White House addresses charges of sexism,' but...oh wait." Deena is reading off her BlackBerry. She pauses and starts typing on her iPhone. "*HuffPo* has a quote in their story from the congresswoman's office. Well, not a quote, a clarification. 'A spokesperson for Congresswoman Wight clarified that she was not referring to the vice president as sexist in her speech.'"

"Nice footnote," I grumble, watching the police motorcycles outside the window. "Damage already done."

"Yes, not much interest in clarification notes," Deena agrees. "Sorry, sir."

"It's fine. They clearly weren't in a hurry to clarify, either. I guess they liked the publicity too much."

Deena, wisely, doesn't agree or disagree, or point out that we told Cindy's people to stay quiet on the topic. She hands me my messages, including a call from the Claytons—scavengers—and one from my mother that says, "I have several ideas for a replacement date for your sister's wedding in August." I crumple it up in my fist. A break-up so public my mother would hear about it is one of the major reasons I've avoided dating in the first place. Her judgment is a stand-in for the American people.

It stays silent in the SUV as my motorcade flies through lights on the way to the airport, where Air Force Two is waiting to take me back to Washington. I'm looking forward to getting home to Thor. Maybe I'll cook, using the ingredients acquired for meals I'd planned to eat with Cindy. They're all going bad rapidly, much like our relationship.

Probably won't, though. I hate cooking for one.

* * *

Cindy

One does not simply turn down an invitation to the White House from the first lady. Even though I want to.

But I spend the whole ride wishing I could have come up with a polite way to ask "will *he* be there?" Having an ex who is one of the most famous people in the world—in *my* world, at least—is going to be difficult. And that's while he's *vice* president. The future, a few years out, is a nightmare.

All those loving feelings that always flamed out in my past broken relationships haven't gone away this time. When I see him, even on the cover of a newspaper casually displayed in my office, I still long for him. I want to know what he's *really* thinking when he frowns on TV. I want to run a soothing hand down his back.

I'm not in a hurry to have a final conversation with him because I don't expect closure. I'm always going to spot him somewhere or have to deal with him and wish, at least a little bit, that I was a slightly different person who could have accepted what he offered.

Who could have made a romantic deal that worked for both of us. It's not solely my fault that things fell apart between us, but I could have tried harder to save us. I'm always going to beat myself up for my negotiation skills failing when I *really* needed them. And for second-guessing every opportunity that came my way.

Parking near the White House isn't worth the stress, so I Uber. The mile from the Capitol to the White House still feels long, given my thoughts are spread out over the many years ahead of me. It won't always hurt quite like this. But I will always have the memory of this hurt to haunt me.

I walk in through the gate for people who have business in the White House, go through security and get a day pass. The near-July sun glares down at me and my silk shirt is growing damp under the sleeves. A member of the first lady's staff is waiting. But so are a few members of the press.

They're standing outside the briefing room on the drive, two men smoking and another woman chatting with them. They all magically pull recorders out of thin air when they clock me walking up the drive.

"Congresswoman, did you break up with the vice president? Are you here to see him?"

"Representative Wight, do these rumors hurt your chances of passing the marijuana bill?"

"Congresswoman, is it more effective to work with your party's leadership than with outside progressive groups?"

Holding up one hand and smiling politely, I walk past them without responding. How long will it be like this? What an indignity to break up with someone and then have to answer constant questions about him; it's like I'm facing a barrage of my own mother.

"Did you *try* hard enough, sweetheart?" my mother had called to ask, after reading the media reports last week.

"No, Mother, I showed him my crazy too early," I'd thought but didn't say. I resent that my mother's voice is the one in my head, wondering what I could have done better.

Anita Meyer meets me inside the foyer and smiles, taking my hand. "I thought you might need a friend who understands the mess you're going through."

A deep breath blows through me at the unexpected words. "Oh. That's so kind." I'd expected to never hear from these people again, except in a professional capacity.

The other woman smiles. "Perhaps a tour of the White House while we talk? Or would you like some tea first?"

"I'd love to walk and talk," I agree, nervous about sitting down to questions.

"Leah can put your bag somewhere safe for now, if you like," Anita says, gesturing at the aide still standing nearby.

"Thanks," I agree, handing over my large purse. I keep my cell phone. Silly, but habit. What call am I going to get that's more important than this appointment?

Anita shows me the East Wing, where her office is located. Its decor is different from what I've seen of the West Wing or in pictures of the Oval Office. Anita used softer colors and high contrast, like an arch of burnt orange painted behind her desk. We chat idly about preparations for July 4, when the president will speak at the Lincoln Memorial before the fireworks set off over the National Mall.

She shows me the movie theater room, which used to be a cloakroom. It's all red and gold with an old-school vibe, like screenings might cost a quarter.

"You should come watch a Zack Ryder movie with me sometime," the first lady says with a smile. "My husband does not appreciate my appreciation of that man."

"He's very charismatic," I agree. "I wasn't romantically

involved with him," I add hurriedly, in case the first lady saw the press.

Anita Meyer raises her eyebrows. "I certainly hope not, given the way Alex looks when he talks about you."

I swallow. "How does he look?" I ask faintly. "Did he look," I correct myself.

"Like a man who knows what he wants." The other woman turns and leads me out of the theater. "I've never seen a movie star look like *that* in real life."

It's not true, I'm too polite to say to the first lady. Alex might know what he wants—but it isn't me. Not the real me. Not the difficult woman who demanded too much of his time and effort.

The other woman pauses, like she senses my doubts.

"We've only known each other five months. It's not enough time to know...anything," I say.

The smaller woman assesses my face. I wonder what she sees, because Anita smiles and says, "Oh, I think you know."

Mercifully, she turns away after cutting me to the bone with that observation. It's too late now.

"I want to show you the bowling alley," the first lady continues, leading the way. "There are two White House bowling alleys. The larger one is in the executive building across the street where the vice president's ceremonial office is. But we have our own private, one-lane alley downstairs." She throws a small smirk over her shoulder. "For when you can't sleep and want to bowl alone."

Because I don't have another choice, I follow. But I'm bracing myself to find out how much worse the comments about Alex will get before the tour is over.

* * *

Alex

I dislike bowling, mainly because I'm not good at it, but if the president asks you to bowl with him, you don't say no. I carry my bowling bag—yes, I keep one with my shoes and ball in it at EEOB, because it's not the first time Tim wanted a meeting while "sporting"—across to the White House along with a copy of the bill the Senate Majority Leader sent me. I need Tim to sign off on the messaging strategy coming from the White House if we're going to unify the party position on the bill.

Toby handed me the folder. "Are you sure you want to back this language, Mr. Vice President?"

Surprised by this unexpected show of conscience, I stared at him. "We want the bill to pass, don't we?"

"The core bill is broadly popular. The provisions the congresswoman wants to include are worthwhile and probably can't pass alone. Now's the time to push them if you want them to pass." He paused and cleared his throat, perhaps embarrassed to be caught advocating a cause. "Besides, people might turn on you if they think you're stabbing your ex-girlfriend in the back."

I had to lean on the edge of my desk for a moment. I wasn't stabbing her in the back; Cindy knew all along the Senate might change her language. But Toby, a master of optics, could pick up emotional signals like reading a heat map. If he thought Cindy would be hurt, she would. That's not what I wanted, but I was driving down a dead-end road on this bill.

"I'll see what the president says," I murmured before I left, kicking the can down the road like any pure-blooded politician would do.

"Mr. President," I sigh now, meeting Tim in the north hall, where we can access the basement. "Must you be such a boomer?"

Tim smirks. "You're only insulting me because you're grumpy. And you're only grumpy because you let a very simple situation become very messy." Not pulling any punches, then.

"Thanks, that's the title of my memoir," I grouse. "If you're done sorting out my personal life, I brought some work with me." I lift the folder in the hand not holding the heavy ball bag.

"We can discuss that later," Tim says, waving me off as we proceed deeper under the north portico. I notice he's not carrying his own ball.

"Wait, is this an ambush? Did you seriously bring me down here to talk about my love life?" I look around at the Secret Service agents tailing us, as if they're going to commiserate. They must *know* how intensely stubborn their boss is, and prone to using his position to meddle in other people's personal lives. Ted raises an eyebrow but doesn't respond. He would never say it, but he probably agrees with Tim that I need some kind of intervention.

"I'm not 13," I continue, unwillingly following because I can't throw a tantrum and abandon Tim in the White House basement. It's part of my job description to follow wherever the president goes. "I don't need you to sit me down and tell me how to treat a lady."

"I'm happy to hear you know how to treat a lady, Alex," Tim says dryly. He pauses outside the door to Nixon's hobby room. "Personally, I like to handle my lady face-to-face, not through a spokesperson."

I pause, because Tim's got me there.

"It just...happened," I say. It's not sufficient. I should have tried again to talk to Cindy myself, even if it meant taking a motorcade down Pennsylvania Avenue to her office. I let other things—important things, though!—stand in the way. And then our relationship became a snowball rolling downhill, melting all the way, until there was no substance left to hold onto.

Whatever had been between us—the "us" we were building —had been such a fragile thing. Between my job and my ambition and my personal fears, I didn't have the time needed to nurture it.

"It is what it is, Tim," I tell him, partly speaking to myself. "Relationships are all about timing. Circumstances aren't right for this one."

"Circumstances?" Tim cocks his head, his hand on the door. "I think I can help with that." He opens the door and gestures me in ahead of him.

I enter the room and spot Anita. It's unusual, but Anita has joined us for a round of bowling before. She's walking toward me, distracting me at first from seeing that Cindy is in the room with her.

Cindy's wearing tight gray pants and a striped shirt with loose sleeves and a bow at the neck that matches her striped high heels. Her dark hair is down and shining in the overhead lights. I stop short. The room is small and I'm closer to her than I've been in weeks.

Anita pats my shoulder as she keeps walking, around me, joining Tim at the door.

"We thought we'd leave the two of you alone to share a constructive activity," Anita says. Tim puts an arm around her waist. "It seems like you might have a few things to talk about."

"Don't do anything I wouldn't do," says Tim, directing Anita out the door.

"Guys..." I protest, following them. Ted stands in the doorway.

"I'm sorry, sir," he says, blocking my way. "I answer to the president and I cannot let you leave until you 'work things out.'"

"Seriously?" Cindy says, approaching from behind. Her heels click on the wood floor.

"Seriously," Ted says, without smiling. He does, indeed, seem serious. He nods politely at us both and closes the door.

I stare at it, alone in the narrow room with Cindy. She smells like oranges. I remind myself to keep my distance. We're not together anymore. Despite myself, a traitorous bubble of hope lifts my stomach. I turn to her. "What are you doing here?"

"The first lady invited me on a tour," she says. "I didn't realize it ended with being locked in the basement."

"What are we supposed to do?" I ask. I cannot be in this room with her without saying or doing or *trying* something that will make our situation worse. I have to escape.

The room is tidy. And narrow—a mere few feet across. There are two blue plush couches on a narrow band of carpet on one side of the room and a wooden credenza on the other under multiple TVs and next to a rack of balls, all stamped "the President's House." Taking up most of the room is the single bowling lane and I fixate on that.

"Maybe we can get out that way." I put down my bag and the folder and half slide, half walk down the lane to the pins. I carefully kneel and try to peer around them to see if there's a back room on the other side.

Cindy curses softly behind me. "This is how you're beheaded. I don't want to watch. This is going to make for some awkward history books."

I can't tell what's behind the pins and she's right that I shouldn't try to crawl through the machine. I stand up and walk back to her, digging in my pockets. I don't have my phone on me, as usual. I can't believe how calm she is. My insides are spinning. Her perfume is overwhelmingly delicious—it's warm, somehow, like touching her skin. "Do *you* want to be stuck in here?"

She frowns at me. "I'm sure they'll let us out in a few minutes. Half an hour, tops. You'll be needed somewhere by then."

"My whole job is to support the president," I reply, voice rising. "If he thinks I can best support him in here, he can keep me here as long as he wants to. No one's going to ask questions."

Cindy stares at me, putting both hands on her hips as she considers this. "Well, someone might notice if the president kidnaps a congresswoman who has criticized him in the past. Eventually."

"Do you have your phone? Call someone. Text Tim. Tell him we sorted it out and he can let us go."

She stares at me. "I don't have *the president's number* in my cell phone." She pulls it out of her pocket and waves it.

"I don't have it memorized," I admit, internally kicking myself. Realistically, the president doesn't answer his own phone any more than I do. I have some choice words for Tim, though. Someday when I write my tell-all book, Tim's mean streak deserves a full chapter.

"I don't have a signal," she says. "Looks like I can't live-tweet this experience."

Humor, when the scaffolding of our relationship is still in shambles around us. I glare at her. "Very funny."

"I thought so." The smile falls off her face. "Can you really not handle the idea of talking to me?"

I flop down on one of the soft blue couches. It feels like velvet. There's a landline phone on the round side table and I pull it toward me, considering.

"It's not that," I say. "There's not much left to say." It's not true, of course. I want to say plenty to her, but I'm afraid. To avoid her pointing this out, I add, "And it's completely inappropriate of them."

Picking up the receiver, I put it to my ear. Dead. Of course it is. "This has got to be some kind of security breach," I mutter, dropping the receiver with a clatter back into its cradle.

"The Secret Service is right outside the door. Unless I kill you with my bare hands, I think you're safe." Her hands are on her hips again.

"Is that a possibility?" I ask.

"I'm considering it," she replies.

Gaze on my clasped hands between my legs, I nod. "I guess I deserve that."

She drops her hands and sits on the other couch, keeping several feet between us. "But you don't plan to do anything about it."

I scan the room again. The machine over the pins at the end of the lane hums a little, but otherwise the room is quiet. "What can I do?" I ask. "We aren't...weren't on the same page. We didn't work out. Nobody's fault."

She doesn't say anything. *At least we agree on that.*

She picks up the folder I dropped on the couch and flips it open.

"Don't..." I say, but trail off because it's too late. Her eyes have narrowed when she raises them to me again.

"You're throwing your support behind the watered-down bill?"

I sigh, letting my shoulders slump forward. She has every reason to be pissed. It is a back-stabbing thing to do, even if it's just politics. "I was going to ask Tim about it. About that scenario."

"You would torpedo our coalition."

"The legislation would still pass. *Your* legislation."

"Shut up," she snaps, tossing the folder aside. "I can't believe I ever thought you were anything more than another politician clawing your way to the top. You don't want a partner, you want a...a supporting actor, a woman who would be happy to play a blank slate for your agenda."

I don't raise my eyes, because there's no way to defend myself from that charge. Is it true? It's possible I don't know how to want anything else. "Hey, don't knock it," I say. "That's the role I play right now."

Her eyes are on me. "That's not who I am," she says. "That's not who I want to be."

"Well, me either," I snap, frustrated. I stand and start to pace in front of her, because that's the only space. "How am I ever supposed to be something greater when my role means I'm not supposed to make any waves?"

She puts a leg out in front of me, stopping my movement. "Your boss is a year into his second term. Who ever said you're not allowed to make waves? Your days of standing quietly in the background are over. You're in a new chapter now."

I turn toward her. It's an off-hand answer when the situation is much more complicated. But her gaze is steady. She's not being glib. She means it. She *sees* me.

"You've got to know what direction you want to go before you start those waves moving," she continues. "That's your problem."

She appears much less agitated than she did a second ago, but I'm the opposite.

"I know what direction I want to go," I reply, gesturing around us at the White House with my hands. *Obviously.*

"But you want more than that," she says. "I know you do. You want to be remembered as more than just a portrait in a museum. You want more than power. If that was all you wanted, you would have had this bill up for a vote by now. Without me."

"So now you're criticizing me for not being ruthless enough?" I run both hands through my hair. I don't know what she *wants.* Did she expect me to take control of our relationship, like I did in the bedroom? In the bedroom, she told me exactly what she wanted first. I'd executed her blueprint, a task I'm familiar with.

"No, I-" she stumbles briefly and then continues, "I want you to find your own voice and use it. I don't want you to use me to make waves for you."

What I *want* is to knock my head against the wall, for all the good this conversation is doing us.

twenty-eight

Cindy

I TAKE the few steps toward the red and blue balls on their rack by the other wall, looking for a distraction. "We should bowl a round, shouldn't we?"

Alex turns and follows me with his eyes. "Sure," he says, voice turning up at the end like it's a question.

What does he expect? We broke up. Even if he's uncertain about what direction he wants to go, *I'm* certain our directions are different. I need independence; he needs a loyal soldier. *Right?*

Unwilling to consider that I might be wrong, I shrug. *It's too late.* "What color do you want?"

"I have my own," he says, pointing at the bag on the floor by the door.

Smiling to myself at this display of nerdiness, I nod. "Great. I'll be red."

So we bowl. Alex is bad at it but I watch him throw gutter balls repeatedly before I offer to show him a few tips. He waves me off.

285

"Tim tried to show me before; I can't be taught. It's my one weakness," he says, self-deprecatingly. "Bad bowler."

I raise my eyebrows, trying not to soften in the face of cuteness. "I can think of a few others, so maybe we better work on the one that can be fixed in an afternoon."

He rolls his eyes dramatically. "Fiiine." But he smiles a little when I wrap my arms around him from behind to show him how to move his shoulder and hips and when to release the ball.

"OK, don't get your hopes up," he says, but he does it exactly how I showed him and earns a spare. He holds his hands up in victory, face incredulous. I laugh; I can't help it.

"You're welcome," I say dryly. "That'll probably make the difference for a voter some day."

Shoulders bowed, he nods. "My one priority," he murmurs.

"Isn't it?" I keep telling myself I shouldn't poke at him, but I have nothing else to do in here: It's bowling or harangue the vice president. And he seems so unhappy, I can't help wanting to fix it. And being angry that I care.

"Well," he sighs and sits down on the couch opposite where I'm leaning against the credenza. "I don't think you get where I am without being a little single-minded about your ambitions. But there are other things I want, too." After a pause, he adds: "I wanted you."

The room is quiet, except for the mechanical humming and the sound of our breathing.

"Just not enough," I suggest.

"Not enough for *you*," he replies promptly.

"Not enough to make time for me," I snap back.

"Not enough to..." he trails off, ending the pointless competition. He sighs. "No, that's fair. I didn't make enough time because I wasn't sure how much time to make. I wasn't sure how long it would last, or what it required, so I didn't dedicate calendar space to it when I should have. And if it's not on my calendar, I feel like I'm messing up—shirking other responsibilities—if I do something."

I nod, wrapping my hands around the edge of the wooden credenza so it digs into my palms. It's what I suspected, but more than I expected him to confirm. Not that it makes a difference. "And the bill...?" I look pointedly at the folder, still on the couch beside Alex.

Running a hand through his hair, he asks, "Well, I *tried*, didn't I?"

"You did the bare minimum!" she snaps. "You don't care how it passes, only that it does."

"That's politics!"

"That's cowardice!"

We fall silent again, the harshness between us unnatural.

Then, because it doesn't matter if I'm vulnerable now, I offer, "I wanted you, too."

Silently, he nods, looking at the floor. We are silent for a beat, except for the humming from down the lane.

"It's hard to build trust," I continue, even though I should leave it alone. "At our age, in our jobs. I'm not sure it's possible. And without trust, everything is a potential betrayal."

He says nothing, but sits up and leans back on the couch. He straightens both legs of his pants, one at a time, and I follow his hands as he does it. He lifts his head.

"I'm sorry for the many tiny betrayals, then," he says quietly, meeting my eyes. It's almost too intimate, the way he's looking at me, when too much sits between us to ever be this close to him again.

My body tensing, I hesitate. I know what I want in this moment, but I'm not sure it's the smart thing. It means breaking down my shields, admitting to vulnerability. At a time when it might be too late. But we'd ruined everything by letting smart become the enemy of going after what we wanted.

"Are there cameras in here?" I ask.

"I don't think so," he says, glancing around.

I push off the credenza and take the steps to the couch so I can slide my legs on either side of his, straddling him. His head turns back to mine, suddenly very close, and his hands wrap around my waist, one palm resting at the small of my back.

"I still want you," I say. "I never stopped."

Then I kiss him. For that moment, it's like we're back in California, standing in the golden sunshine on the beach amid the soft music of the waves. He tastes like spearmint gum and smells like spice. His lap is warm and his shoulders are hard against my hands.

This time, I don't want him to take control, to roll me under his body and have his way with me. I flip his tie over one shoulder and unbutton his shirt enough to slip my hand inside, then under his undershirt, over his warm chest.

I'm in awe of the fact I get to feel this—the vice president's heart, buried under layers of clothes and protocol—and he lets me. One of his hands is on my back and the other is at his side, like he understands I'm driving on this particular journey.

I kiss him again, an unhurried meeting of our lips like we have all the time in the world to explore one another, again or for real this time. We spend what could be an hour like that, making out slowly, like adults who care about each other rather than frantic like teenagers. It feels like it could be the first time we're together. His body is still new to me. The way the pulse in his neck beats and the sharpness of his breath against my neck are still surprising.

It changes nothing. But it means everything.

"I meant it," he whispers, the first thing he's said since I kissed him. "When I told you I loved you." His eyes catch mine and I can see almost to the beating heart of him, to the sincerity at his core.

"I know," I say. "Me too."

Someone knocks on the door.

I jump, feeling the tent in his pants as I do, and meet Alex's eyes, panicked.

"Just a minute," he calls out. I carefully slide off him.

"Sir," Ted says from outside the door.

"OK," I call back, once my clothes are adjusted and Alex has taken off his jacket and covered his lap. The room smells like arousal. But the Secret Service has probably seen it all.

Ted opens the door and pokes his head inside, zeroing in on Alex, who is rumpled but covered, shirt once again buttoned. "Sir, the president sends his apologies but you're needed in the Situation Room."

"Thanks," he says, and leaps to his feet. He visually checks in with me, and I nod, because what else can I do? National security comes first. "I guess we managed to deflect a serious conversation again," he says. And then he's gone, out the door and possibly out of my life. He's right that we had our chance and did nothing with it.

There isn't anything I can do about it. I can't chase him through the halls of the White House. I've reached my limit on vulnerability for one day.

"Ma'am? Whenever you're ready, I can lead you out." A female agent, now standing at the open door, is much more put together than I am right now. I hear the sound of people down the hall laughing. It's just another day in the office for people working here.

I nod and sit down to put on my shoes.

He's not what I need. I repeat it to myself as I'm following the agent through the White House toward the exit, thinking about how Alex went from disheveled on the couch with me to some national crisis in the West Wing without batting an eye. About how he told me in so many ways, even if it wasn't always verbal, that he wants me as much as this job he's worked for for years.

The farther I walk away from him, the more my body floods with adrenaline.

Nothing about this is right. I'm giving up what I want for the sake of a goal that I can't say for certain was ever out of reach when we were together.

I imagine running back through the White House to find Alex. Breaking into the Situation Room. Getting killed by some Secret Service agent. *This isn't a rom-com, Cindy, this is real life.* I might know what I want, but sometimes, wanting—and even needing—are not enough.

twenty-nine

Alex

MY WEEK GOES on like any other, like I haven't discovered something irreplaceable is missing in my life. Like I haven't realized the goal I've been single-mindedly running toward isn't quite—isn't *all*—I wanted, after all. Like I don't have to live with that knowledge the rest of my life. Even if I become president, it will always be *almost* but not enough.

The only thing I have to look forward to is showing off my 1967 Corvette on Friday for a pre-taped segment of a late-night talk show. We had it driven out here from California especially for the show. Any excuse to see it again.

I approve the details on my trip to Philadelphia for July 4— the vice president gets to celebrate at a smaller city's parade rather than attend the chaotic festivities in Washington—and I pick the local business I want to "surprise" visit while I'm there. I mark up the draft of my speech and finally call my mother back.

On the phone, I insist on changing my RSVP to my sister's wedding to no plus one. Mom protests, and I wouldn't put it past her to invite someone meant for me "just in case." Then she gets quiet and tells me she's sorry it didn't work out. She does sound very sorry. My mother wants grandchildren; the more of her children are married, the better her odds.

After I talk to Tim, who agrees, and Toby, who eventually nods, I make some calls to Capitol Hill. I have Deena write a statement about the cannabis legislation, but tell her not to release it until someone asks. I want Cindy to take the lead on this.

I talk to my campaign manager about setting up an exploratory committee, the first step toward running for president. She and Toby have worried that there's something wrong with me—that my ambition is flagging in the face of the job. I don't think that is it; my ego is still big enough to imagine myself as president. I have the skill and experience for the job. I also know there are not enough aides to hire in the world to fill the role of a partner.

I'm stuck between what I need and want, but I won't give up one dream just because I can't have another.

"Let's do it," I tell her. I can remake the presidency. I just have to win it first.

Anita comes to see me the day after locking us in the bowling alley. Tim took one look at me that day in the Situation Room and recognized I didn't want to talk about it. We focused on business, ignoring emotions like men. But Anita won't be so easy on me.

"No hard feelings?" she asks, standing halfway in the door of my office.

"I'm honored that I have such a loyal friend," I answer. My tone is flat instead of teasing, but I can't help it. She notices.

"I take it it didn't go well," she says, coming farther into the office.

"It went fine," I reply. "Didn't change anything."

She "hmms," sympathetic. But then she hits me with one of

her tough love observations: "Then maybe you need to try harder."

* * *

Cindy

Whatever has Martin bouncing into my office like it's his lucky day, I'm primed to oppose it. But he says, "Have you heard? The White House threatened to veto the Senate bill."

I exchange glances with Lizzie, who is sitting in the chair in front of my desk. I pick up my "Best Boss Ever" coffee mug and take another sip to hide my reaction from Martin, who doesn't need any encouragement.

"What about the House bill? With Cindy's provisions in it?" Lizzie asks.

"Yes," Martin confirms. "They only support that version. It's in the *Post*."

Sitting back in my chair, I grip the mug between both hands. This isn't *definitely* Alex sending me a message, but it's not nothing, either, for the White House to pull back from an easy win.

Lizzie is pulling up the story on her phone. "'This is a historic bill, led by Representative Cindy Wight, and we expect it to pass with historic support," she reads.

"They used my name in the statement?" I ask, sitting up and putting my mug down on the desk, my hands too numb to hold it. He might as well have bought a billboard outside my office. *He finally took a stand.*

"They did," Lizzie confirms, raising her eyes to mine with a little smile. "They're handing it back to you."

Lizzie gets it. Martin doesn't. "This is insane!" he says. "We need to act fast to shore up support before they change their minds."

"He's not going to change his mind," Lizzie says, standing and taking Martin by the shoulder to direct him back out the door of my office. "But go ahead and start shoring up support, Martin. I'll check in with you later."

"He?" Martin repeats, before Lizzie closes the door on him.

"You're going to get asked about this," Lizzie tells me, as she sits back down. "We should call Max."

Still staring into my rapidly cooling coffee, I pull out my phone and text the *Post* link to Max, and then to Kari and Sara.

"But more importantly, how do *you* feel about it?" Lizzie asks.

I smile a little, grateful to be surrounded by women who can switch back and forth between competent strategists and sympathetic friends. Max, who dealt with most of the fallout from my near-disastrous breakup *and* interfaced with the overprotective White House team over it, texts me every day to make sure I'm able to get out of bed in the morning.

"It's great news, obviously," I say. I sound like a robot, but processing emotions quickly isn't my forte. "I want this bill to be something I point to as a huge success on my record."

Lizzie nods, but she's clearly unimpressed by my assessment. "I think he loves you," she says, gently. It's the kind of thing I gave her implicit permission to say as a senior member of my staff, as well as someone I consider a confidant.

My phone buzzes twice with responses from two other women I trust the most.

Kari: Wow! It doesn't get any more 'grand gesture' than this in that town.

Sara: This is going to make a great behind-the-scenes book someday.

Unable to keep sitting while talking about this, I stand. I take a deep breath and try to focus on the bubble of emotion in my gut, the one that is going to pop if I examine it. I go to the window and gaze down at Independence Avenue and Longworth, the House office building next door.

It's nearly lunchtime and it's beautiful out, so the sidewalk is full of congressional interns and staff. They're all in formal business clothes. Tooth-achingly young. All of them are full of ambition and dreams. I take deep breaths.

"I think he does, too," I answer Lizzie. *Love.* I've always thought of it as intangible, easy to say and then steal back. But this love...this is something concrete. Kari is right. "What better way to show love than to give up leverage, in this town," I murmur.

Lizzie snorts. "It's true."

"But what about my leverage," I add, gaze still focused out the window. I'm standing in an office I fought hard to win. "Do I have to give that up to love him back?"

Lizzie doesn't say anything at first. We've both poured sweat and tears into building my status in this job and don't want to tear that down. It's so hard to see the future. The decision I make now could be one I regret the rest of my life. Or it could be one of the *best* of my life. There is no in-between.

"What would happen if you just gave it up...*with him*?" Lizzie asks. "I honestly don't know the answer," she adds.

"Leap of faith," I murmur. "What a terrifying thought."

Even though the words are flippant, I'm scared. My hand is shaking a little as I put it on the window.

"Totally," Lizzie agrees. "Most people aren't worth the faith, in my experience."

I sigh and nod. I've taken the leap before and painfully flopped. "In my experience, too."

"But," Lizzie adds. "I guess we have to be open to being surprised once in a while."

Glancing over my shoulder, Lizzie is still sitting there in front of my desk, waiting for me to decide one way or the other. My decision affects all of my staff.

I'm scared, but the right path is obvious. It's to walk toward the challenge, not run away from it. If I'm going to take a risk, it's going to be reaching for an opportunity, not avoiding it.

* * *

Alex

I'm filming a video in the East Room of the White House for social media. It's one of my least favorite activities, because it requires a lot of effort—make-up and production values and time—for a few minutes of content that I suspect less than a million people watch.

While I wait for the production team to prepare, I'm reading the print editions of the major newspapers that Kaylee, all smiles, brought me. "VP pushes White House to the left," reads one headline. The story includes a section high up that gives me credit:

> Vice President Drake worked behind the scenes to urge the president to collaborate with a progressive coalition that has worked for years on the bill, according to two senior White House officials familiar with the matter.

"He said the win only matters if we do it right," one official said, citing multiple meetings between the vice president and the firebrand freshman congresswoman who wrote the bill. "He made multiple direct calls to senators to urge them not to take a nibble when they could have the whole apple."

Toby threads his way through the excessive number of people in the room setting up equipment and nods at the paper I'm holding. "I have more good news."

"Really? That's your 'good news' face?" I fold the paper and sit forward. Toby's face is impassive. "Tell me. I could use some."

Toby raises one eyebrow. "Getting credit for giving credit to someone else isn't enough for you?"

I smile. "It was a heroic effort by Kaylee and her team to reframe what happened. They did an excellent job, despite going *entirely* against my wishes." I raise my voice on the last part for the benefit of Kaylee, who is talking to Maggie and Deena behind the camera set-up. She gives me a thumbs-up. Somehow, I've come out looking like the good guy in the press, despite how close I came to stealing Cindy's win.

It turns out making waves is surprisingly fun.

"They did what I asked," Toby replies, shamelessly calm about contradicting my instructions to *quietly* direct attention back to Cindy and the House version of the bill. "For the greater good." He slaps a folder down in front of me. "New polling."

I grimace. "Let me guess, the good news is everyone is OK again with the status quo."

Toby waits, somehow making it clear without saying a word that he's exercising extreme patience with my attitude. "We ran the same questions we did a few weeks ago, with one addition accounting for success with the cannabis legislation."

"Really?" I sit forward and open the folder. "Why?" I don't care why; I'm morbidly curious about the answers. I run a finger down the topline results and have a jolt of excitement before I remember that this hypothetical poll is meaningless now.

"People don't like compromise, but they love results." Toby shuffles his feet, the equivalent of rolling his eyes. "And your successful professional risk has the ricochet effect of approval for you taking personal risks."

"Relatable," I say, paging through the poll results to see how the individual questions were worded. "I don't like compromise as a concept, either. Just sounds like selling out until you sit down and hammer out a bill that can become law."

"Good line for the video!" Kaylee pipes up from across the room.

"What is the theme of this video again?" Toby frowns, creating deep lines on his forehead. "I thought we were focusing on Independence Day this week."

"Coalition-building is patriotic, Toby," Kaylee says, walking toward us. "We thought we'd try something and see how it goes."

"Waving flags in the background, rah rah?" Toby asks, deadpan.

She smiles. Kaylee is young and blonde, but she can hold her own against Toby. "Let's leave the visual strategy to me, shall we?"

If only my staff included a relationship strategist who could manage my dating life as well as these two manage politics and messaging for me. Maybe then, this poll really would be good news, and not a sign that in hindsight, I should have been less cautious.

I glance at Deena, who holds my phone, and almost ask again if Cindy called. But she would have told me immediately.

So I stay silent, and promise myself: *Next time I'll make it clear what I want when I have it.*

But I'm afraid there won't be a next time.

* * *

Cindy

A press availability with the Speaker and the Whip means standing in a stuffy, windowless room in the Capitol. I'm on display with my colleagues in front of a whole army of reporters and cameras and nothing but a podium and mostly unwritten rules separating the two groups.

The Speaker murmurs to me before we go into the room, "Nicely done on the bill. Getting the White House to stand down is no small feat."

I feel a little flutter at the rare compliment, even though I'm aware that the rest of the leadership team left me on my own to pull off negotiations and didn't expect me to succeed. "Thank you, Madame Speaker," I say, swallowing down the negativity. *Baby steps.*

"I spoke to the Judiciary chairman," the Speaker continues. She raises her eyebrows and I brace myself for the worst. "And Randy can stuff it. This is your win."

After that affirmation, I float into the room. The Speaker has my back in front of the press, too, telling them the cannabis bill is scheduled for hearings within the month and will be "brought to the Floor in a timely manner."

Then I get the questions Lizzie predicted.

"Congresswoman Wight, do you believe you pushed the White House to the left on this legislation?"

"Congresswoman, do you know why the White House pulled back their support for the Senate bill?"

The Speaker and Whip make room for me at the podium, where the microphones are.

"They made their own statement about their reasons and I won't guess beyond that," I reply, and take a step back. It's the answer Max suggested on the phone as I rushed here, running late. We'd tried to plan for every scenario, but now that I'm faced with this room, I'm uncertain.

I know the expectations surrounding this legislation, and at this event I'm supposed to stand in the background and let party leadership pretend they've supported me all along. There's a line and I'm willing to cross it, but I'm not sure when is appropriate.

"Congresswoman, have you spoken to the vice president about the bill?"

Reluctantly, I step back up to the podium. "I have not." I pause. "In a few days." I step back again.

"The *Post* is reporting he plans to launch an exploratory committee for the presidency next week. Did the two of you discuss his plans?"

The last bit of doubt in my heart lifts so suddenly, my insides jump. Alex is going after what he wants. He listened to me. I'm not just a prop. I'm someone he listens to on the big decisions.

I glance at the Speaker and Whip, who have retained their neutral expressions for the sake of the media but are shuffling their feet a bit as this turns into the Cindy Wight press conference.

Time to go with my instincts.

Straightening my spine, I lift my chin, and step back to the podium once again. "I'll make a simple statement," I say, and the reporters' hands all go down and back to their pens and notebooks. The room falls silent but for the sound of tension.

"The vice president and I worked closely on the cannabis legislation to ensure it included the provisions most important to the communities it impacts. The vice president impressed me with his forthright communication style, his negotiation skills, his ability to multitask, his love of his dog and his kindness to everyone around him. He was an excellent partner in the negotiations over this bill."

I take a breath and then I say it: "And I'd vote for him. Every time, every office."

Stepping back as the room explodes around me, I watch reporters yelling questions without waiting to be called on. I raise my eyebrows at my colleagues, mouthing, "That's it."

We gather in a huddle and leave, surrounded by aides.

"Taking party unity a bit far, aren't you?" the Whip murmurs. The Speaker meets my eyes and just smiles a little, the smile of two women letting a man think what he wants.

As we're leaving, someone asks: "Do you think the vice president will be our next president?"

And someone else calls out: "Are you going to marry him?"

thirty

Alex

REMEMBER TO SMILE. Smiling is what vice presidents do on late night talk shows. The host's politics match mine, there's a beautiful car sitting in front of us, and I have no reason —that people know about—not to smile.

The host, an amiable man known for his dad jokes, already teased me about how my hobbies—old cars and legal marijuana —make me some kind of "Ron Swanson but with real power."

Instead of getting uptight about being reduced to one issue, I responded that Ron Swanson could move the cogs of city government much faster than a vice president can change the country.

"He moved at the speed of fiction," I joked.

My Corvette is parked in the circle drive in front of the White House. Thor is curled up on the grass. The sun is out, but the humidity is low for once, so it is a nice day to be outside.

If only I was having more fun with this than I am. My team told me that I need to do more media to get Americans used to my presence and the idea of me as a leader. I'm going through the motions, uncertain I've got a clear runway toward a goal anymore. I don't feel like a leader; I feel like roadkill.

"Communication strategy is about repeating the message," Toby keeps saying, and I keep hoping that strategy will work on *myself*.

According to Toby, there's some book coming out in which a former White House staffer refers to me as "the boy wonder" and it's important to get out in front of the idea that I'm just Tim's sidekick. More solo appearances, "more kicking ass in headlines like you did this week," more *personality*, Toby had told me.

"Having hobbies makes me a man?" I'd asked.

"Having a cool car makes you *Bat*man," Toby replied dryly.

Once Toby makes me laugh, it's hard to disagree with him.

So here I am, filming a segment in which I climb behind the wheel for the first time in five years. The Secret Service is out in force, surrounding us although we're on White House grounds and I've been warned not to hit the gas. I only have a few yards of driveway, so there's little danger of me gunning it through security like some kind of attempted escape back to the real world.

Keep smiling. I smile as I climb in my car and the host climbs into the passenger seat, putting Thor on his lap. I visually check on Thor, who loves strangers and seems content enough to sit on one. I buckle my seatbelt and wait for my passenger to do the same.

"Safety first," I say, mugging for the camera poked in my window. Another one is affixed to the dash. That glue better come off.

I start the engine and rev it a little for the sake of the show. The host laughs, joking, "Is that the engine or is she just happy to see you?"

"It's been awhile." I'm not allowed to drive on the open road as vice president. If I become president, I basically won't be allowed to drive myself for the rest of my life. "It's a real disincentive for the job," I add.

"I'll say!" the host agrees. "Driving like a maniac is as American as apple pie. Can you even be a true American without experiencing road rage?"

"Don't get me wrong, flying through traffic in a motorcade is a perk, too," I tack on, not wanting to complain too much and ruin my relatability on national television. Toby would kill me.

The host leans in. "Ever gotten up to anything in the back seat of one of those limos?"

I keep my smile lit. I absolutely don't want to relive one of my best personal moments as vice president on TV. "Let's just say the other disincentive is the Secret Service is always watching," I deflect, earning another easy laugh.

"Are we ready for this?" the host demands, shouting it out the open window like he's at a NASCAR race. We've already gone over what the show wants from the segment, so I go through the motions.

When I put the car in neutral, it rolls forward slowly as the cameras follow it down the asphalt driveway away from the White House. For comedic effect, I bet the show adds the sound of a revving engine in post-production.

Inside the car, Thor gives a yip.

"That'll put the wind in your hair," the host says, straight-faced, as we inch forward. I laugh a little, because yes, my life is ridiculous.

Glancing at the rear view mirror, I expect to see a mix of TV production crew and Secret Service agents. What I see is Cindy Wight, wearing blue and standing with her hands on her hips amid a bunch of suits.

I hit the brakes, jerking us to an unexpected halt. I murmur an apology and climb out of the car, walking back to her. She meets me half-way between the car and the group of people watching.

"How did you get in?" I ask, ridiculously, because I don't know how to ask what I'm thinking: Why are you here? Did you change your mind about us?

"I know the owners," Cindy replies. It takes me a second to realize she's being funny. She smiles at me, like everything between us is fine.

"Are you here for me?" I mean it as a question of fact, but it comes out painfully vulnerable. I look around. The cameras are still aimed at us, and likely still rolling. I lower my voice. "I'm in the middle of shooting."

"I know, and I am," she replies. She seems different: More like the Cindy that I first met here at the White House than the Cindy I've been dating. Sure of herself, her eyes on a goal. "Alex, are you going to become president?" she asks.

Both because of our surroundings and because she's never asked me that question directly before, I hesitate. "I don't know," I reply, and then I decide to be honest. "I'd like to have a partner first."

She smiles, with only a little surprise in it. "This country needs you."

"This country can wait." I mean it. If I have to wait a few more years to take this office, I will. There are other things in this world I *need* right now.

"Maybe you can have it all."

I tilt my head at her. Something hopeful is bubbling between us, something I can't examine yet. "Can I?"

She keeps smiling, like she knows something.

Behind her, the crowd is growing. The press is trickling out of the wing where they have offices under the briefing room. This whole conversation is likely being live-posted on social media along with photos of the two of us standing close together, clearly having a personal conversation. But I wouldn't put this talk off for a world of bad optics.

I gesture at Cindy to follow me back to the car.

The host is standing on the other side of the Corvette. Thor runs up to Cindy as she approaches and she bends down to pick him up.

"Do you mind if we steal this back for a few minutes?" I ask the host, already sliding in on the driver's side.

"Hi," I hear Cindy saying, as she walks around to the other side. "I love your show."

"I'm a big fan of yours, as well," he replies. "I caught the video this morning."

If she responds, I can't hear it. She slides into the car beside me, putting Thor on her lap.

"What happened this morning?" I ask, after the host closes her door and steps away.

She glances at me and then at the camera on the dash. I grimace. I wonder if I can cover it up or mute it. Asking the crew to take it out seems like a big hassle that would cost me time when I feel so much urgency to have this conversation now.

She must see in my eyes that I don't care if we're still being watched. She puts Thor down in the foot well and turns to me in her seat. "I basically declared my love for you at a press conference," she says.

Blinking, I'm trying to take this in on multiple levels. First, I can't believe my staff didn't already brief me. Second, I can't believe the *press* didn't brief me. Third, is she saying she *loves* me? Present tense?

"I love you, Alex," she says, confirming it. "And I think, if we're on the same page on that, and we're honest about what we want, we can figure out the rest."

The crazy mess buzzes around us—the people waiting to pounce in the driveway, the cameras, the White House and all the responsibility it represents, the tourists standing behind the fence down the driveway, aiming their phones at us. But Cindy's eyes are focused on me and not any of that stuff. *She's right.*

"I love you, too," I say.

Her expression doesn't change so much as settle, accepting this and our new reality. We gaze at each other, and then at the camera on the dash, mutually agreeing not to give the whole world a glimpse of us making out. We've already given the world enough pieces of us.

"Take a ride with me?" I ask, quietly. I put all the hope I can in the words, along with all the understanding that the future will be a winding road. She puts on her seat belt. Safety first, even for a leap of faith. I grin.

I turn the key and roll over the engine. I see the Secret Service come running toward us in the rear view mirror. I rev the engine, like we're a couple of rebels instead of people who've carefully weighed this decision.

We take off for a very short drive down the White House driveway and into our future. Together.

epilogue

Cindy

5 years later

IT'S NOT COLORADO, but the rolling hills and nothing in sight but the rocks and green trees of northern Maryland are still enough to insulate me from the pressure of constant notifications and meetings.

I stand on 1,400 feet of rocks and close my eyes, smelling the air that carries nothing more than nature. Pausing at the summit, I take 15 minutes or so to eat my packed lunch, letting the sweat dry on my back where it gathered under my day pack. I have to be back in an hour, or alarms will be raised. But this morning can be leisurely, without the multitasking required of my usual schedule.

Other than the Secret Service agents, there might not be another person around for miles in Catoctin Mountain Park. I left my protection on the ground when I climbed up here, assuring them I have my panic button should things go epically wrong.

It's unlikely, up here at the top of Chimney Rock where I have panoramic views of the national park.

This park gets remarkably few visitors, considering it's barely more than an hour from Washington and 10 degrees cooler while the city is a swampy hellhole right now in mid-August.

Eventually, I gather up my banana peel and sandwich wrapper and stuff them back into my pack, throwing it back on over my shoulders. I stand for another long minute, enjoying the view.

If only Alex could be here, but his hiking is limited to the 200 acres that encompass Camp David and then it's a big production to make it happen. The Secret Service searches the area first as thoroughly as if a child is missing.

I'm reluctant to head back, but not out of dread. I love my life, despite its many pressures. I just don't know when I'll have a chance to do this again. So I take a last, long look out over the valley before I turn back to the Jeep.

When I arrive at the Camp David compound, Louise is up from her nap. The day nanny, Alice, has her sitting at the table eating her afternoon snack of blueberries and cheese.

"Hi, Lou-who," I say, kissing my daughter on the top of her soft, dark-fluffed head. "How was your nap?"

"Good," she replies, one chubby hand squishing a blueberry. "Mama working?"

I smile. Alex and I have worked hard for consistency when it comes to explaining work demands to Louise. As often as possible, we block off both of our calendars for "Louise time," a chunk of time when we are parents first and any interruption had better involve nuclear missiles. Louise understands the difference between that and "working" time.

"Mama's on a break right now, so I can't stay," I say. "We'll have Louise time later, after your daddy's done working. OK?"

"OK," Louise agrees, distracted by her food project.

Alice nods and waves from nearby as I stand to go to my study.

"The president stopped by earlier," Alice says. "He said he'd try to check in again around 4."

I nod. "Thanks, Alice." Alex is meeting with the joint chiefs, which I expect will run long. Later, we have plans to watch the latest movie where Zack Ryder plays a newly-sworn-in president. It's a decent time for me to accomplish some work of my own. I have Martin's notes to read on legislation up for a vote on Monday, and Max sent me a draft of the op-ed we're submitting to the *Journal* about my proposal to include more street lighting and closed-circuit security cameras in the infrastructure bill.

And yet every time I hand over Louise's care to someone else, I still have to remind myself I'm not failing. I'm there for meals and naps and baths and bedtimes—just not all of them. Juggling priorities is an endless challenge, for both Alex and me.

One of the reasons we went ahead and pulled the trigger on IVF almost immediately after getting married was because—as I'd told Alex—he shouldn't have the presidency as a reason to avoid getting up with the baby.

"I'm not going to feel guilty for making you go sleepless in case of a national crisis," I'd said. As a member of Congress and vice president at the time, our jobs were on more equal footing. We suffered equally for a year after Louise's birth, trading shifts and sharing joys. Then Lou finally slept through the night during Alex's intense campaign, when he was on the road most days. Louise and Thor and I joined him whenever Congress recessed.

I seriously considered retirement, or at least a break, but Alex urged me to keep my job and I coasted to re-election almost without trying, clinging to Alex's coattails as an incumbent candidate with one of the highest approval ratings in recent history. His popularity was thanks to his role in passing stunningly popular legislation, as the cannabis bill turned out to be once jobs were filled by people with expunged records and dispensaries were able to freely take credit card payments.

Tim campaigned for him, and so did Anita. Thor appeared in a campaign ad that went viral. Louise took her first steps during an interview with Oprah. He won by a landslide.

Now it's tricky. Even I can't argue "my job is just as important as yours" to the leader of the free world. Thank God for good nannies. And for the second gentleman, the husband of Alex's vice president, who regularly picks up my slack on hosting duties for White House events. We share staff and I trust him with all the major decisions on decor and State Dinners and—thankfully—the annual Easter Egg roll.

I still calculate, often, whether taking a break from my job in Congress would be smart. I could still run for Senate in a few years, while Alex is in his second term and after Lou starts school.

My editor is begging for another book, after the success of my first one, and I don't have time to work on it while juggling two jobs and trying to preserve time for my family. But a book by a sitting first lady that elevates the voices of women and minorities, the voices once silenced by cannabis prohibition and still silenced by fear of harassment, could do a lot of good. It'd be a return to my activist roots, in some ways. I've started an outline for it that I work on for a while that afternoon, after emailing back Martin and Max.

Alex interrupts my daydreaming after 4 p.m., coming up behind me at my desk and kissing me on the temple.

"How's Afghanistan?" I ask, turning to him.

"Still there," he replies. "You smell like nature."

"I didn't shower yet," I admit. "But it was so nice. I took a picture for you."

Alex darts a glance around us. We're alone. He kisses me on

the lips and pulls me out of my chair. "Are you done with work?" he asks, belatedly, recognizing he interrupted.

"For now," I agree. "You?"

He makes a face. Alex is never "done" with work. "I have long enough for a shower, at least."

I laugh and let him drag me upstairs. Visiting Camp David always makes Alex a little reckless. He persists in his delusions about midnight sexcapades although usually we're both so tired we fall asleep without a goodnight kiss.

He ends up taking a call, of course, so I shower alone, but by the time I'm toweling off, he's back. He licks my neck, where it's still wet below my ear. I shiver from it, meeting his eyes in the mirror above the sink. For once, we're both wide awake.

"Come out here," he urges. "I locked the door and told Ted we're not to be disturbed for at least half an hour. We'll still make it to dinner with Lou."

Laying back on the bed, pulling me with him, I drop my towel and follow his guidance until I'm sitting on the face of the most powerful man in the world.

He opens me up using his fingers, and licks inside me. My nipples harden and I hold onto the bed frame. He brings me to the edge, taking his time—and it does take more time, now that we're both older, but the gift of half an hour feels luxurious— and then I slide down his body and take him inside me.

Rolling us over, he raises my hands above my head and places my palms against the bed frame. "Don't move," he says, and fucks me the way I want him to while I hold on.

My orgasm is gentle, rippling through me like the tide coming in rather than slamming into me like a wave. We lay side by side, holding each other, for long minutes after, Alex still inside of me. We revel in the miracle of stolen time, right in the middle of the afternoon.

There are sounds of people outside the room, staff preparing dinner and agents communicating about the perimeter. Louise is laughing somewhere outside, probably playing with Thor, who barks twice in response. The dog's obsession with her began when she was a newborn.

But right now, it's the two of us, looking into each other's eyes. Regular check-ins, either silent and spontaneous or planned and out loud, have become our way of making sure we're still aligned. It's become increasingly important as our time to talk in private has become more compact.

"I think I might retire this term," I murmur. "But not for you."

"Hm?" he says. "You really want to?"

"So I can work on my book."

Considering this, he nods. "What can I do to make it easier?"

Smiling, I lean in to kiss him, a brush across his lips to let him know I appreciate him. My decision affects both of us, but he would never make it less than mine. It's a difficult choice, but there are upsides. "Maybe we can start working out together again. If I'm around more during the day."

He wraps his arms around me and shifts a little, pulling me closer. "I like that idea." He pauses, running his fingers up and down my naked spine. "You'll talk to Maggie about the messaging? You know people will think you're giving up your career."

I nod, tucking my head under his chin, my nose in the hollow of his neck where I can smell his skin. He smells smokey, from the fire they built in Laurel Lodge during his last meeting. "I know. I'll remind them you've only got another six years or so of work in you and I plan on a much longer career so I'm pacing myself."

He laughs once, a bark muffled in my hair. "Don't make me sound old. I'm not ready for the shuffle ball court just yet."

"I noticed," I tease, rolling my hips against him. He grins, sliding one hand over the curve of my bare bottom. We might not have time for this kind of intimacy often, but when we do, we still know how to make it count.

"Of course, we'll need to put a shuffle court in at the White House once *you* become president," he continues, his usual tease about my future. I have no desire to run for president—yet. "I can't spend all my time picking out china patterns."

I smack him on the ass in return. "Shut up, you."

"Excuse me," he says, mock-serious. "The Secret Service could shoot you for hitting the president."

I snuggle further into him. His arms are comfortable now, familiar, but never less than amazing to be in. Sometimes, as in this moment, all the work we put in daily falls away and I cannot believe how lucky I am to have a partner I love so deeply and have built such a rich life with.

"Shut up, Mr. President," I say, and I can feel his smile against the top of my head.

* * *

Thank you for reading *My Secret Vice*! Reviews help indie authors.

Read Max's story in *Breadcrumbs*, Kari (the reporter)'s story in *Photograph Me*, or Zack Ryder's story in *Leave No Trace*.

acknowledgments

I worked as a political journalist for about six years, often covering the settings in this book. (I took some liberties regarding Air Force Two.) I never thought I had this book in me until the pandemic forced me back into my parents' basement to write it.

This book would not be what it is without the people who helped edit it: Valerie Pepper and Kat Saturday. My early readers also directed future revisions: Regina Black, Vanessa King, Sarah T. Dubb, Jessica St. Hollis, and Jonathan Easley. Thanks to you all, and to the community of other indie authors that support me in so many ways.

Thanks also to the many political journos I worked with—many of whom are still in the business—including Brooke, Emily, Justin, Meg, Nikki, Mary Tyler, Daniel, Josh, Judy, Avery, Morgan and Lauren.

about the author

Alicia Wilder is many things: a romance author, a journalist, a geek who loves cosplay, a cat mom, and a triathlete. She's split time living between Washington, D.C. and Denver. She writes happily ever afters for imperfect people.

Sign up for her author newsletter at aliciawilder.com/newsletter and get freebies, news and behind-the-scenes info.